JORY STRONG

ZOË'S GIFT

ELLORA'S CAVE
ROMANTICA PUBLISHING

An Ellora's Cave Romantica Publication

www.ellorascave.com

Zoë's Gift

ISBN 9781419960369
ALL RIGHTS RESERVED.
Zoë's Gift Copyright © 2009 Jory Strong
Edited by Sue-Ellen Gower.
Cover art by Syneca.

This book printed in the U.S.A. by Jasmine–Jade Enterprises, LLC.

Electronic book publication May 2009
Trade paperback publication January 2010

The terms Romantica® and Quickies® are registered trademarks of
Ellora's Cave Publishing.

ZOË'S GIFT

෨

Acknowledgments

හ

It's only fitting that with this, my 30th story for Ellora's Cave, I acknowledge my editor, Sue-Ellen Gower, who picked *Fallon Mates: Binding Krista* from the "slush" pile so many years ago and set my career as a published author in motion. My stories continue to be richer and fuller for passing through her hands, and her praise and encouragement still challenge me to make each story better than the previous one. Thanks, Sue-Ellen! This one's for you!

Trademarks Acknowledgement

හ

The author acknowledges the trademarked status and trademark owners of the following wordmarks mentioned in this work of fiction:

Big Mac: McDonald's Corporation

Kentucky Fried Chicken: KFC Corporation

National Enquirer: American Media Operations, Inc.

Qwirkle: MindWare

Star Trek: CBS Inc.

Styrofoam: Dow Chemical Company, The

Prologue

Kaylee Ripa, formerly of the planet Earth and not yet ten years old, knew one thing with complete and utter certainty. Bossy boys were a million times worse than a shot in the butt. A trillion times worse than the strictest nurse she'd ever had to deal with and a zillion times worse than the meanest doctor. And that was a saying a lot considering she'd been in and out of hospitals for most of her life and would have died if Zeraac and Komet hadn't come to Earth and brought her to Belizair.

She peeked around the bush she was currently hiding behind and gauged the distance to the archway separating this courtyard from the next one. Then she checked the sky to make sure everyone was playing by the rules she'd insisted on before the game started—no flying when you were *it*.

That was part of the problem with the two bossy boys who were a million times worse than a shot in the butt. Just because *she* didn't have wings, they thought she needed to be watched over constantly.

Well, she didn't. And she shouldn't *have* to sneak away from the game like this either. But there was something she had to do and she had to do it alone because it was a secret task the golden lady had asked her to do.

If it hadn't been a secret, then Kaylee would have asked her mother or her new fathers, Komet and Zeraac, to take her to the Council building. But since it *was* a secret mission, she had to wait until she was out playing with the friends she'd made in Winseka.

Winseka was where all the humans had to live when they were first brought to Belizair. Not that there were many humans. And except for her, there were no human children.

All her friends were either Amato or Vesti. The Amato friends looked like angels, though the feathers on their wings weren't always solid white like in the picture books on Earth. Her Vesti friends were darker skinned than most of the Amato and they had suede-soft wings that looked like bat wings.

This was the longest she'd ever managed to be alone. So far every time she'd tried to go off by herself, The Bossy Boys had stopped her. They said it was their job to protect her and keep her out of trouble because one day she was going to grow up and be their wife.

That was *not* going to happen! *Some* boys were good to have as friends. But she wasn't even old enough to have a boyfriend yet. And even if she had been, it would *not* be one of The Bossy Boys.

Kaylee checked the sky one last time and raced for the archway leading into the next courtyard. She wasn't sure if Miciah d'Vesti was in the Council building or how she'd get to see him, or even if he'd want to see her, but she had to try.

Miciah was a powerful Council member. He was one of twelve people who made the laws on Belizair. But more importantly, he was a genetic match for her mother, and if he'd wanted to, he could have had Komet and Zeraac sent away. He hadn't done it though. He'd let her mother keep Komet and Zeraac as husbands which meant Kaylee got to keep them as her daddies. And as far as she was concerned, they were the best daddies in the entire universe!

She thought that's why the golden lady wanted to help Miciah find a human female to bring back to Belizair. Because of the Hotaling virus, it took one Amato, one Vesti, and one human to form a family and make babies. Unless Miciah found a genetic match or got asked to be a co-mate, he'd never have children.

Today was the last day she had in order to do what the golden lady wanted and go see Miciah herself. When she'd given Jeqon d'Amato the strands of hair she'd found in her mother's keepsake box, she hadn't told him who they belonged to. But in exchange for Jeqon testing them, she'd had to agree to tell him where they came from if one of them had the Fallon gene sequence in it.

When the hair she was hoping for was the one that came back positive, she'd begged him to keep it secret from the other scientists and to not tell her mother or fathers for just a few more days. Now her time was up.

A shout sounded several courtyards away. Followed by another. And then a whole chorus of voices was yelling her name.

Kaylee grabbed her backpack straps and sprinted even harder, covering the remaining distance to the Council building like she had wings on her feet instead of her back. She darted inside, running past two Amato women and an Amato man.

She thought maybe they said, "Halt", but she ignored them and rushed into the Council chamber. Just inside the doorway she stopped and held her breath so she could listen if anyone was chasing her. They weren't.

Kaylee exhaled quietly and looked around. The room resembled a courtroom on a TV program, except there were no benches for spectators and no seats for jurors. When the twelve Council members were listening to a complaint or making a judgment they sat behind a long, slightly raised judge's bench made of crystals.

In the middle of the judges' table was a set of scales. Her mom called it The Scales of Justice.

All along its base and arms were carvings of winged creatures. Zeraac had told her they were just some of the different forms the Fallon—the ancient winged ancestors of the Amato and Vesti—could take.

The scales seemed to tower above everything else in the room and Kaylee couldn't keep herself from walking over to them. She touched her finger to one flat tray and watched the scale tilt, remembering the day the Council members had voted on whether or not to hear the challenge that could have broken up her family.

Each council member had placed a token on either one side of the scale or the other. And in the end, it was Miciah's vote that decided.

Kaylee walked toward the door the Council members used. Thanks to her mom, she knew how to find Miciah's office if she went through that door.

She looked down at the wristbands she wore. They sparkled with the Ylan stones called the Tears of the Goddess. The sight of them made her square her shoulders. She had an important task to do and she wouldn't let the golden lady down.

Chapter One

ℒ

Miciah d'Vesti turned away from the window. He was restless, on edge. He felt worn down by the endless discussion and behind-the-scenes maneuvering, by the crushing responsibility that came with trying to guide Belizair through this time of devastation and change.

Hidden hostilities lying dormant between the Amato and Vesti for centuries now threatened to boil to the surface, and yet now more than ever, there was no place for anger or grudges. Not when the Hotaling virus would ultimately lead to their extinction if they didn't work together. Live together. Join together and form mate bonds with those humans carrying the Fallon genetic markers.

The Council scientists had found a solution for the unmated males. They'd also found a small measure of hope for the unbound females — though only a few knew of it and the Council hadn't decided on a course of action.

There was no hope for those Amato and Vesti who had bonded before the Hotalings struck. It was their fate that grieved Miciah more than any of the others.

He returned to his desk, stretching his wings as he contemplated what he should do next. He longed to be back in his home set high in the trees.

From his balcony he had only to launch himself into the sky to soar above a region of Belizair populated almost entirely by Vesti. From anywhere in the house he could enjoy the view, the dense forest for as far as the eye could see in one direction, the red mountains separating jungle from desert in the other direction.

11

A knock on the door made him sigh. Miciah said "Enter" without bothering to reach out mentally or read the display that would tell him who his unexpected guest was.

He was unprepared for the sight of the Earth child, Kaylee. A stab of regret pierced him, a sense of loss.

She could have been his daughter. And with her mother as his mate, there would have been additional children.

He hid his emotions behind a mask, retreated into politeness. "This is a surprise. Are you lost?"

Kaylee scowled at him and just as quickly as he'd felt the sting of pain, his emotions swung to the edge of smiling. "Then you were seeking me?"

His amusement deepening when Kaylee's lips pursed as though having found him, she wasn't exactly sure why she'd sought out his company.

"I need to talk to you," she finally said, coming to stand on the opposite side of his desk.

He waved toward the chair, wondering as he did so if the Earth females grew tired of sitting on furniture built with little or no backs and at a height to accommodate the winged Vesti and Amato. "Take a seat. Would you like something to eat or drink?"

Kaylee shook her head and let out a breath. He was different than she'd expected. Less stern. Maybe he only seemed fierce and scary when he was sitting in the Council chamber.

Before she'd actually *gotten* here, she'd known exactly what she was going to say to him. She'd rehearsed it a hundred times in her head. But now that she was standing this close to Miciah, she was afraid she was wrong.

What if the golden lady who visited her in her dreams wasn't the goddess of the Amato after all? What if the message she thought she was supposed to give Miciah was just wishful thinking?

Kaylee chewed on her bottom lip. She'd overheard Komet and Zeraac talking about how Miciah was the only child of an important Vesti clan-house. Now that she was looking at him, she didn't want to be wrong about what she had to tell him.

Miciah didn't know what to make of the child. Her expressions changed so rapidly he was left with only an impression she was worried about something, and yet no clear idea of what it was and why she would come to him, unless...

He stiffened and closed his mind to that avenue of speculation, though he went as far as to ask, "Is your mother still happy with Zeraac and Komet? Do they treat the two of you well?"

Kaylee face went from uncertain to indignant. "That's not why I'm here! Mommy and I love Zeraac and Komet!"

She pulled a knapsack from her shoulders and placed it on Miciah's desk. "I'm here because of you. I think I know how you can get a mate."

Miciah coughed to hide his startled amusement, thinking in that instant how well Kaylee and his mother would have gotten along. From the time he'd reached manhood, his mother had been parading Vesti females in front of him. Then the Hotaling virus struck.

When he'd first seen Ariel, he'd been tempted to claim her for the good of his clan-house, whether she was willing or not, whether she loved another or not. He'd been tempted even as they spoke privately in this very chamber. But in the end he'd made the only choice he knew he could live with. He'd let her go.

Miciah watched as the small human emptied her knapsack. It contained a thin bound book, a locket, and what looked like a folder full of papers.

She fussed with the contents then finally opened the book to reveal the photographs inside. "Mommy doesn't know I've got these things. They all belonged to her mother."

13

Kaylee flipped through the pages. When she found what she was looking for, she turned the book toward Miciah. "This is my grandfather and my grandmother on their wedding day. I never knew either of them. They didn't stay together for very long. Grandma died. Mommy says she can barely remember her father. She says he couldn't stay in one place very long. He liked to gamble and stay out all night. These are all the pictures there are of him, except for the newspaper clippings."

She reached for the folder and opened it. They showed her grandfather at various casinos, pictured with stacks of paper money in front of him.

"My grandmother saved all these clippings telling how he kept getting rich in Las Vegas then losing it all. For a while he had fifty million dollars." Small lips pursed in disapproval. "He didn't even put a single dollar of it in the bank. Then he lost it all in one week by playing dice."

Kaylee began shuffling through the articles. On more than one occasion, the man featured in them was accompanied by the same woman, a willowy dark-haired beauty who was very obviously pregnant in a later photograph. Her image made Miciah think about his own preference for dark hair and darker skin when it came to women.

True, he'd reacted to Ariel with her blonde hair and blue eyes. He would have happily mated with her and, no doubt, have experienced the full effects of the Vesti mating fever if she hadn't already been with Zeraac and Komet. But seeing the woman in the newspaper clipping…

A disgruntled sigh drew Miciah's attention back to Kaylee. She was frowning again. "Did you hear what I said?"

Miciah felt the heat rise to his face. An embarrassed laugh escaped before he could prevent it. "I'm sorry. I was immersed in the articles you were showing me."

His answer mollified the small human. She smiled and nodded. "Okay then. That's all right. I was just saying Mommy finally admitted that part of the reason her mother and father didn't live together was because he liked to be with different women but he didn't like to stay with any particular woman for very long."

Her earnest little face scrunched up as she captured his gaze. Miciah felt his heart melt and ache at the same time. What a fine daughter she would have made.

"Do you think this woman is pretty?" Kaylee asked, a delicate fingertip settling on the very image Miciah had been contemplating.

"Yes. Very."

The answer seemed to satisfy his imperious visitor. She nodded on some private thought and said, "There was another paper I wanted to show you but I couldn't find it in time. You'll just have to believe me when I tell you what it says."

Miciah only barely suppressed a smile. "Of course."

Kaylee pushed the open folder aside and reached for the last item she'd placed on his desk, the locket. She opened it gently and revealed the pictures inside.

Ariel's father was on the left, her mother on the right. A strand of hair from each of them was curled underneath the portraits.

"Jeqon d'Amato tested their hair for me," Kaylee said in such a matter of fact manner that Miciah couldn't resist a smile at the thought of this small boss bullying one of the Council's own scientists into working for her. "My grandfather was the one with Fallon genes."

Kaylee looked at Miciah intently, but when he didn't comment she looked pointedly at the picture of the dark-haired woman then flipped through the newspaper clippings until she got to the one where the woman was pregnant. This time Kaylee's small fingertip landed on the extended belly.

"The paper I saw was from a private investigator. It said this baby turned out to be a girl, Mommy's sister. I think Mommy meant to find her, only I got sick and then my first

15

daddy started always being at work. Mommy's sister would be your match, that's what I think."

Kaylee's revelation staggered Miciah, not because he thought there would be a match for him, but because she'd worried enough to try to find hope for him. "Kaylee..." he began only to trail off for lack of words.

"You can't give up," the small general said, her expression and tone fierce. "You've got to look for her. The golden lady wants you to."

He was almost afraid to ask. "The golden lady?"

Kaylee thrust her arms out so the Ylan stones on her wristbands glittered in a swirl of purple and green and red.

Miciah had heard the tale of how Komet and Zeraac's bands had merged with the Tears of the Goddess so all in their family unit had the same stones at their wrists, but he had not seen it for himself. Now he studied Kaylee's wristbands and felt an unnerving hope build in his chest.

The Amato placed great stock in the Ylan stone called the Tears of the Goddess, not just for the extraordinary healing properties the stones possessed, but because they believed those who held the Tears had been favored by their Goddess.

The Vesti valued the stones not because they played in to their religious beliefs, but because they were rare. Even so, Miciah did not discount Kaylee's claim or her reason for coming to him. It wasn't common knowledge, but the first pregnancy to occur since the Hotaling virus was introduced onto Belizair, came because of an Amato's dream.

"I will speak to Jeqon about this matter," Miciah found himself saying. "I'll have him set some of our bounty hunters to work in an effort to find your mother's sister."

"She'll be your mate," Kaylee said with utter confidence as she slipped the empty knapsack onto her shoulder. "I'll leave all this stuff with you. But you've got to take care of it, it belongs to Mommy."

"I will do so."

"Good. When you go to Earth, will you do something for me?"

Miciah found her happiness and hope contagious. "What?"

"Bring back a carton of chocolate ice cream. The biggest one you can find so I can share it with Mommy."

"I will make every effort to bring some back," Miciah promised.

"Okay then. I've got to go. I've got to get home before The Bossy Boys find me."

Miciah held his laugh until the little general left, then it burst out of him, filling him with a lightheartedness he hadn't experienced since the Hotaling virus was let loose on Belizair.

When his laughter finally subsided, he gathered the items belonging to Kaylee's mother and put them away. A touch to the flat screen on the surface of his desk confirmed what he'd guessed. Jeqon was on Belizair, in Winseka, waiting as the majority of Council scientists were, for the birth of the first children since scientists had found the Fallon gene sequence in selected humans.

The early pairings had yielded no results. It was only when Laith d'Amato shared Cyan, the female he was matched to, with his Vesti work partner and friend, Rykken, that a pregnancy took.

Cyan carried twins, as all the women did who'd been joined to a male of each race after the success of the first sharing. But whether her twins would be winged or not, was unknown, just as it was unknown whether they would be Amato or Vesti—or human whose link to the Fallon remained internal, present only in their genes.

Miciah tapped the keys allowing him to reach Jeqon. The scientist responded immediately.

Jeqon's face filled the screen and there was no mistaking the amusement in his expression or his voice when he said,

"Am I correct in thinking you had an unexpected visitor today?"

"Yes."

Miciah dared not allow his hope to show though his heart raced with it.

"Will you put off a trip to Earth until after Cyan's children are born?" Jeqon asked.

Everything inside Miciah stilled. "There's reason for me to go to Earth?"

Jeqon's smile held the answer. "Yes. I thought it appropriate to let Kaylee be the first to tell you of a possible mate. But after her initial visit to me, it took only a few words with Komet and his subtle questioning of Ariel for me to send word to the bounty hunters on Earth."

"They've located Ariel's sister?"

"Her name is Zoë Andreadis. Would you care to see a picture of her?"

"She's mine?"

"If you choose to claim her." Jeqon's expression became somber. "You're alone?"

"Yes."

"I used the experimental parameters in searching for the male with the greatest right to claim her, as the Council authorized us to do after Kaylee and Ariel's arrival on Belizair led to the discovery that there can be more than one match. Of the Vesti candidates, you share the most markers in common with Zoë."

A hard knot formed in Miciah's chest. "And among the Amato?"

"Only one was close. He scored almost as high as you did, well within the parameters if the old standard was applied."

The potential for future problems and added conflict between the two races made Miciah's muscles bunch with tension. At every turn, there were decisions to make, turbulence

18

to navigate. He resisted the urge to massage the tightness from his neck. "Who?"

"Iden, of the Cathetel clan-house."

Iden. It had to be Iden.

The image of the white-winged Amato with black hair and blue eyes flashed into Miciah's mind, infusing his cock with forbidden heat. Same sex liaisons were taboo among the Vesti, and he more than many others had something to lose if his desire was made public.

"Do you want me to send the picture of Ariel's sister and the information the bounty hunters gathered?" Jeqon asked.

"Yes."

Miciah hardly dared to breathe as the screen on his desk went dark rather than splitting into two transmission areas, signaling Jeqon's intention to afford him privacy when viewing the female for the first time—a gesture Miciah appreciated when an instant later, his cock went completely hard and his skin flushed with the beginnings of the Vesti mating fever at the sight of Zoë.

The resemblance to the woman pictured in the newspaper clippings the small general had shown him was there, but the daughter's beauty eclipsed the mother's. And Miciah's reaction to it nearly dropped him to his knees.

He gripped the edge of his desk to keep himself from grasping his cock as he devoured her with his eyes, taking in the willowy frame, the breasts that begged for a man's hands to cup them, a man's lips to suckle, the face surrounded by a riot of dark curls cascading downward to her shoulders.

A light sheen of sweat coated Miciah's chest. His fingers itched to comb through the silky locks. To feel it brushing against his thighs, his cock, and use it to hold her in position beneath him as he thrust into her and filled her with his seed.

The rising heat of the Vesti mating fever was reason enough to claim her. "Next image," Miciah said, before he disgraced himself by panting or bringing himself to relief, the sounds of it traveling through the audio link.

A map of Earth replaced the picture of his mate. As he watched, the map telescoped to become what he now recognized as the United States, and then the west coast of it, where several transport chambers existed. Finally zooming in on a place called Auburn.

"This is where she lives?" Miciah asked.

"At the moment, though the bounty hunter who located her thought it possible she was planning on leaving. Apparently she's a wanderer by nature."

The possessive instinct of the Vesti rose along with the mating fever, making it difficult for Miciah to keep his voice free of inflection. Males of his kind claimed one female and took her completely, totally, possessing her in every way so she would never crave another's touch. And even then, it was often impossible to allow her to be unattended and in the presence of an unmated male.

"She's being watched?"

"No. There is no apparent danger to her. I thought it better to authorize a tag in this case."

"Good," Miciah said, calming. On occasion, when there was fear of losing a potential bond-mate, Council scientists were allowed to send a bounty hunter to implant a tiny tracking chip. It was done at a distance, with a special device, so the female was not frightened or forewarned. The sting was no more painful than the bite of an insect and the chip was easily destroyed once she was claimed and mated, dissolving regardless during transport to Belizair.

"Transmit the frequency information as well as what's known of her daily activities and living arrangements. I will leave as soon as I've made the necessary arrangements."

"Done," Jeqon said and signed off.

Miciah left his office moments later, justifying what he was about to do with logic. There were political reasons for asking Iden to be his co-mate he told himself, closing his mind to any fantasies beyond that of sharing a woman with the Amato priest whose clan-house was one of the oldest and most powerful on Belizair.

Tensions had escalated as the birth of Cyan's twins neared. Despite the scientists' optimism that her pregnancy, as well as the others, would result in an Amato and a Vesti child for each bonded threesome, there were no guarantees.

Wings didn't manifest until after a baby was born. They emerged only when the wristbands were placed on the infant and a portion of the Ylan stones from the parents bands migrated to the child's.

It was a private moment, one to be witnessed only by close family members. It would be no less so for Cyan, Laith and Rykken, though all of Belizair would wait in agony for the outcome, both dreading the future it might define, and hoping for it.

So much rested on the first sharing. The first births.

The Amato feared their race was destined for extinction. They feared that in the end Belizair would belong to the Vesti because always before, when the races mixed to produce children, *all* those born were Vesti. And those offspring went on to produce only Vesti children, meaning the Amato clan-line was lost.

The Vesti feared their culture and beliefs would die out. Already they'd been forced to adapt.

Unlike the Amato who bonded in whatever variation was agreeable to those involved, sharing a female was unheard of among the Vesti. It was only one of the many differences between the two races.

There were those of both races who didn't agree with the current solution, who resisted change, who opposed introducing humans to Belizair because they feared what such a thing would mean. It made for a delicate balancing act, one Miciah understood completely.

Change needed to be managed. To be kept to a minimum, and where it was inevitable, held to a rate that smoothed the transition, allowing both Vesti and Amato to kept as much of their culture and traditions as possible.

Miciah stepped from the Council building. He unfurled his wings and launched himself upward, heading toward the Amato temple where he would find Iden.

The warm air caressed his bare torso and legs, teasing over the thin material of his loin covering where his cock remained hardened from its reaction to Zoë. He didn't will his erection to subside. Polite custom dictated it wouldn't be noted or commented on by anyone he encountered, and should there be private speculation, word of his departure for Earth to claim a mate would silence it.

Familiar anxiety settled into a hot, pulsing throb in Miciah's gut. He refused to let it slip lower, into his testicles and shaft, just as he refused to contemplate why he hadn't considered, even for an instant, a different Amato co-mate.

It was only right he offer Iden the chance to claim Zoë. Like him, Iden was an only son and had been under intense pressure to take a mate from an early age. Beyond that, Iden was well respected among the Amato and if one of their priests visibly embraced the sharing of a human mate...

Chapter Two

ℰℭ

Miciah landed in front of the temple built to serve the Goddess and Consort of the Amato. It was made entirely of Ylan stones. But unlike the elaborate places the humans often built to worship in, it was small, created to serve individuals and family groups.

He didn't look to the Amato Goddess and Consort for aid in his life's journey, but Miciah could feel the power radiating from the Ylan stones. He could understand how those who *did* believe felt a direct link to the Goddess and Consort while in their temple.

The door opened and Miciah stilled as a fellow Council member stepped out of the temple. He became hyperaware of the thick bulge of his cock pressing against his loin covering and his pulse rate sped up as he wondered if Iden had ever spoken of him to the Amato High Priest who also served on the Council.

Jarlath's raised eyebrow was his only response at seeing Miciah there. Mercifully, he passed with a tiny nod of acknowledgment, allowing Miciah to enter the temple without comment.

Iden stood behind a low altar. Diffuse, golden light bathed him, making the muscles of Miciah's stomach grow taut and his cock harden further. He forced himself forward, stopping when he reached the first of the pillows scattered on the floor for kneeling and sitting.

Incense wafted upward. Candle flames danced, inviting closeness and the sharing of secrets.

"Why was Jarlath here?" Miciah asked.

"His reasons are his own." Iden's gaze swept downward, lingering boldly on Miciah's erection before lifting. "It's not like you to allow yourself into my presence in such a state."

Miciah's nostrils flared at the taunt and the satisfaction in Iden's voice. But he preferred not to cross verbal swords with the only male he'd ever desired physically.

A touch to one of his wristbands and Zoë's image was projected onto the glossy surface of the low altar. Iden reacted as quickly to the human female as he himself had, the golden material of his loincloth no more hiding his sudden erection than the dark blue of Miciah's did.

"Who is she?" Iden asked.

"Her name is Zoë Andreadis. She's the sister to Zeraac and Komet's mate, Ariel. I've been matched to her."

"Congratulations."

Iden crossed his arms and widened his stance. A challenge? A defensive posture? His expression gave nothing way.

Tension coiled and knotted in Miciah's stomach as he was forced to admit to himself just how much he wanted Iden as a co-mate and how little it involved politics.

The Council had not decided on an official policy when two men were an exact match for the same human. Few outside the Council and its scientists knew that the parameters for matching the gene sequences had been experimentally broadened to avoid such a thing, with successful results.

Miciah resisted the urge to copy Iden's posture, but he shared the truth with him. "You are also a close match to her."

The dark eyebrows raised in silent query, forcing Miciah to elaborate, to say the words. "I'd like you to claim her with me."

Sensuous lips curved upward. "Am I your first choice?"

Miciah clenched his jaw as his cock spasmed in reaction to the smooth purr in Iden's voice. A telltale drop of arousal leaked, making him glad he wore a dark loin covering and the light in the temple was diffuse. "Yes."

By the Goddess, the human female was beautiful, Iden thought as he skirted the altar, stopping when he was inches away from Miciah. But would she accept his needs? Would Miciah finally admit to his own? Even for a mate and the possibility of children, Iden knew he wouldn't live a lie.

His heart thundered in his chest, making it difficult to appear unaffected by the situation. If he'd been the one presented with the possibility of a mate, he would have approached Miciah.

Iden moved further into Miciah's personal space, close enough so their hardened cocks nearly touched. Satisfaction scorched through him at the tightening of Miciah's features and the flash of need he couldn't hide.

"You seem to be forgetting something about me," Iden said.

"I'm not forgetting anything."

"And you're prepared to accommodate my desires? Or are you hoping our being inside our mate's body at the same time will be enough? That it will stop there?"

"If she's repulsed —"

"Then perhaps I'd better wait for a better match," Iden said, risking everything by stepping away.

His retreat was stopped by Miciah's hand gripping his arm. The firm fingers sent a hot bolt of lust straight to Iden's penis as he imagined that same hand clamping around his shaft.

"Come with me to Earth," Miciah said, as close to begging as he would allow himself. "Meet her."

"And if she's as open-minded as the Amato when it comes to coupling?"

Miciah's other hand clenched at his side. Perhaps this moment was inevitable, the end result of a desire he had never been able to fully suppress despite attempting it.

Images of Iden had slipped into his dreams from the first, breaking through cultural inhibitions just as the lust he'd experienced when they met shocked him to his core and sent him reeling for days afterward with the realization that he wanted another male.

Curse Iden for forcing him to say the words. For making him openly admit what would happen if Zoë found it erotic to watch or participate as her two mates also enjoyed each other.

Such a thing wasn't spoken of or acknowledged among the Vesti. But in the privacy of the home he would share with Zoë and Iden, Miciah knew he wouldn't say no to the needs Iden stirred in him. "Whatever happens when we are alone in our quarters, I will accept it as natural for our mate-bond."

"Good enough," Iden said, his gaze lowering to where Miciah's cock throbbed against the thin material of the loin covering. "For now."

* * * * *

The petite blonde across the table from Zoë looked up from the tea leaves she was studying and said, "You've been holding out on me."

"Is that an opinion? Or is it part of the reading?" Zoë teased.

"Oh, it's in the tea leaves all right."

Destiny's mischievous smile made Zoë fidget. When it came to seeing things, Destiny's talent was as accurate as her own, though in her case, she avoided the gift rather than embrace it.

"Chicken," Destiny said, correctly reading Zoë's thoughts.

Zoë did a fair imitation of a chicken clucking. "That's right."

26

Destiny shook her head, sending the feather and bead earrings swinging. "Doesn't matter, I'm going to tell you anyway. You want the 'bad though you might not think it's bad' news first? Or the, 'I'm so envious I want to scratch your eyes out' news?"

"Hmmm. Tough choice. Let's get the bad-but-maybe-not over with."

"Your wandering days are about to end."

A chill slid down Zoë's spine and she shivered. Okay. That could bad. The longer she stayed in one place, the stronger her out-of sync psychic gifts became and the more careful she had to be about where she went and who she touched.

"Now you know why I never let you read for me," Zoë joked.

"Trust me. Settling down is a small price to pay for the other thing I'm reading in the tea lives."

"Do we need a drum roll here?"

Destiny laughed. "Maybe." She glanced at the other patrons in the tearoom then leaned forward to whisper, "You remember the last time we sat in the hot tub drinking strawberry daiquiris and talking about fantasies?"

Zoë tensed, not from those memories, but from the dreams that had plagued her for the last week, making her wake up each morning covered in sweat and with her hand between her legs. "I remember."

"That's what I see in your future. Two men. As in a threesome. You and them." Eyebrows lifted and lowered dramatically. "And maybe even the two of them together, with you watching. Sound like anyone you know?"

If the dreams weren't just dreams, she could describe exactly what they looked liked. Black hair past their shoulders. One man darker skinned than the other. Both of them dominant, ultramasculine. The stuff of fantasies.

They hadn't done each other in her dreams. But if they wanted to, it was a definite turn-on for her.

Her cunt spasmed at the image. She shivered again, this time from heat, and clamped her legs together.

Across the table, Destiny's eyes widened then narrowed with suspicion. "Tell," she said, in a determined voice Zoë knew only too well. Destiny's dainty, petite body housed a tiger when it came to getting what she wanted.

"I've been dreaming about the same two guys for the last week," Zoë admitted.

"As in premonition?"

Zoë blushed. "I thought it'd been too long since..."

Destiny snorted. "Tell me about it. I could take on a football team myself."

"All hundred pounds of you, I'd like to see that."

"Voyeur. But that could come in handy if the guys like doing each other. Do I know them?"

"No. Neither do I."

"Tall, dark, and handsome?"

"With long black hair and bodies to drool over."

Destiny licked her lips. "Yummy. So are the dreams the reason you've suddenly decided to pump up the RV tires and roll out of town for the Sol Celebration? Have itch, need to scratch it. Not that I blame you. I think I might leave town too if I'd end up in a threesome with a couple of gorgeous guys."

Zoë shook her head. If her visions were *only* filled with hot sex and happy ever after, she'd be content to stay in one place. The trouble was that her gifts seemed to lock onto intense emotion, of the dark, depressing kind.

"No, the thing I told you about—my psychic gifts kicking in if I stayed in one place too long—happened. It'll only get worse if I don't move on."

Destiny nibbled on her bottom lip. "Maybe these guys are the answer. Didn't you say an old fortuneteller in Greece saw a future where you could use your gifts to help others? What were the words exactly?"

"When your heart is finally captured, the ability to see and feel will become one gift. Your touch will offer hope to those who have lost it."

"This could be it. I mean, she didn't specifically limit it one man. Did she?"

Hope fluttered through Zoë like a butterfly, creating a buffer against the memory of the old man whose hand had touched hers when they both reached for the same loaf of freshly baked bread at the grocery store the morning before.

He ended up in possession. She ended up smothered by despair that lasted all day and only ended with a vision at sunset, of him sitting next to a bedside, tears streaming down his face as his wife took a final breath after begging him to help her die rather than to exist in a state of helplessness and pain.

Once the door opened in the mental shields she'd learned to erect in order to survive her empathic psychic gift, there was no closing it. All it took was the touch of her hand to someone else's for their grief and sorrow to be hers—but that wasn't the worst of it.

Seeing where their dark emotions ultimately led when there was nothing she could do to prevent it or change the outcome was what she hated the most. If only her gifts were in sync. If only she could feel someone's sadness, or the darkness surrounding them, and see what it meant for the future *right then*, instead of getting the vision only when it was too late to change anything.

Hours could pass. Days or months before the unintended psychic link closed.

Her stomach churned, remembering strangers whose suicides she'd witnessed in her visions after a casual touch. Guilt followed, though intellectually she knew she couldn't have prevented those deaths.

She'd tried more times than she could count. And failed each one of them.

The only thing left was to keep moving, never staying in one place long enough for the door in her shields to open. She'd known a week ago that it was time to leave Auburn, but the dreams...maybe that's why she'd stuck around, because subconsciously she'd been waiting for the two men to show up.

Destiny tapped the side of the teacup, drawing Zoë out of her thoughts. "I bet you'll meet them at the Sol Celebration. I mean, it can't be coincidence. You seeing them in a dream. Me reading about them in the tea leaves. Under the circumstances, I'll even forgive you for holding out on me, especially if you send a picture of them, preferably full body and naked."

Zoë laughed. "What if I ask them to send a couple of their friends instead?"

"That works for me."

Silence descended and Zoë felt her throat close up as the time for saying goodbye drew closer. They lingered for a few minutes longer then stood and hugged.

"May wanted you to stop by her shop before you leave." Destiny wiped at her eyes. "I'd go with you and follow you back to the campground, but..."

"I know. This way is easier."

A final hug and Zoë left before they both broke down in tears. She walked past one historic building after another, thinking about Destiny's reading and all the psychics she'd visited, first with her grandparents and then solo, as she tired to turn her empath ability and *sight* into something useful.

Zoë rubbed her chest. Despite the hope, there was a sense of loss at the thought that her days on the road might come to an end. It's what she knew, and the articles she wrote about the places she visited paid the way.

She loved meeting people and learning about them. Loved observing them and getting the "feel" of each new place she parked the RV and called "home for now". Her grandparents had been the same way, right up until a heart attack had taken her grandfather and months later, a stroke killed her grandmother.

Thankfully she hadn't *seen* either death coming. But then, except for the dreams she'd been plagued with for the last week, she'd never caught glimpses involving own future.

She didn't know for sure where the gift of *sight* came from, most likely she'd inherited it from her biological father. It'd make sense given his lifestyle. Not that she'd ever met him.

Her empath ability came from her grandmother. Grams had been able to touch the full spectrum of emotion. In comparison, Zoë seemed programmed for darkness, while her mother seemed to be a thrill junkie—again, not that Zoë had a lot of firsthand knowledge.

She'd only been in the same room with her mother three or four times that she could remember. The majority of her impressions about her parents came from what she'd seen in newspaper clippings—Mom with a taste for high rollers, dangerous men and a fast lifestyle. Dad, the big-time Las Vegas gambler, who won and lost millions and always had a new woman on his arm.

Neither of them had been even remotely interested in being a parent. Luckily for her, her grandparents had been willing, more than willing despite being fifty-one and fifty-six when she came into existence.

They'd packed up and gone to Las Vegas the day they'd learned of their daughter's pregnancy, then stayed there until Zoë was born just to be certain their daughter didn't change her mind about letting them raise the baby and decide to abort or place their grandchild up for adoption to the highest bidder.

Zoë's throat tightened. Her grandparents had been gone for three years and she still missed them.

She pushed thoughts of her parents and grandparents aside. Moving on always stirred them up.

May's Trash and Treasures came into sight when Zoë rounded the corner. Tourists emerged from the shop as she reached it. They were ecstatic over the purchase of an old bottle and a ceramic plate.

A cowbell announced her arrival. May looked up from a cardboard box coated with dust and cobwebs and leaving streaks of the same across the denim overalls and flannel shirt she wore. Her wrinkled face blossomed into a toothless smile. "Good! Destiny remembered my message."

May stepped away from the box and gave Zoë a hug. "I've got something for you. A small gift. Business is booming thanks your article!"

Zoë glanced at where a copy of the article now hung in an old frame on the wall behind the cash register. "You don't have to give me anything."

"Of course not, but I want to. Now do me a favor while I fetch your gift. See if you can spot my dentures. Damn things got away from me again. Meant to put them on first thing when I got here but I set them down somewhere instead. Then James stopped in with some stuff he picked up at a yard sale, and right about the time he left, Sasha showed up with a rocking horse, and then..."

Zoë laughed. "Are they in the red case or are they loose and poised to bite whoever locates them?"

"That'd be something, wouldn't it? Might cost me a pretty penny in a lawsuit if it happened, but you could write up an article for the *National Enquirer* and get the money back." May cackled. "That'd really put Trash and Treasures on the map."

She disappeared behind the cluttered counter with its antique cash register and collection of knickknacks. Zoë began searching the area just inside the front door.

"Are you missing your keys too?" Zoë asked a moment later, holding up a paper bag full of well-used stuffed toys in one hand and a ring of keys in the other.

May straightened. In the short time she'd been behind the counter, wisps of gray hair had come loose from her bun. "Damn. Did I set those down somewhere too?"

Zoë jingled the keys. "Looks like it."

"My teeth with them?"

Zoë crouched in front of the chair where she'd found the keys underneath the bag. Sure enough, the familiar red case was on the floor. "Here they are."

"Good," May said. She spritzed something in her hand with a small water bottle she kept near the cash register for cleaning up trash and treasures alike, then folded the item into a cloth to dry.

Zoë took keys and dentures to the counter and set them down. "I'm not leaving until I see you pocket the keys and put the dentures in your mouth."

May laughed. "Probably a good thing. Now close your eyes and hold out your arms. No cheating."

Zoë did as she was told and felt a bracelet go on one wrist then the other. Strange, she thought, feeling a subtle tightening, as if her body heat had warmed the metal so it molded and clung to her skin.

"You can look now."

Zoë's breath caught at the delicate bands fashioned as though a string of butterflies flew in a narrow silver meadow. She brought her arms up for a closer inspection, marveling at the fine craftsmanship. The electric blue stones with streaks of black seemed to flow unbroken from one butterfly to the next.

"I love them," Zoë said, meaning it and hating the thought of parting with them. But she had a feeling they were valuable, priceless if they were offered to the right buyer, and May was old. "I know someone in San Francisco who deals in high-end jewelry, May. I—"

"Nonsense. They're on your wrists and that's where they belong. Say another word about them ending up somewhere else and I'll set my teeth on you."

Zoë glanced at the case with the dentures in it and laughed. She leaned across the counter and gave May a hug. "Thank you."

"You're welcome."

Zoë ran a finger along the bracelet on her left wrist. She couldn't find a latch for removing it. It was the same with the band on her right arm.

Weird, Zoë thought, but given May's threat and her own lack of desire to remove the bracelets, she didn't ask where the clasps were. She'd figure it out later.

"How'd they end up at Trash and Treasures?"

"Otis brought them in. Found them when he was prospecting. You know him, if it's not gold, he doesn't see the value."

Zoë grinned at that. Over the years she'd written a lot of articles on how the dream of finding gold in the Sierras wasn't dead, not by a long shot. Executives sporting thousand-dollar suits for most of the year, college students on break, families with children of all ages—during the summer the dream of hitting a vein or pulling up a pan loaded with nuggets had them all heading for the mountains.

Then there were the old-timers like Otis, who discovered just enough gold to keep them looking for "the big one". They were men in heavily patched clothing who drove beat-up old cars and hunted or fished for most of their food, who kept the location of their current camp a secret and only came into town when necessary.

"I'm glad he brought the bracelets to you," Zoë said, tracing the seamless flow of stones with a fingertip before sighing as the moment she'd been delaying for the last week arrived. "I better get going. I want to get to the desert and settled in before dark."

Chapter Three

ε⊃

Iden smiled as he viewed the gathering in the canyon below where he and Miciah stood. It spread from one end to the other, a brightly colored city of tents and campers and cars. It hummed with life and music and human energy.

He understood completely why the Fallon had been drawn to Earth over and over again. There was a passion in humans, a craving to create for its own sake. To get in touch with emotions whether they were dark or light and expose them, using their lives as both a canvas and a source of inspiration.

Those below had come together, not to worship a deity, but to celebrate art in all its forms, and in doing so, they pulled power from the land and sky around them. The Ylan stones on Iden's wrists pulsed with it, feeding and being fed in turn by his anticipation of descending into the mass of humanity below and finding Zoë. Of taking a mate...and taking Miciah.

A glance to his right and down revealed the hard outline of Miciah's cock against the front of what the bounty-hunter who'd met them when they emerged from the transport chamber called cargo shorts. Iden grinned. He definitely approved of the cargo concealed in Miciah's garments. He had no doubt their soon-to-be mate would approve of it as well.

He'd bluffed in the temple, needing to hear Miciah admit to the attraction between them, preferring open consent over seduction. Since arriving in Winseka to serve the Amato there at the request of Jarlath, and meeting Miciah, Iden had known that ultimately his future and that of the Vesti representative from the jungle region would be entwined.

He replayed the moment when their eyes met as they touched their bands together in formal greeting for the first time, when mutual desire pierced the mental barricade Miciah had no doubt spent his entire life erecting in order to hide the truth of his sexuality from himself. He'd felt Miciah's shock, his self-denial as his cock hardened. And he hadn't been the least bit surprised when Miciah avoided being alone with him from then on, even as Miciah unconsciously sought him out.

Whether Zoë initially accepted that her two mates would also be lovers didn't matter to Iden. In the end she would not only accept it but find immense pleasure in it.

He believed it completely. Totally. With a sureness that had only deepened when Miciah told him about Kaylee's dream of a golden lady.

He'd never met the Earth child, but he knew she wore the Tears of the Goddess at her wrists. He glanced down at the bands on his wrists. Two were his own, placed on him at birth by his parents. The remaining bracelet, empty of Ylan stones, was meant for Zoë.

They'd been allowed to transport from the chamber to this location, but from here on out, they were on foot. He rolled his shoulders, finding the weight of the small backpack strangely comforting, a sensory replacement for his transmuted wings.

"Shall we go claim our mate?" Iden asked, speaking out loud as was his custom even on Belizair.

Miciah turned his head and their eyes met, making Iden's cock throb. By the Goddess, what was it about this particular Vesti that made him want to conquer and be conquered?

He'd had male lovers before, all of them Amato, all of them seeking tenderness and caring. They'd been friends before passion turned them into bedmates, and remained friends afterward when they'd drifted into other couplings, same-sex and otherwise.

Such wouldn't be the case with Miciah. But then Miciah exuded the raw possessiveness of his race, the primal need to thoroughly dominate. It was there beneath the veneer he wore in order to serve his people and his region as a member of the Council.

Iden couldn't wait to see it stripped away, though at the beginning of their erotic dance with their mate, he fully intended to concentrate his efforts on Zoë. She was the nucleus of their joining, the all-important center. Without her, their future and Belizair's were greatly diminished.

"Primitive," Miciah muttered, making Iden laugh.

"I was thinking the same thing," he said, though instead of the nature of their yet un-begun sex life, he knew Miciah meant the lack of technological development here that was about to force them into a long walk.

Miciah's gaze dropped, as if picking up on Iden's thoughts. His nostrils flared and his jaw tensed at the sight of Iden's cock pressed rigidly against the Earth garments.

"Let's go," Miciah said, adjusting the pack he wore. "We'll be lucky if we get to the camp by dusk."

Iden refrained from reaching out to touch Miciah. Miciah might have agreed to becoming lovers, he might crave it as much as Iden did, but he wasn't comfortable with it and probably wouldn't be until they lay with Zoë.

"After you," Iden said, tilting his head in the direction of the narrow trail leading downward. "It's fortuitous Jeqon had her implanted with the tracking chip, otherwise I suspect nights of sleeping on the ground and days of searching for her wouldn't improve your mood."

* * * * *

The air was as much of a canvas as the paint-splattered one the artist in front of Zoë was using. It smelled like desert sage and diesel, held the scent of burning wood and hints of hashish, barbequed meat and homemade wine as well as incense and patchouli.

Zoë lifted her face, letting the last of the sun's rays caress her skin. It felt good to be here. Right to be here. And maybe—

"Hey, beautiful, long time no see," a man's voice murmured in her ear from behind her an instant before masculine lips touched her neck and firm hands gripped her hips, holding her against a lean, familiar body.

"Jason," she said, smiling, turning to give him a hug and noticing as she did that he'd gotten rid of the dreads in favor of a clean-shaven scalp and another eyebrow piercing.

He flashed a devastating grin. "In the flesh."

She stepped back and studied what wasn't hidden beneath cutoff shorts. His body was a testament to his work as a tattoo artist. Every picture was his own creation, part of a dreamscape of winged creatures.

Zoë lifted her hand and twirled her finger. He obeyed her command and turned slowly.

"You're running out of room," she said when he was facing her again.

"That's what reincarnation is for, babe. Fresh body, fresh slate."

She grinned. "I don't think it works that way. Next life you could end up a soldier or a boxer."

"Not me. I'm a lover. Not a fighter." Jason made a show of looking around. "You here by yourself?"

The image of the two men she'd been dreaming about rose in her thoughts and sent a ripple of heat downward, through her belly and cunt. "For now."

"Right off the top of my head I can think of at least three guys who'd be just your type." He grinned. "Separately or all together."

She shook her head. "I'm good."

"Okay. But if you change your mind, I'm camped over in the indigo section." He pointed to where a temporary flagpole sporting an indigo flag bearing the letter *I* hung.

"I'm in yellow."

"They give you a map and the official schedule when you pulled in?"

Zoë nodded. The camp was divided into twenty-six sections with bathrooms, water and power sources, first-aid and security stations marked, along with main stages and any other important locations. The schedule covered only the big events. It'd be impossible to pin down any others since most of them were spontaneous—a jam session that turned into a dance, a paint-making demonstration that turned into a discussion of tribal artwork and tattooing.

"Don't miss the band. They're amazing." Jason glanced at where the sun was disappearing behind a mountain. "Speaking of which, I'd better go collect my current significant other so we can stake out our piece of ground near the stage."

Zoë gave him another hug before he disappeared into the throng of people. She noticed others packing up their art and putting it away or heading in the direction of the night's entertainment with blankets tucked under their arms and coolers in their hands.

She lingered for a while, going down an alleyway where jewelry makers had gathered, pausing in front of each campsite to look at the work on display, before turning a corner to find the focus had shifted to weaving and making clothing.

Shawls and sweaters made of alpaca yarn hung side by side with those made of sheep wool and colored with plant dye. Wooden spinning wheels whirled and women of all ages gathered at looms to share stories and knowledge.

They'd welcome her if she joined them. It was one of the things she loved about the Sol Celebration. It was Woodstock without the emphasis on drugs and music—though there was an ever-present background of guitars, drums and singing, along with plenty of "free love".

The inner muscles of her channel clenched, dampening her panties with arousal. Whether they were part of the fortuneteller's prophecy or not, she wouldn't say no if the men who'd shown up in her dreams turned up in her reality. It'd been a long time since she'd invited anyone back to her bed or accepted an offer to visit someone else's.

She left "Weaver's Alley" and wandered through an eclectic mix of artisans on her way back to where the RV was parked. Because she was late to the gathering, she was just about as far away from the stage where tonight's featured band was playing as possible.

Not that it'd matter in terms of finding a place to spread out a blanket and lie beneath the stars. The camp city hadn't been allowed to grow beyond the main stage. There was plenty of desert to occupy, and for couples, enough space to afford privacy for enjoying more than the music and the nightscape.

Zoë stopped long enough to buy a gyro at a food stand, and finished eating the spicy sandwich by the time she reached her campsite. Except for unrolling the awning, she hadn't done anything to turn it into a gathering place. The long drive from Auburn had made her too antsy to get out and walk around.

On a whim she changed into a long skirt and a loose peasant blouse. They were definitely shades of the Sixties, but she always felt sensuous and sexy in them.

Of course, that might have a lot to do with the lack of a bra and the thin scrap of material impersonating panties, she thought with a grin. But she could get away with a hell of a lot less in the way of clothing here and tonight she wanted…

Her heart raced with the sudden insight that she was dressing for the men she'd been dreaming about. Why was she so sure they'd show up?

Zoë caught herself tracing the stones flowing unbroken from one butterfly into the next. It wasn't the first time. It had happened repeatedly while she was driving, so many times she must have rubbed off a layer of grime she hadn't been aware they possessed.

Their color seemed deeper, more vibrant. Warmer. As if they'd absorbed her body heat and come alive because of it.

Zoë laughed at her own flight of fancy. It was definitely time to head for the opposite end of camp and lose herself in music.

* * * * *

If humans had appealed to the Fallon, it soon became obvious to Iden that those on this planet were equally drawn to the Amato and Vesti descendents of the Fallon. Even with their wings transmuted into unseen particles by the Ylan stones, every step was a battle. Men and women alike found a reason to stop them, some offering sex with a subtle glance or touch, others with bold words and equally bold hands.

Iden took it in stride and found immense enjoyment in watching Miciah confront what he least wanted to confront, the dual nature of his sexuality. Had Zoë known what awaited her, their mate couldn't have picked a better place for them to meet for the first time and explore what they would soon mean to each other. There was an openness here, an atmosphere of celebration and experimentation and acceptance Iden doubted would easily be found elsewhere.

He grinned when a young male wearing eye makeup and extremely tight pants approached Miciah. But rather than let the scene play out, he spared the boy and used the moment to reinforce a message.

"He's with me," Iden said, closing the small distance between him and Miciah so their bare arms touched.

Desire surged between them, as it had from their very first meeting. Miciah tensed but didn't pull away. *Progress,* Iden thought, satisfied for now.

Miciah's stomach tightened into a knot even as his cock pulsed at the contact of skin against skin. He felt as though he'd been dipped in one of the lava pools found on the jungle planet of Farini, yet at the same time, he felt speared by ice.

Was his willingness to couple with another male so obvious? Had some barrier hiding the nature of his sexuality fallen when Iden forced him to admit the truth of what their relationship would be if Zoë was accepting of it?

Never had he been approached with such confidence and propositioned so blatantly by members of his own sex. It was disconcerting, terrifying if he allowed himself to worry at what it meant for his return to Belizair.

He pushed forward, noting how yet another human squinted, though the sun had long since disappeared and it was very nearly full dark. He thought back to how often he'd glimpsed a surprised, disbelieving expression as he and Iden passed, as if their wings were visible, at least for an instant, until human minds hid them as something that couldn't exist.

Such a reaction indicated the presence of Fallon genes and there seemed to be a higher percentage of them *here*, among those with an artistic nature, than in the general population. Relief poured into Miciah then as he desperately latched on to the reason he'd been propositioned so many times by men. They were drawn to him because he, too, was a descendant of the Fallon, and not because they'd guessed at his fantasies of Iden.

Miciah relaxed and made a note to himself to speak with Jeqon about his observations. Bounty hunters should be sent to gatherings like this one. There could be dozens of matches…

Worry returned in a rush, of a different nature. Despite the desperate situation on Belizair, integrating large numbers of humans all at one time risked adding to the already increased tensions. Change to their world needed to be controlled. It—

Enough, Iden said, the word slicing across Miciah's thoughts. *If I were to guess I'd say you're consumed with deliberations regarding the fate of Belizair. Forget your duties as a Council member while we are on this planet. Forming a mate-bond should take precedence. No one will fault you or judge you for focusing all of your attention on what we are trying to build for ourselves. Do you want Zoë to believe she is only a means to an end and has no value in her own right, if she'll have us at all?*

Denial screamed through Miciah—both at the thought she'd reject them and the possibility she would believe they didn't want her for herself. Upon seeing her image he'd nearly dropped to his knees as heat surged through him with the stirring of the Vesti mating fever. When they finally reached her, it would take all his control not to pounce.

You are correct. From this moment on, I will close my mind to thoughts of Belizair or my duties there.

Good, Iden said, but his reply was lost in a roar of lust as they pushed through the last of the standing humans and glimpsed Zoë in the distance, kneeling as she unrolled a blanket and smoothed it flat on the sandy desert floor.

Need such as Miciah had never known shot through his cock like a lightning strike. A growl escaped before he could stop it when Iden moved forward purposely, his attention completely focused on Zoë.

Primitive urges assailed Miciah, the Vesti need to fight any rival who would lay claim to a chosen female. He struggled against the desire to put himself between Zoë and Iden, to warn Iden away from her then take her to place where he could mount her repeatedly and possess her thoroughly, until his name was the only one imprinted on her heart and soul and body.

Are you coming? Iden purred into his mind.

With the words came an image of the two of them taking Zoë at the same time. It was enough to deflect the seething possessiveness brought on by the Vesti mating fever, turning it into a violent need to be inside her, his cock rubbing against Iden's as the three of them became one.

Yes, Miciah said, easily catching up to Iden and matching him stride for stride as they maneuvered their way around couples and groups of humans sitting and lying on blankets, some of them engaged in the very activity Miciah planned to be doing shortly, lovemaking.

His jaws clenched against the need to immediately press his mouth to the tender spot at the base of her neck and let his mating teeth finally slip out of their hidden sheaths for the first time in his life. He shuddered in anticipation of the heightened pleasure that would occur at the moment of climax, when the serum making a female easy to track and that had once helped bring about pregnancy in the Vesti, would flow through his fangs. His hands fisted and unfisted as he imagined piercing her, both with his cock and his mating teeth, sinking into her body and marking her with his scent and his bite.

As if sensing their presence and their carnal intent, Zoë glanced up. Miciah felt the impact as their eyes met.

His heart thundered in his chest. His cock screamed in protest when her attention shifted to Iden.

"Exquisite," Iden murmured, lust coiling in his belly and snaking down through his shaft until each step was sweet torture.

He'd known on Belizair that she was the one he wanted to bond with. But even knowing it, he hadn't anticipated her true effect on him. Desire such as he'd never known crashed through him, opening a place only she would be able fill.

"We won't leave her side until she agrees to return home with us," Miciah said, his voice holding the unwavering resolve of a Vesti in the grip of the mating fever.

"Agreed. She is ours to pleasure and protect."

There was no turning back now.

Chapter Four

ॐ

The band onstage and the people who'd gathered to listen to it faded from Zoë's consciousness. She forgot what she was doing though her hands kept moving, shaking slightly as they rubbed over the blanket, ensuring there were no rocks underneath it.

Her cunt wept and her stomach quivered as the two men approached. Looking away from them was impossible.

She'd *known* they were going to be here, and yet a part of her hadn't dared to really believe it. A part of her still didn't.

They were a fantasy moving toward her with predatory intensity, with hungry expressions and a masculine perfection that tightened her nipples and sent spasms of need through her. It was like her dream, only more so.

A soft moan escaped as they neared. She bit her bottom lip to keep another one from doing the same.

Her mouth went dry. Her breath short.

"May we join you?" the lighter-skinned one asked.

She managed a nod and only barely suppressed a shiver as they sat on either side of her, swamping her with their heat and scent.

"I'm Miciah," the darker one said, his golden eyes making her think of a large cat, a mountain lion or leopard.

"And I'm Iden," his companion said.

"Zoë," she said, her voice coming out husky, like an invitation to push her onto her back and cover her with their bodies.

It was a good thing she'd already accepted that she wouldn't say no to them if they turned up in her life. After a

45

week of dreaming about their touch, of waking up with her hand cupping her mound and her fingers jammed into her channel as she desperately sought relief, she was primed for them.

She licked her lips and struggled to come up with a complete sentence, wanted to turn her thoughts away from sex long enough to get to know them first. They made it impossible by leaning in as if they intended to kiss her at the same time.

Zoë suppressed a whimper at the image of their mouths on hers, their tongues tangling. They exuded raw sensuality, all of it directed at her so she didn't know if they also felt it toward one another.

Miciah's nostrils flared and the color of his eyes intensified, turning molten and making her curl her legs in an effort to ease the throbbing between her thighs.

The blue of Iden's became a dark sea of desire. "You are beautiful," he said.

"I could say the same about the two of you," she managed, fighting to keep her fingers from combing through the black waves of Iden's hair and the straight length of Miciah's, from grasping it and pulling them to her so she could touch her lips to theirs.

The press of her hard nipples against the peasant blouse attested to just what they did to her. Wet inner thighs and the scent of desire made her feel like a primal woman in search of mates. Images of going to her elbows and knees in an invitation for them to mount her had her cunt clenching and heat climbing up her neck and into her cheeks.

Miciah's gaze left her face and traveled downward. She fisted her long skirt in her hands to keep from arching her back and thrusting her breasts forward at the hungry expression on his face as he looked at her chest.

"Beautiful doesn't do you justice," he said, his voice so low it rumbled out like a growl. "I'm glad we found you here by yourself."

Because she'd dreamed of them, the possessiveness in his tone was darkly thrilling instead of unsettling. It sent a shiver of erotic fear through her, deepening the desire instead of chilling it.

She glanced at Iden and found him studying her, measuring her reaction. He pulled her hand away from her skirt, lifted it to his mouth and pressed a kiss to her palm, letting her feel the slightest caress of his tongue.

"A few minutes later and we would no doubt have had competition," he said, his eyes narrowing suddenly as his attention shifted to the bracelet on her wrist. "How did you come by these?"

She noticed the bands he wore then, three of them, though one was unadorned by gems. Instead of butterflies, his were engraved with...falcons maybe, something winged and fast. But it was the stones that sent a little ripple of surprise through her.

They weren't the same color as hers, yet their texture, the way they seemed to swirl with life made her think they could have come from the same place. In the fading light, the black stones held a white glitter, like the Milky Way at night.

Miciah grasped her other hand. The contact made her body tighten further. She shivered, assaulted by the image of them holding her down as they tortured her with their mouths and hands. More arousal slid from her channel to coat her inner thighs.

Their grip on her firmed, as if they'd read her fantasy and caught the scent of her desire. She forced her attention to Miciah's wrists and saw he wore similar bands, two with gems and one unadorned.

The stones were the same black with hints of white. But instead of birds of prey, the creatures looked like Pteranodons, one of her favorites when it came to prehistoric creatures.

It fit Miciah, just as the falcon fit Iden. There was an elegance to Iden, and though she imagined most saw a civilized veneer on Miciah, just underneath the surface of it was a man who would just as soon drag his woman off to the cave and fuck her than take her out to dinner as part of seducing her.

I'm good with both, she thought, suppressing a smile when Miciah proved her theory by leaning in, his voice holding a promise of violence as he demanded to know who'd given her the bracelets.

As if worried Miciah's approach might scare her off, Iden leaned in and whispered kisses along her jaw to end at her ear. His fingers explored the bracelet on her wrist as if looking for the clasp.

Given his own bands, she wondered if he'd accomplish what she couldn't, and find a way to remove the bracelet. Not that she intended to let him.

Despite owning the bracelets for only a short period of time, they already felt like they were a part of her. Maybe it was because they were now wrapped up in memories of Auburn, of Destiny's prediction as well as her own dreams. On the drive to the Sol Celebration, she'd come to see them as symbolic of the hopes she had, that one day her psychic gifts would evolve like a butterfly from a cocoon and be unified into something beautiful, something she could use to make the world a better place.

"The stones and the butterfly imagery seem familiar to me," Iden said, his lips grazing her ear and making her shudder with need. "But I can't remember where I've seen them before. How did you come by them?"

His breath and the proximity of his mouth and tongue to her ear made her breasts swell until they ached. If they hadn't been holding her wrists, she wouldn't have been able to keep her fingers from going to her nipples, or dragging their hands to her chest.

"May gave them to me before I left Auburn."

Her answer caused Iden's eyes to widen with speculation and Miciah's to narrow with determination. Molten eyes bored into hers as Miciah's free hand cupped her chin. "I can share you with Iden, but not with anyone else, not even another female. You desire us. Your body doesn't lie. And we won't leave you unsatisfied."

Lust and embarrassment hit Zoë in equal measure. It added heat to her face and made her glad the last of the daylight had disappeared.

The darkness and tolerant atmosphere found at the Sol Celebration granted everyone the illusion of privacy. Though between the moon above, and the flickering candles nearby filling the night air with incense, she could still make out Miciah's features.

"May is a friend," Zoë said. "Nothing more." And because Miciah was closer, she closed the distance between them and teased him with the touch of her tongue along the seam of him lips. "Besides, I like men. Always have, though I have no problem with women who prefer other women."

A hot fury of lust scorched Miciah. It burned away all thought, leaving behind only raw need and the desire to explore his mate's body until no part of it was left untouched.

On a growl his mouth opened and his tongue found hers, twining and tangling in a dance of dominance that could only end in one way, with her complete submission. Her soft moan fed his hunger. Her sultry scent nearly had him freeing himself from the confining Earth clothing so he could force her hand to his cock. Or her lips.

The very thought of her taking his cock that way sent a shudder through Miciah and had him struggling not to break off the kiss and urge her mouth downward. Iden's hand sliding around to cup Zoë's breast, brushing against his bare chest and nipple in the process made him moan and harden further. The exquisite touch of Iden's skin to his and the heady deepening of Zoë's scent at being caressed by both of them threatened his control.

Between them her body vibrated with need. Soft sounds of pleasure slid from her mouth into his, feeding the fever in him.

Though he'd asked Iden to be his co-mate, at the moment they'd pushed through the crowd and he'd seen Zoë, part of Miciah had wondered if he could truly stand the sight of another man touching her, of another man making her cry out in pleasure.

Now he knew. With Iden he could. With Iden, the desire was heightened.

He was intensely aware of Iden's mouth trailing kisses along her neck and ear, of Iden's hands on her breast and side. It aroused him to be claiming a mate with Iden, to be working toward the ultimate goal of gaining her love and seeing her grow heavy with their children. Because of her, there would be true intimacy, something more than a sating of lust when he and Iden finally acted on their attraction.

Lost in passion, they'd freed her hands. Miciah moaned as Zoë's fingers combed through his hair. He closed his eyes, imagining her caressing the edges of his wings and sliding underneath to the sensitive places where they joined to his body. Almost reflexively he rid himself of the backpack, setting it at the edge of the blanket as Iden did the same.

He cursed the necessity of hiding his true form from her. The Fallon had once walked freely in this world, as had the Vesti and Amato long ago. They'd been viewed as deities by humans, but at the moment, it was Miciah who wanted to do the worshipping. He wanted to start at her lips and move to her breasts before burying his face between her thighs and tasting her.

50

In perfect accord they eased her backward onto the blanket then settled on either side of her, their thighs touching as they wedged their legs between hers, their torsos blocking their actions from view as they each braced themselves on an elbow and looked down at her.

At the sight Iden's fingers stroking the smooth, tanned flesh of Zoë's belly and dipping into her navel, arousal escaped from the slit in Miciah's cock head. His hand joined Iden's on her abdomen, only higher, just beneath where her blouse had bunched underneath her breasts, the soft material doing nothing to hide taut nipples and rapid breathing.

On Belizair women wore only thin trousers made of the same cloth as a male's loin covering. They didn't cover their breasts or bind them, as if what they represented — sexual maturity and the ability to provide nourishment for their young — was something to be ashamed of.

Miciah pushed his hand underneath her blouse. He paused to caress the silky underside of her breast before covering her nipple possessively.

Mine.

The claim reverberated through him, savage and primal. The mating fever of the Vesti burned hotter, turning his mind into a churning red sea of conflicting emotion and instinct.

Despite his willingness to share Zoë and his enjoyment of it, Miciah fought against instinctively baring his teeth and forcing Iden away from her.

Zoë's gasp drew his eyes back to her belly. As Miciah watched, Iden's hand slipped beneath the waistband of her skirt just as their mental connection opened, flooding Miciah with exquisite sensation and erotic images.

A bolt of heat arrowed through his cock. His palm rubbed aggressively over Zoë's nipple and he drank in her cry, savored it like a man who'd been lost in the desert for a lifetime.

Iden nearly came as his fingers glided over Zoë's erect clit to find swollen folds and slick, hot woman. She was so wet, as ready for them as they were for her.

He'd felt an instant of unadulterated fear when he'd noticed the bracelets she wore. For the span of a single heartbeat, he would have sworn the Ylan stones at his wrists pulsed in recognition, like to like.

Impossible, he told himself. He'd never seen that shade of blue streaked with black on Belizair. And though there was something familiar about the bands with their butterfly device, the knowledge fluttered at the edge of his memory.

Later, he thought. There'd be plenty of time when they returned to Winseka to study the bands. At the moment he was engaged in a delicate dance with Miciah as they found the rhythm necessary for sharing a woman and building a life together. For now, he wanted only to study the woman he would soon mate with.

Iden felt the effort it took for Miciah to hold himself still as another male lowered his head to claim Zoë's lips in a first kiss. Not to strike, when she opened for another, her tongue greeting, sliding sensuously in an invitation to plumb the depths of her mouth.

Iden moaned. His hips jerked as his cock urged him to replace his fingers with it, to let it slide through her lower lips and be surrounded by wet heat.

Where Miciah had shown Zoë dominance, Iden fought to show her tenderness, to demonstrate with his actions that between them, they could see to her needs. She would learn he could be as demanding a lover as Miciah, just as she would no doubt learn Miciah was capable of gentleness, and in the end, they would be *all* to her.

Satisfaction surged through him as her back arched and she gave him the sounds of her pleasure as she'd done with Miciah. Her fingers tangled in his hair, holding him to her though nothing could have made him retreat now that he was in possession of her lips.

She was everything he'd ever dreamed of in a mate. Uninhibited, unashamed of taking and receiving pleasure.

The Ylan stones at his wrists vibrated subtly, growing denser in preparation for the binding, when half of them would migrate to the bands he and Miciah would soon give Zoë. He was aware of Miciah's hand stroking downward, over her belly, joining his between their mate's thighs.

A shudder went through the three them, physical desire coalescing into a tight gathering of lust. There was no differentiating between seducers and seduced.

"Will you let us have you?" Iden whispered against her lips when the need for breath forced an end to their first kiss.

"Yes, but not here."

He became aware of the music then. Heavy rock pulsed through the air and ground. The smell of marijuana mingled with that of incense. Rhythmic grunting behind him marked a place in the darkness where another couple fucked and he was glad she preferred privacy for their mating.

"Take us back to your campsite," he murmured, nibbling on her bottom lip. "Let us prove to you that no one else can satisfy you as we can."

Her smile was a caress to his heart. "I'm already convinced. The two of you are the stuff of erotic fantasies."

"Only your fantasies," he said, running his tongue along the seam of her lips. "Those are the only ones we care to be in."

Zoë opened her mouth and touched her tongue to Iden's. They'd been in her dreams for a week. She didn't understand the why or how of it, but the reality was so much better.

She wanted to see them, touch them, spend all night making love to them.

And in the morning…

Zoë pushed away thoughts of it. She'd deal with tomorrow when it arrived.

Her hand joined theirs, sliding beneath skirt waistband and panties into humid heat. She'd meant only to urge them away from her cunt while she still had the will to wait until they got back to her trailer before going further, but her fingers tangling with theirs inflamed them.

Iden's tongue plunged into her mouth, taking charge of the kiss. Their hands covered hers, forcing her palm to strike her clit as her fingers delved in and out of her clit as they made her fuck herself. Their breathing matching hers, fast and shallow.

She cried out when wet lips claimed her nipple and Miciah began sucking hungrily, his rhythm in perfect sync to the plundering of Iden's tongue and the hard rub of her palm over her clit. Her heels dug into the sand beneath the blanket, lifting her toward ecstasy, hips canting so her fingers could slide deeper into her channel.

Their hands were masculine and controlling, communicating without words that despite her touching herself, the pleasure came because they gave it to her, because they willed it. Mindless need reached up to consume her and she gave herself over to it, uncaring of the desperate sounds she made as her heart thundered in her chest and her body climbed toward release.

It came on a shimmering wave, a cresting that had her gasping, her toes curling and her fingers tightening in Iden's hair before she relaxed into boneless satisfaction.

Iden's kiss gentled. His tongue twined with hers in a sensuous promise of more to come, one given voice against her mouth when the kiss ended. "That was just a small demonstration of what Miciah and I can do for you. Unless you want another one, I would suggest we leave."

She nodded, intensely aware of their rigid cocks pressed against her thighs. Miciah lifted his head, his lips retaining possession of her nipple, elongating it and sending renewed spikes of heat to her cunt until it finally popped free.

A small thrill went through her as she felt how reluctant they were to pull their hands out of her panties. Iden managed it first, rolling away with a small groan before getting to his feet and snagging his pack.

Miciah rose above her, claiming a kiss that threatened to become something more as his hand dislodged hers to cup her mound and his fingers found her slit. He bucked when her passion-slick palm touched his chest, gliding over his nipples. Growled when Iden crouched down next to them and said, "Is this really what you want? To join with others present and have them share in our pleasure even if the darkness hides the full truth of it?"

Zoë was grateful for the reminder though she couldn't stop a small murmured protest from escaping when Miciah levered himself away from her and got to his feet. Another minute and she would have allowed him to pull her skirt up and her panties down, she would have freed their cocks and hurriedly guided first one of them and then the other to her opening.

Not that she would have regretted it. The night offered a measure of privacy and the Sol Celebration an atmosphere of freedom. But a soft bed and flickering candles allowed time to explore, to savor and capture every nuance of pleasure, and that's what she wanted with them.

Chapter Five

ജ

It was all Miciah could do not to order Zoë to take off her clothes and get on the bed the moment they entered her recreational vehicle. Instead he held himself ready, waiting for her to finish lighting candles and give them some indication of *how* she wanted to proceed.

Tomorrow you will have time alone with her. Iden said, his mental voice thick with amusement. *You can play Vesti games of dominance and take her as often and quickly as you desire. I, on the other hand, am enjoying every moment of this sweet seduction.*

A shudder passed through Miciah, a hot wash of sensation as he acknowledged to himself that he was being seduced along with Zoë. When they took her together, he and Iden would touch, casually, inadvertently. With each brush of skin to skin, with each shared moment of pleasure, the need for sexual contact between them would build despite his cultural inhibitions against it.

Zoë turned then, the last of the candles lit. In the RV, it took no more than a few steps for her to reach them, and Miciah's intentions to hold himself in check disappeared in a heartbeat. "Strip, Zoë."

Her husky laugh was a challenge. Her bold perusal nearly drove his hands to the front of his shorts so he could free his cock from its painful confinement.

"Putting it like that almost begs for disobedience," she teased, making Miciah's nostrils flare and his instincts threaten to take over.

"Perhaps there's room for compromise," Iden said, moving behind her and pushing her hair to one side. "I'll remove your clothing so neither you nor Miciah loses face."

He kissed her neck, his hands sliding around to gather up the hem of her blouse. "What do you say, Zoë?"

"Yes."

Her answer was little more than a whisper, but it lashed across Miciah like a fiery whip. Iden's interference should have outraged him, but there was no room for anything but lust as inch by inch her body was revealed.

The soft light of the candles allowed Miciah to see clearly what the moonlight and stars had only hinted at. She was exquisitely formed, made for a man's pleasure. For his pleasure.

He couldn't look away from her dusky areolas, one of them already marked by his passion. Iden's hands went to her breasts, cupping them as if in offering.

His thumbs brushed over the hardened tips, reminding Miciah of what it felt like to take her nipple between his lips and suck. Iden's fingers took possession of the taut points, tugging, twisting, squeezing, making her arch her back and shudder in pleasure.

"That feels so good," she whispered, pressing against Iden's hand, rubbing against his body behind her.

Miciah's cock spasmed. Without conscious thought he shed what he was wearing.

Her eyes went immediately to his rigid length, sending a wave of heat through it. Her lips parted, as if she hungered to take him in her mouth.

He widened his stance, intensely aware of his testicles hanging free and heavy beneath his throbbing penis. His fingers circled his cock, tightened when he glimpsed her tongue.

"I wish I could take a picture of you just like that," she said, her scent deep and lush, utterly intoxicating. "I think I could look at you all day long."

"The best is still to come," Iden teased in a husky voice, finding their love play incredibly arousing.

His hands left her breasts and slid down to the waistband of her skirt. "You haven't yet seen what I have to offer."

When she would have turned he bit her in gentle warning then loosened her skirt, enjoying the taut hunger on Miciah's face, the way his hand worked up and down on his shaft. In his mind's eye, Iden saw the dark suede of Vesti wings, quivering as a result of Miciah's need to touch and be touched.

Iden let Zoë's garment slide down shapely legs to pool at her feet. He savored the feel of her sleek buttocks, the wet evidence of her desire as he teased all of them by tracing along the edges of her almost nonexistent panties.

Miciah stepped forward, his erection glistening where semen escaped from the tiny slit in his cock head. "Finish it," he said.

Beneath his hands Zoë shivered. It pleased Iden that she responded to Miciah's dominance. She'd experience his brand of it on another day, when there was time to more fully explore her willingness to submit.

He slipped his thumbs under the miniscule waistband at each hip and tugged slowly, complying with Miciah's command, but on his own terms.

A moan escaped from Miciah as her mound was reveled, a tiny triangle of dark hair above glistening, swollen folds. The panties joined the skirt on the floor and Miciah sank to his knees in front of her.

Iden took possession of her breasts, covering them with his palms as his mouth sought her shoulder, her neck, her ear. He opened his mind to Miciah, sharing his pleasure at having her naked between them.

Her gasp as Miciah's lips settled against her lower ones poured molten lust into Iden's bloodstream. He cursed the material separating his groin from her smooth buttocks, but he couldn't force his hands away from her breasts long enough to rid himself of his clothing. *Soon,* he told himself, wanting Miciah to have her first, as a balance to what would come later, when Miciah broke with his culture and allowed himself to be taken by another male.

"You are perfect for us," he told Zoë, loving that she reached behind her to tangle her fingers in his hair, the movement pressing her breasts harder against his hands.

Iden explored her ear with his tongue, fucked in and out of it as he knew Miciah was doing to her cunt. He imagined sliding his length between her thighs, bathing in her wetness and having Miciah pleasure him with his mouth too, and afterward, guiding her hands and body forward to brace against the table so he could enter and take her while Miciah sucked her clit.

Zoë's breath caught. No fantasy could compare to what they were doing her. She'd thought their touches were devastating when they'd been on the blanket, but those barely counted as foreplay against what they were doing to her now.

Miciah's wicked tongue swirled around her clit before rasping over its naked head and sending icy-hot blasts of sensation all the way to the bottoms of her feet. He growled when she lifted on her toes—the pleasure almost too much to bear—followed her, taking the stiffened knob between firm lips.

She panted then, her hips bucking in a silent plea for him to suck. He licked instead, hard presses demonstrating who was in command.

"Please," she begged, rubbing her cunt against his face, trying to entice him into giving her what she needed.

Iden's fingers tightened on her nipples, making it feel as though a heated wire ran from them to her clit, blending pain and pleasure. "We wish only to please and protect you," he whispered in her ear. "Tell us you are ours to command."

His words stirred the darkest of her desires, the things an independent woman wasn't supposed to want. It was easy to imagine giving even more of herself to them, allowing them to dominate her more thoroughly in the name of pleasure.

Already she'd behaved differently with them. Always before her lovers had been friends, the sex playful or comforting or simply a physical release between two people who cared about each other but weren't meant for each other.

Miciah and Iden made her feel enslaved by desire, powerless against it. Need ravaged her, raw and frightening in its intensity, equally exhilarating and freeing.

She wanted to belong to them, wanted to be theirs to command. "Yes," she whispered.

"Say the words," Iden demanded.

Erotic fear shivered through her. "I'm yours to command. For tonight."

Iden's fingers tightened on her nipples in protest of her limited surrender. His mouth and teeth settled on the spot where her neck met her shoulder, marked her. Against her cunt Miciah growled, *for always*, before sealing his lips around her clit, sucking, striking it with his tongue.

Sensation ripped through Zoë as they eradicated the ability to think with their hands and mouths. She writhed between them, caught in a vortex from which there was no escape.

They tore away all barriers, reduced her to a helplessness she'd never known. She begged for them to let her come, cried for them to never stop as they intensified their heated touches. Screamed for them in release when Iden lifted his mouth from her neck and said, "Now."

Now! Miciah echoed, sending the message mentally to Iden, along with the image of them fucking her.

Iden answered by picking Zoë up and carrying her the short distance to the bed. Seeing her there, legs spread to reveal her slit, her swollen folds still quivering from the pleasure they'd given her nearly made Miciah coat his own belly in seed.

He squeezed his cock mercilessly to prevent it, went to her with no thought other than to get inside her. But as he reached the bed she slid off to kneel at Iden's feet.

Her fingers caressed Iden's erection through the fabric of his clothing before going to the waistband of his shorts. "Your turn," she said, a siren and not a supplicant despite her position. "Let me take you in my mouth."

It inflamed Miciah. He grasped her hair, nostrils flaring when he saw the mark Iden had left at the base of her neck.

"Undress him. But you won't touch him until you're given permission."

Defiance flashed in her eyes.

"Don't think I won't punish you," he said, the words escaping before he could prevent them.

He expected a silent rebuke from Iden, a warning of caution. Instead Iden said, "Obey him, Zoë."

Iden's response settled around Miciah's cock like a hand. It scorched away all remnants of Vesti resistance when it came to sharing a mate. They would be equals, allies and competitors in a mate-bond where mutual satisfaction was the ultimate prize.

She licked her lips, forcing Miciah to tighten his grip on his cock to stave off release. In another minute, even the pain of viselike fingers would no longer be an effective deterrent.

"Zoë." It was little more than a growl.

She unsnapped the top of Iden's shorts. Unzipped them. Freed his cock.

It rose against his belly. Dark. Thick. Its length equal to Miciah's.

"Please," Zoë whispered, her eyes lifted to meet Miciah's, begging for his permission to love Iden.

"You haven't done what I told you to do."

Somewhere along the way Iden had kicked off his shoes. She tugged the shorts downward and they fell to the floor, leaving him as naked as they were.

Her palms rested on Iden's thighs, framing the heavy globes of his testicles. Everything about her spoke of true submission and in that instant Miciah knew she'd enslaved him completely.

The law, his duties to the Council and his clan-house, they were secondary to her. He would never be able to part with her.

His gaze met Iden's and he saw the same emotion in them. *Do you wish to accept the pleasure she offers you like this? Or do you want it while I take her?*

Iden's fingers circled his cock, stroking up and down. "Get on the bed, Zoë. On your hands and knees."

She complied with provocative grace, her very obedience commanding them to follow her, to position themselves in front and behind her. Miciah had the thought to plunge immediately into her sultry depths, to feel her sheath fisting around him in hungry welcome. But he was mesmerized by the sight of Iden's penis only inches away from Zoë's mouth.

"Take him," Miciah growled, then shuddered, panted when her tongued darted out, laving, tasting, exploring Iden's hardened length before her lips followed.

It was arousing to witness it, darkly carnal to take pleasure in the sight of Iden's face taut with sensual agony, his hand clenched around his penis as his hips thrust in time to her sucks.

Miciah slid his fingers into her opening, groaned at the feel of her hot core and flooded channel. He fucked them in and out of her in the same rhythm as she worked Iden's cock with her mouth.

His breathing became as shallow as theirs, barely enough to sustain him given the fire roaring through his veins, building in his testicles and warning that when he covered

Zoë's body with his, there would be no gentleness, no awareness of anything other than the need to claim her.

Iden had thought it torture to hold Zoë as Miciah knelt in front of her and pleasured her with his mouth, but that torment paled in comparison to kneeling in front of her himself and feeling the pull of her mouth, the hot lash and smooth slide of her tongue.

Lust burned through his veins, unlike any he had ever known. The promise of ecstasy was a siren song that grew louder and louder as Zoë forced his hand back and took more of him into her mouth.

His thighs bunched as lips and tongue concentrated on his cock head. Need pulsed through him, raw and urgent.

His buttocks clenched in a desperate attempt to keep his thrusts shallow, slow, to stave off the moment of orgasm. He shook with the effort to draw out the moment. The harsh, ragged sound of his breathing marking his struggle, testifying that he was losing it.

They'd come to this planet to claim her, but they were the ones being claimed. The instant she'd touched her lips and tongue to him, she'd addicted him to the feel of them, turned them into a craving he was powerless against.

"Zoë," he moaned, her name a surrender of self as she began sucking harder, faster, leaving him helpless against the shuddering, merciless pleasure that came with the lava-hot spill of seed.

He pulled from her mouth and collapsed on the bed. Sensation rippled through him, but despite his release, he was held captive still by the scene playing out in front of him.

Miciah mounting her, thrusting hard and deep, phantom wings made up of barely visible particles spread behind him in a glorious, primal display during mating. His face a mask of feral possessiveness.

Iden's cock hardened as he watched. He'd known when he marked her how it would affect Miciah, how it would add to the intensity of the mating fever of the Vesti.

He heightened the lust further by sliding closer, by capturing Zoë's lips as Miciah continued to forge in and out of her channel. She tasted of him and it excited Iden, satisfied him even as it made Miciah more savage.

Miciah's growl rumbled through Iden's mind, but he didn't retreat. His tongue tangled with Zoë's and her moans of pleasure slid down his throat to add to the fullness of his cock.

He claimed the sharp cry she gave when Miciah's mating teeth pierced her flesh where her neck met her shoulder. Yielded her lips only after her orgasm sent Miciah tumbling over the edge.

My turn, Iden said, his arm curling around Zoë, extracting her from Miciah grasp and guiding her onto her back so he could cover her with his body.

He'd waited. He'd been patient, sacrificing his ego and suppressing his own desire to mate in the interest of beginning their bond with Miciah truly reconciled to sharing Zoë as well as himself.

A moan escaped when he lay along her length, her skin pressed to his, her legs parting voluntarily, her heated mound and dripping slit enticing him to take her.

"I need you too," she whispered, lifting her head and touching her lips to his, slipping her tongue into his mouth, tempting him to mimic the action, to slide his cock into her channel.

In the future he would deny her, make her beg for him to enter her. But denying her now was impossible, not when his cock throbbed with urgency at being so close to her opening, not when he found it unbearably pleasing to have her underneath him.

Iden lowered his torso. His hands held hers to the mattress. Behind his back he could feel the phantom spread of his wings, their edges rigid with tension.

Ecstasy shimmered through him as he joined his body to hers, knowing Miciah watched as he took her, as his cock claimed the same channel Miciah's had claimed, bathed in seed and feminine arousal.

Zoë. Always and forever it would be her name that sang through him when he needed a woman's body, a woman's touch.

He fought against movement, wanting to savor the feel of inner muscles spasming hungrily on his cock. But he lasted only until she canted her hips and thrust upward, taking him deeper, claiming him as thoroughly as he intended to claim her.

His hips bucked, jerked. And with the first thrust and retreat, there was no stopping. There was only mindless pistoning, the satisfaction of having her writhe and cry out his name in release, the frenzied climb until he filled her with his seed as Miciah had done.

Zoë murmured appreciatively as Miciah and Iden settled on either side of her. Their warmth made it unnecessary to free the comforter, for which she was grateful. She was loath to give up the view of their firm bodies.

Miciah was hard again, from watching Iden fuck her. Just as Iden's cock had filled moments after she'd sucked him to orgasm, as he watched Miciah take her from behind.

She loved having their warm skin touching hers, loved the lazy way hands smoothed over her breasts and belly, as though they enjoyed petting her as much as they'd enjoyed the foreplay and sex. She could get used to having them with her.

The soft glow of candlelight reflected off their bands, drawing her attention to them again. Her hands captured their wrists. She brushed her fingertips over the carved designs, the

Pteranodons and falcons, the identical stones that reminded her of the Milky Way.

Curiosity stirred and was further aroused by the subtle tension vibrating through both men. An earlier thought returned, how well the two of them were matched, like a perfect pair.

From her studies she knew some psychologists believed that when two men shared a woman, the woman served as a substitute for them having sex with one another, a way to be together without admitting or acknowledging homosexual desires.

Zoë couldn't suppress a smile. Even if it were true in their case, she'd volunteer to be their sexual substitute any day of the week.

"What are you thinking?" Iden asked, punctuating the beginning and ending of the question with a soft kiss.

She studied his face and liked his open expression. There was masculine satisfaction there, but caring as well, a desire to stay connected rather than disengage.

Her gaze shifted to Miciah. Her eyes were met by his possessive ones.

His expression said he didn't intend to leave her side anytime soon. It made her forget Iden's question until he repeated it, punishing her with a sharp bite to her earlobe.

It would have been easy to turn back to Iden and gauge his reaction. But it was Miciah's hard length pressed to her thigh, Miciah's inherent dominance that made her watch him as she said, "I was wondering if the two of you are lovers."

Her answer came in the flush spreading across Miciah's cheeks, the pulse of his cock against her leg, in Iden's sharp inhalation before he answered in a warm whisper next to her ear, "Miciah and I have never been intimate, but we desire each other. When we decided to approach you together, we agreed to act on our attraction, if you were accepting of it."

Heat slid through her, pooling in her labia and breasts. She believed him, completely—both that he and Miciah had never had sex with one another and that she was somehow a catalyst bringing them together. She'd been dreaming about them both for a week.

Iden pulled his wrist from her grasp and cupped her cheek with his hand, turning her attention back to his face. "Does the thought of Miciah and me being lovers repulse you, Zoë? Or does it arouse you?"

"Let me show you," she said, taking his hand, guiding it first between her legs so he could feel her stiffened clit and leaking slit, then across her hip and down, to Miciah's hard penis.

"Stroke him," she dared. "Let me see you make him come."

Miciah's moan was echoed by Iden's soft one. Beneath her hand, Iden's fingers circled Miciah's length, squeezed, moved up and down just enough to make Miciah quiver.

She shifted onto her side, snuggled her back against Iden's chest so she could feel his increased excitement as he worked Miciah.

Iden's heated lips touched the place where both he and Miciah had bitten her. "Help me, Zoë," he said. "Play with his nipple."

A shiver of pleasure went through her, at being included, made part of their first intimate encounter. She leaned forward, licked over the tiny dark areola, took it between her teeth and tugged.

"That's right," Iden said. "Suck him. Mark him as belonging to us."

She moaned, not just at his words but at the slide of his cock into her channel. It throbbed, deep and hard inside her, and she fucked herself on it with subtle movements, timed to the stroke of his hand on Miciah's cock and the sucking of her lips on Miciah's nipple.

It was heady to hear Miciah panting, to feel the tension vibrating through him as if he fought some internal battle, not quite willing to come with another man's hand on his cock. With a hard sucking bite that left him marked, Zoë's fingers replaced her mouth on his nipple so she could watch the battle between Iden and Miciah.

"Do you like what you see?" Iden asked, his lips brushing her ear.

Her cunt answered first, clenching on him, making his hips buck as a moan escaped. "Yes," she whispered, mesmerized by the sight Iden's hand gliding up and down on Miciah's length, by the savage expression on Miciah's face. He wanted the pleasure as desperately as he tried to keep from surrendering to it.

In that instant she understood Miciah was the reason they'd never acted on their attraction—until now, and only because of her. It was heady knowledge, power unlike any she'd ever experienced. She leaned forward, her lips nearly touching Miciah's, remembering how he'd commanded her, used words to drive her need for them higher.

"Next time it won't be his hand. It'll be his mouth. We'll take turns sucking you, then he'll fuck you, and I'll come with my fingers, pretending its one of you between my legs."

Her words roared through Miciah like molten fire. The fingers that had been gripping the comforter tangled in the silky strands of her hair instead, forcing her to close the distance and holding her prisoner as his lips and tongue promised carnal retribution for stripping away the last of his barriers.

Images bombarded him, of Iden's mouth, of Iden's cock. Of him taking Iden in the same way he wanted to be taken. Of Zoë witnessing it, her fingers wet as she thrust them in and out of her slit.

Pleasure scorched through Miciah. He could no longer stop himself from fucking through the tight fist of Iden's fingers, from moaning at how good if felt to finally feel them on his shaft, firm and hard, masculine and knowledgeable.

They tightened each time he was near release. Refused to grant it so the need built to the point he might be willing to beg for it.

Sweat coated Miciah's chest. His testicles ached and burned.

It was impossible to differentiate between his breath and Zoë's.

He would have begged if Iden had demanded it. But mercifully, Iden didn't need that final surrender.

"Do you want to see him come?" Iden asked, and Miciah allowed Zoë to escape their kiss so she could give her answer.

"Yes."

"Then watch," Iden said, stroking until hot semen jetted from Miciah's cock, coating his belly in a wash of ecstasy and leaving him shuddering in the aftermath as Iden's hand left him to fondle Zoë's tiny clit, to make her come as Iden spilled his seed into her channel.

Chapter Six

ഌ

Iden woke slowly, content to savor the moment and the memories of the previous day. He'd never known such pleasure, and yet it would pale in comparison to what they'd have once the three of them were bound together by the Ylan stones.

Against his chest, Zoë stirred and he nuzzled kisses along her neck, inhaling the flower scent of the soap from her shower. He was very much aware of how his arm draped over her side so his hand settled on Miciah's chest, his fingers idly rubbing across Miciah's nipple.

There was tension beneath the smooth skin and hard muscle. Its presence made Iden hide a smile against Zoë's shoulder. It would have been too much to expect Miciah to permanently surrender to the desire between them, especially when there was so much more to explore and experience.

Iden's cock hardened as he thought about Zoë's whispered words to Miciah. It had added layers of ecstasy to their first encounter to have her watch and to know she found the sight of her two mates touching erotic.

The tiny shower in her RV hadn't allowed them to do more than enter singly and cleanse themselves, but in the quarters waiting for them on Belizair, the walls could become mirrors and restraints could be called forth to turn bathing into a sensual celebration of wet pleasure.

They'd take her there, where she could watch as he and Miciah touched her intimately. And though it wasn't his preference, it was a measure of her power over him that if she asked it of him, he'd allow himself to be bound and made helpless so she and Miciah could do anything they desired with him.

Heat coiled in his testicles and his cock pulsed as he imagined it. The hand on Miciah's chest drifted downward, only to be halted.

The denial didn't spring from Miciah's reluctance to have Iden's fingers curled once again around his cock. Instead, at the touch of Miciah's wrist band to his, Iden became aware of the heavy weight and throb of the Ylan stones.

They were close to separating and migrating in recognition of a mate bond. And while he and Miciah both wore the bands they'd crafted for Zoë, they risked an exclusive bonding, one that didn't include her.

They could slip the stone-free bracelets on her wrists as she slept. There was no law against it. But even as Iden thought it, he realized he wanted her to accept the band he'd made for her willingly, in a private moment shared by only the two of them.

Their time for convincing her to return home with them was running out. Once Zoë wore the bands, and they contained the Ylan stones, then there would be no hiding their true form from her.

Only a bond-mate could be given such proof of Vesti and Amato existence, and only then, in the transport chamber. But by Council law, human females found to be a match to a male on Belizair had to agree to a binding ceremony and to return home with their Vesti and Amato mates first.

Sounds drifted in, along with the smell of cooking food. Iden rose onto an elbow, intending to meet Miciah's eyes. His gaze traveled downward instead, visually caressing skin darker than his own and a cock equally engorged and with moisture glistening on its tip.

In defense — or unconscious offering — Miciah's hand went to his shaft, his fingers circling it, almost begging for Iden to lean over and take him into his mouth. There was no hiding his desire, so Iden sent an image of what he wanted to do, along with a warning.

If we're lucky, we can each take her once more before the Ylan stones migrate from our bands to hers. I suggest we do so separately. If we both remain in bed with her...

He didn't need to add what would happen when she woke and asked them to touch each other, when she whispered how much she wanted to see one of them mount the other. Only sated sleep had kept her from it the night before when she'd returned to bed after her shower.

I agree, Miciah said, surprising Iden by leaving the bed, though he remained next to it, his hand gliding up and down his shaft as his eyes roved over Zoë's sleeping form, then Iden's body when Iden rolled to his back. *I will leave to purchase food for us to break our fast with.*

Only the heavy, throbbing weight of the Ylan stones at his wrists kept Iden from delaying Miciah's departure by waking Zoë, knowing that if he did so, she'd draw Miciah back to bed and the pleasure they both wanted.

Iden waited for Miciah to dress and depart before easing Zoë onto her back, then waking her with nuzzled kisses and the weight of his body on hers.

She moaned and stretched like a contented cat, her thighs splaying and her hips lifting, rubbing her mound against his hardened length. "I could get used to this," she murmured.

"Both Miciah and I would like that very much."

"Maybe we should practice waking up together."

Her smile and the feel of her fingers combing through his hair to scrape lightly down the length of his back nearly undid him. His buttocks clenched and there was no resisting the urge to thrust against her tiny clit. Her gasp was his reward, as was the obvious effort she made to present her opening so he could penetrate her.

He resisted. Barely.

This was their first time alone together. It would be their last until she agreed to join her life to his and Miciah's and return home with them.

"Practice should be done slowly," Iden said against her lips before sealing them with his and pressing his tongue into her mouth to tangle sensuously with hers.

Zoë gave herself over to the pleasure. It felt so good to have his hard body pressing down on hers. He was heat and strength, passion given physical form.

Beneath her hands his muscles rippled as she dragged her fingers through the long, wavy locks of his hair. Despite its length, there was nothing feminine about him.

"Where's Miciah?" she asked, left breathless by their kiss.

"Getting food for our breakfast and allowing us time alone."

The answer sent a skittering dance through Zoë's chest. It satisfied something primal in her, even as it surprised her how much she liked knowing they wanted her separately as well as together.

"Then we better not waste it," she said, sucking gently on his bottom lip and feeling an answering throb where his penis pressed hard against her clit. "Put your cock inside me."

His hands tangled in her hair on a moan as he halted her teasing with the savage claiming of her lips and dominant thrust of his tongue into her mouth. He gave her more of his weight, rocked against her but denied her the thing she wanted most, his thick length filling and stretching her.

"Please," she whispered when he finally freed her lips. "Come inside me."

"After I know your taste as thoroughly and intimately as Miciah does."

He paired action with his words, kissing down and capturing a nipple, his hands pinning her wrists to the mattress.

73

Her cunt clenched as he suckled, not in a gentle nursing, but with the hunger of man who intended that his claim burn its way into every cell.

He gave equal attention to both breasts. Sucked her love-abraded nipples deep into his mouth, each pull sending more and more arousal escaping from her slit as her pleas became a litany of desire.

She writhed, lifting her hips and wetting his belly with her need. A moan escaped when he left her breasts and kissed downward.

Her cunt lips were flushed and swollen, already parted in anticipation of his mouth and tongue. "Let me take you the same way," she said. "Let me pleasure you the way I did last night while Miciah fucked me."

Iden shuddered in response. His fingers tightened on her wrists. "I won't last."

"You don't need to. Let me take you in my mouth."

He shuddered again, panted.

"No," he said, ending their conversation by lowering his head and thrusting his tongue into her sheath.

Her hips lifted on a moan, driving him deeper.

She cried out as he plundered her channel with the same thoroughness as he'd taken her mouth, making her shiver and plead for release. She whimpered when he left her slit and captured her clit between his lips.

Fire streaked downward to the soles of her feet. Her toes curled and only his hands holding her wrists to the mattress kept her from rising off it as he alternated between lashing and sucking the small nerve-filled knob.

She fought. To get closer. To get away.

He held the promise of release just out of reach until finally commanding it, demanding that she come for him and leaving her no choice but to obey.

Satisfaction raged through Iden as the bed shook with the force of her orgasm. He nearly purred at the way she was left boneless and sated, softly compliant.

All thoughts of placing her on her hands and knees and mounting her left him as he crawled up her body. He wanted her to see his face, to know in every fiber of her being that *he* was the one pleasuring her to ecstasy.

He positioned her unresisting arms above her head, holding them there with one hand as the other covered her breast possessively. "I can share you with Miciah," he said, rubbing his hand over her nipple and feeling it harden against his palm. "But my claim to you is equal to his."

Her eyes widened slightly. He wondered if his words were ill-advised, but discarded the thought. There was no turning back, not with the Ylan stones in his bands growing heavier with each passing moment.

He freed her breast and wrists, only to entwine his fingers with hers against the sheet. A hot throb of warning went through his penis when his wristbands touched her bracelets. It was accompanied by the same flash of fear he'd experienced when he first saw the blue stones with their streaks of black.

"Spread your legs," he ordered, unwilling to be diverted by his uneasiness over the unfamiliar stones.

He was rewarded by the darkening of her eyes, by obedience that testified to how much she enjoyed a dominant male. Pleasure rippled through him. He didn't desire it exclusively, but he needed her submission as much as he needed the balance of having both Miciah and her in his bed.

The feel of her wet slit against his cock made him shudder with need, and this time, he had no intention of denying himself. He slid into her on a moan, nearly came when she whispered, "You feel so good inside me."

Good didn't come close to describing the sensations coursing through him with each thrust and retreat. Her channel clung to him, resisted him, made him fight to enter and work to escape.

His testicles drew up tight and hard. His hips pistoned faster and faster in a fevered rush to fill her with his seed.

He sealed her lips with his, swallowing the sounds of her enjoyment as he lay heavily on her. He wanted to meld so completely to her that there would be no separation between them, that they would become one being forced to live in separate bodies except in those joyous moments when they joined in passion.

Her fingers tightened on his. Her legs wrapped around him as though she were driven by the same need.

What little control he had disappeared in a searing flash. He thrust harder, deeper, and found savage ecstasy when her channel clamped down on him mercilessly in her release.

He came, his heart and soul flowing into her with the hot wash of his semen. His body shuddered as wave after wave of pleasure rushed through him, leaving him with only enough strength to roll to his side when his testicles were empty.

Even then, he couldn't bear to separate from her. Couldn't stop kissing her. Shallow, quick touches of mouth against mouth as their breathing slowed and steadied.

"I definitely like your way of starting the day," Zoë said, smiling against his lips. "But it creates a big problem."

"What?"

"It makes getting out of bed hard to do."

She nudged him onto his back and sprawled out on top of him, her channel rippling against has softening cock. "I could stay here all day. Maybe when Miciah gets back, that's what we'll do. I want to see the two of you together."

There was no hiding what her words did to him, not when he was still inside her. He began hardening again, her expression revealing just how much she liked knowing he and Miciah desired each other as well as her.

Blood pulsed into his cock in a subtle beat matching the heavy, throbbing energy of the Ylan stones as they grew ready to separate and migrate. Even the fear of that happening didn't make it easier to retreat from her slick, heated depths.

He rolled so she was once again underneath him, then had to force himself off her.

His penis screamed in protest at the loss of her wet heat. It ached with the need to return to her slit.

Instead of lying next to her and tormenting himself with temptation, Iden sat. Relief swept through him when Zoë did the same. And yet it was still all he could do not to pull her onto his lap and begin kissing her.

It wasn't inner strength that saved him, but her hand on his chest, her fingers glancing over his nipple and drawing his attention downward, to the bracelet she wore. He covered her hand with his, stopping her teasing.

He leaned forward, nuzzling her cheek and ear. "Will you accept a gift from me?" he asked, sucking her earlobe into his mouth to ensure her answer was the one he wanted.

She shivered and moved into him, her nipples pebble-hard against his chest. "Yes."

He moaned as the fingers of her free hand curled around his cock. In desperation he reached out mentally for Miciah and found him only steps away.

Get it done, Miciah growled, the instant sharing of images and thoughts allowing him to know the situation inside the RV.

Iden captured Zoë's tormenting hand and carried it to his chest. "Behave," he said. "Miciah will be here in minutes."

"And you don't want him to walk in and find us this way? Naked and ready to have him for breakfast?"

He laughed despite the erotic picture she painted. He could well imagine having Miciah stretched out between them, their mouths and hands making it impossible for Miciah to escape the true nature of his desire.

"Behave," Iden repeated, this time giving her earlobe a sharp nip. "Promise me you will so I can free my hands."

The breeze brought the smell of baking bread into the RV. Her stomach rumbled and she laughed. "I guess I'd better. I'll behave. But only until after I've had breakfast."

"You'll be Miciah's problem then." He pressed a kiss to her lips before she could protest. "It's only fair he have time alone with you."

"And afterward, will you join us in bed? I want you both. I want one of you to fuck the other."

He shuddered. "Soon."

Her tongue darted out to trace the seam of his lips. "Was last night really the first time the two of you have been intimate?"

A throb of searing heat pulsed through his cock. "You're cheating," he said, carrying her captured hands down to his penis before he could stop himself. "This isn't behaving."

Her laugh was sultry, her eyes filled with wicked intent. He moaned when she rubbed her thumb over the crown of his cock, smearing the liquid she found there into his heated skin. "It's hard to behave. You and Miciah are like something out of an erotic fantasy."

"You're our fantasy as well," Iden said, somehow finding the strength to reposition her hands so they rested on his thigh.

The feel of her bracelets beneath his palms helped steady him, as did the menacing, growling presence of Miciah in his mind, threatening to enter the RV regardless of Iden's desire to make the gift of the wristband a private moment.

When Iden was sure he could trust her, he took his hands from hers and removed the band he'd crafted in anticipation of a mate-bond. Its edges held the device of his house, the elegant sand-colored birds of prey found in the desert region known as the Cradle of the Goddess.

Words crowded in, eloquent declarations and heartfelt promises. But he remained silent. Until she agreed to go home with them and lay on the bed in the transport chamber, held between them as they finalized the bond, she couldn't know the truth of what the gift represented.

She was their hope. Their future. The woman who meant life itself to them.

Meeting her eyes, he lifted her left hand and pressed a kiss to her palm. "Accept all that I offer," he murmured before placing the band on her wrist and closing it, locking it into place so that none could remove it.

Zoë's heart rabbited in her chest. His gift and his words felt significant, binding, and yet it wasn't fear of them that had her pulse racing.

She touched a fingertip to the bracelet, tracing one of the birds and noticing as she did so how snugly the band fit to the butterfly embellished one she already wore. Delicate wings overlapping silver edges, falcon and butterfly so the two bracelets seemed like a single piece of jewelry.

"It's beautiful," she said, leaning forward and offering a kiss of thanks.

His hand cupped her cheek. She would have melted into him, tumbling them both backward to lie across the mattress so their bodies could join as intimately as the two bands—except for Miciah's entrance. The force of it sent the door crashing against the side of the RV.

"Someone's impatient," Iden said with a laugh, rising from the bed and tugging her along with him.

Chapter Seven

ഏ

Miciah hadn't bothered with either shoes or shirt. The sight of him in the doorway, burnished skin and taut, masculine features, made Zoë's breath catch and her clit stiffen.

She excused herself to visit the bathroom, donning a comfortable robe hanging on the back of the door before leaving it.

Miciah's eyes narrowed as soon as she stepped into view. And when she reached the table, he stripped the gown off her.

"I want you naked," he said, pulling her against his chest.

Her cunt wept at his dominant tone and sexual demand. Refusal didn't enter her mind.

His hand cupped her mound, his fingers finding slick heat. "Mine."

"And Iden's." The words came automatically, without conscious thought.

Miciah's nostrils flared but he didn't deny them. He gave her a quick, savage kiss then stepped back, leaving her feeling needy and fighting the urge to touch herself.

She sat, and found it incredibly erotic to be naked while they both wore the loose, multi-pocketed shorts favored by so many of the men who came to the desert Sol Celebration.

Spread out on the table was an assortment of fruit slices along with bread and cheese and a small pot of honey. Rather than sit across from her, or at the table's sides to her left and right, they turned their chairs, crowding her so their thighs pressed against hers and sent small spikes of heat straight to her clit.

Zoë pressed her legs together, her color heightening as she felt the seat growing wet with escaped arousal. Miciah ate her with his eyes, his gaze roving over her possessively, stopping to focus on nipples that were love-bruised and stiffened.

When she would have escaped the intensity of his focus by eating, they captured her hands in concert and held them against the table. "We will feed you," Miciah said. "You are ours to pleasure and protect."

There was an underlying formalness to the words and she couldn't deny their effect on her. She'd never felt so desirable, so alive, so connected to a lover — to two lovers. The hunger for food was replaced by the hunger for touch and praise, for an intimacy that reached the heart and soul.

Iden's expression was as possessive as Miciah's, his features as taut. He picked up a slice of orange and held it to her lips. She took it, slowly, sucking both fruit and juice from his fingers, her tongue caressing him, tormenting him, reminding him of her earlier offer to take his penis between her lips.

"It's my cock you'll have next," Miciah growled as if guessing at the silent conversation taking place between her and Iden. He picked up the honey dipper, but rather than hold it over a slice of bread, he held it above her breasts so the honey streamed downward to first one nipple and then the other.

"Arch your back," Miciah said, putting the dipper aside. "Offer yourself to me."

On a moan she obeyed. And he rewarded her by leaning down to suck the glistening honey off her skin in the same slow torment as she'd taken the fruit from Iden's fingers.

Any hope of conversation over breakfast was lost in their sensual feeding. Iden's mouth replacing Miciah's, Miciah's replacing Iden's as she took food from both of them, filling her belly even as her cunt spasmed and dripped, needing to be filled as well.

She made a small keening sound when Iden stood abruptly and said, "I will leave you now."

His penis was a hard, rigid line at the front of his shorts. His eyes blazed with carnal need. She opened her mouth to tell him to stay, but his kiss stopped her, and her protest of his leaving was burned away by his whispered promise. "The next time Miciah and I will take you together, we'll both be inside you, our cocks rubbing against each other as we pleasure you."

He left then and Miciah stood. With the same casualness as he'd stripped her robe from her, he undid his shorts.

They dropped to the floor, revealing his hardened length with its glistening tip. She shivered when he took his cock in hand. The sight of his dark, masculine fingers wrapped around his flushed, swollen penis was incredibly arousing.

She licked her lips, and felt a powerful surge of satisfaction at the way his fist tightened and his breathing grew more ragged. "You know what I want," he said, command in his voice.

Without glancing away from him she picked up the honey dipper and dribbled its sweet gold onto his cock head, murmuring appreciatively as it slid down the shaft to pool on top of his fist. "Mmmm, looks like a treat meant for adults," she said, leaning forward, her tongue darting out, lapping honey from his length.

His hips bucked and his knuckles whitened. His moan ended on a growled, "Take me in your mouth, Zoë."

She touched the tip of her tongue to the tiny slit in his crown instead, rubbed over it, coaxing more arousal into escaping. Her hand slid between his thighs, cupping his testicles as her finger stroked the skin between the velvety globes and his back entrance.

It excited her to think of Iden fucking Miciah, just as it excited her to think of one of them filling her cunt while the other slid into her ass. She closed her lips around his cock head, sucked quickly then released him.

His free hand tangled in her hair. His eyes were the molten gold of lust that wouldn't be denied. "Now, Zoë, or everyone outside this RV will hear the sound of my hand as it strikes your buttocks repeatedly. They'll all imagine your skin reddening and filling with fire."

She considered defying him, and let him see the thought. Dominance games had always been a part of her fantasies, as had the idea of being punished with a spanking.

His fingers tightened in her hair. His nostrils flared. "Do it," he growled, his expression telling her he would find equal pleasure in the obedient sucking of his cock, or in the opportunity to drape her over his knees and discipline her.

Only the thought of encountering knowing glances when she left the RV, of having word of her punishment reach her friends, most of them male and ruthless when it came to teasing, kept her from pushing Miciah into delivering the promised spanking. She lowered her eyes, hiding them beneath her lashes in a signal of her submission—for now. There would be another time, away from the crowded desert celebration, when she'd make a different choice.

Sheer ecstasy surged through Miciah when she took him into her mouth, sucking his exposed length with pulls that filled his veins with liquid fire and made him pant and moan. Her lips glistened, wet from the honey captured by his fist.

The delicate line of her spine, the fall of her hair brought every possessive instinct surging forward. *Mine.* There was no room in his thoughts for Iden or their future on Belizair. All that mattered was claiming his mate as a Vesti would, having her in every way a male could take his female.

He leaned forward, no longer able to stand without bracing his hand against the back of her chair. "More," he commanded, loosening the fingers around his cock so she could take him deeper, and only barely maintaining enough control to avoid hurting her in his passion when she obeyed with fevered intensity, her moans testifying to the pleasure she found in having him take her mouth as he'd already taken her cunt, as he would soon take her ass.

His testicles burned with the need for release. His breathing was little more than shallow gasps timed to the thrust of his hips.

He wanted to make it last, to spend his seed in her mouth and watch her swallow it in a primal acknowledgement of who she belonged to. But with each suck, each plunge of his cock between her lips, the Ylan stones grew heavier, pulsed in a warning announcing how close they were to separating and moving to the waiting, empty bracelet Iden had placed on her wrist. With a groan Miciah forced himself away from her, but only long enough to scoop up his shorts and retrieve the tube of ritzca oil from a pocket.

He ordered Zoë to stand and turn around, to brace herself against the table. She complied, willingly leaning forward and spreading her legs, presenting him with her woman's opening.

It was almost his undoing.

His first instinct was to step forward and sheath himself in her heated depths. Even as he denied that impulse, his hips bucked and fire lanced through his cock.

There was no fighting the need to coat himself in her juices, but he didn't dare rub his penis back and forth over her parted, swollen cunt lips. He cupped her mound instead, shuddered as his fingers and palm grew wet.

He gathered the moisture, stroking her clit and pushing his fingers into her hot slit. Reveling in the way she rocked backward, in her panted, whimpered pleas begging for him to put his cock inside her.

When she was shivering uncontrollably, his fingers left her channel and went to the puckered rosette of her anus. She tried to evade his touch and felt the sting of his hand against her buttock.

"It's not too late for me to punish you," he said, caressing the curve of her ass with his knuckles, then returning to her back entrance, coating it with the slick juices of her cunt before pausing to thumb open the tube of ritzca oil and squeeze the lubricant onto his fingers.

It heated on contact, but the feel of it was nothing compared to the fiery need it created when applied to penis, or slit, or puckered anus. It spread, heightening the senses, lubricating, turning lovemaking into fevered ecstasy and blending pain into pleasure.

Zoë gasped when he coated her anus with it. Within seconds she was pushing against his fingertips, pleading for what she'd tried to evade moments earlier.

He pressed into her with his fingers, stretched and prepared her for the width of his cock as she begged him to put it inside her. Sweat coated his body as he fought against impaling her in a rough claiming.

Delaying was agony and ecstasy. He was shaking with need by the time he placed the head of his cock against her back opening and joined their bodies, pushing into her slowly despite the ritzca oil's assault on his penis and the feel of her clamping down on him, making him fight for every inch.

He gave a low, tortured moan when he was finally in. And then there was no choice but to fuck. He gave in to the demand to thrust in shallows digs, then longer, harder ones, the fire of the ritzca oil driving them both to heady release.

Zoë sagged forward, only barely managing to shove the remains of their breakfast out of her way before her upper body sprawled on the table. The wood was cool against her skin compared to Miciah's heat against her back.

His lips brushed over the bite mark on her shoulder, scorched their way up her neck. "You're okay, beloved?" he asked, sending a flutter through her heart that she felt in her belly as well.

"Yes."

"Good."

The single word held such a wealth of masculine satisfaction that Zoë couldn't help but smile. She pressed backward, subtly rubbing her buttocks against him and feeling him start to harden inside her.

"Behave," he growled.

She laughed. "Iden told me the same thing. I'll tell you what I told him. It's nearly impossible to behave when the two of you are straight out of an erotic fantasy."

Hers in fact, though she wasn't quite ready to share how she'd dreamed about them for a week before they entered her life.

His hand pushed between the table and her body to cup her breast possessively. "You are the only woman whose fantasy I wish to star in with Iden."

She smiled. "Hmmm, then maybe we'd better take showers so we'll be ready when he gets back."

Miciah shuddered and pulled out of her. He continued to stand behind her, trapping her between his body and the table as she pushed herself upright. It didn't surprise her in the least that where Iden asked, Miciah simply reached around and snapped the gemless bracelet engraved with Pteradons onto her right wrist, the act accompanied by a single, growled word. "Mine."

As with Iden's band, Miciah's fit snugly against the butterfly one she already wore. The intricately crafted wings overlapping an edge of silver, one band to the other, prehistoric creatures and butterflies making it seem as though the two bracelets were a single piece of jewelry.

"It's beautiful," she said, then dared to ask, "They mean something, don't they?"

Miciah's lips touched the spot where her shoulder met her neck, where they'd both bitten her the night before. "They mean something," he agreed, hugging her to him. "We'll talk more about it later. For now, let's shower. Singly, because I can't trust myself not to take you again and I've promised myself not to do so until Iden and I can both be inside you at the same time."

Her cunt spasmed at the thought of it. But when she emerged from the shower after Miciah had finished with his, she found Iden had returned and both he and Miciah were dressed. Despite the fantasy of spending the day in bed with them, she wasn't disappointed when they suggested leaving the RV and exploring the festival.

It would be good to be outside in the sun, to have a chance to talk and enjoy their company. *And* to recover from their lovemaking—though it didn't stop her from teasing them by making a show of putting on nearly transparent panties and bra before covering them with a short flower-patterned skirt and a delicate tank top that clung to her in a way that had their eyes heating as their attention was drawn to her breasts.

The thin bra and tank top did nothing to hide taut nipples pressed against fabric. Rather than make Zoë feel self-conscious, it made her feel sexy and desirable, especially when Iden and Miciah closed the distance, crowding her, each of them claiming a breast possessively, their heat sweeping through her and making her cunt lips swell and part.

"You need to be taught to behave," Miciah said, his fingers going to her nipple, tightening so she moaned and arched her back.

"I agree," Iden said, his eyes and voice holding the same fierce dominance as Miciah's, his fingers equally punishing on her nipple. "Her lessons can begin as soon as we get her home."

Zoë trembled at the fantasy they were weaving around her. Good intentions and the desire for sunshine and companionship melted with their touch, as did her worries about what those camping around her would hear.

"We can start now," she said, imagining herself draped over Miciah's knees, her buttocks bared and Iden watching as Miciah administered the spanking he'd threatened earlier.

Iden's hand slid downward, beneath the waistband of her skirt and panties. She shivered when he rubbed over her stiffened clit and caressed her weeping slit with his fingertips.

"Let's go back to bed," she whispered, needing them again with an intensity that bordered on addiction. "You promised to take me at the same time when the three of us were together again."

Desire made Iden lightheaded. It throbbed through him, demanding with each beat of his heart that he give in to her plea. His fingers delved into her slit, thrust deeply and were welcomed with the hungry gripping of her channel and the wet heat his cock craved.

Her moan made him shudder and grasp his cloth-covered erection. Miciah snarled a warning. *We fuck her to orgasm where she stands or we won't get out of here without binding her to us.*

More than anything Iden wanted to bind her to them, to lie with her between them, their cocks deep inside her, separated by only a thin barrier as the Ylan stones on their wristbands split and moved to hers, enabling them to share thought and feeling and have a life together. His breath escaped on a pant imagining it, but he forced himself to heed Miciah's words.

He tangled his fingers in her hair, as did Miciah, their grip angling her face so they could kiss her, their lips brushing against each other's as they alternated in claiming hers.

Lust poured off them at the contact, Zoë's fast breathing and fevered moans reinforcing how erotic she found it when her men touched.

Her men. Iden didn't try to deny it. They belonged to her completely, in all ways despite there being no Ylan stone binding.

He struck her clit with the palm of his hand as he pumped in and out of her with his fingers. The link with Miciah allowed for perfect, unconscious timing as they made love to her with their mouths and hands, fought to give her a release even as the stones at their wrists warned just how dangerous their behavior was.

Her keening cry and clinging, shuddering orgasm sent them both over the edge, flashing fire through their cocks, then heated embarrassment into their cheeks at having come like boys first discovering the pleasure of spilling their seed.

Zoë's eyes held sultry satisfaction when they pulled away and she saw the glistening evidence of their lack of control spewed on their bellies. Somehow both he and Miciah had managed to open their shorts and free their cocks, though Iden didn't remember it happening.

Without a word Zoë pulled out of their grasp, retreating to the bathroom long enough to emerge with a washcloth. Iden's hips pumped subtly as she pressed the warm cloth to his skin. He closed his eyes against the sight of her bathing him, fought against hardening again as she cleansed his penis and testicles.

He couldn't endure much more. They were lucky to have escaped the consequences this time. But that didn't keep him from opening his eyes and watching as she left him to refresh the cloth, then returned to tend to Miciah.

The struggle for control was written on every line of Miciah's body. Conversation between them wasn't necessary. They both knew how desperate the situation with Zoë had become.

Iden closed his mind to the sensual memory of his mouth brushing against Miciah's as they'd kissed their mate, and the fevered need heightened by it. He refused to linger on the knowledge that Zoë wanted to witness the sexual surrender of one of them to the other.

He didn't give her a chance to tempt them again. A word, a touch, would be enough to drive them to the bed if they stayed in the RV any longer. As soon as she put the washcloth away, he placed his hand at the small of her back and urged her toward the door. "Let's explore."

Chapter Eight

ဆ

Zoë went willingly, pausing only long enough to grab her purse. Once outside, surrounded by people, Iden found himself relaxing.

Different types of music battled for supremacy, filling the air with sound. It was a restrained violence, but against the tranquility of Belizair, the constant bombardment provided yet another reason to get Zoë away from the Sol Celebration and to the closest transport chamber as soon as possible — not that they needed additional inducement.

He smiled when Zoë slipped her arm through his then did the same to Miciah, her body language openly proclaiming they were both her lovers. It pleased him to have a bond-mate who was comfortable and confident in her sexuality.

A wry smile twisted his lips as he spared Miciah a glance. Having one bond-mate who had yet to fully embrace his sexual cravings was enough of a challenge, especially when coupled with the urgency in which they now needed to get Zoë to commit herself to them.

He'd thought they would have days of lovemaking away from their world and the shadow of Vesti cultural disapproval. He'd thought there would be plenty of time for him and Miciah to become lovers in the fullest sense of the word before they returned to Belizair. Looking back on it and remembering his reaction to Zoë's image, he should have guessed that once they came to Earth, the need to claim her would make everything else secondary.

He couldn't resist the urge to lean over and brush a kiss against her cheek. "You're beautiful. More than one male is wishing he was standing at your side."

Her laugh filled his chest with warmth. "And more than one woman is wondering what she'd have to do to get you to abandon me in favor of her."

Iden cupped Zoë's face and forced her gaze to his. "Nothing could entice us away from you. Nothing."

Her eyes darkened and he cursed himself when her tongue darted out to wet her lips, inviting him to prove his statement with a very public claim. He didn't dare.

"Say you'll come home with us," Miciah said, springing Iden from the trap of his own creation but setting a snare for himself when Zoë responded by asking, "Where's home?"

Iden held his breath. He understood at a gut level what he'd only understood intellectually before, how difficult a task the Council had set before those willing to be matched with a human female. It was against their laws to tell the truth about their world or their appearance until they were in the transport chamber and the female bound to them.

Still, he fought a smile, knowing Miciah had been one of the staunchest of believers when it came to the necessity of creating and enforcing laws with respect to those who might be brought from Earth. Jarlath, who served as both High Priest and Council representative, had ranted many times that when it came to change, Miciah often made him think of a thick, immovable *letakbra* tree with roots deep in the past.

"Winseka," Miciah shocked Iden by saying, then impressed him by touching his mouth to Zoë's briefly and adding, "It's not a place you'll find on any map."

"Sometimes those are the best kind of places," Zoë said, thinking of the photo essays and travel articles that stood out in her mind as the best she'd ever done. Almost all of them had been about places off the beaten track, small towns whose names held no significance except to those who lived in or near them.

"Say you'll come home with us," Miciah murmured against her lips, making her ache to agree.

Cautious hope filled her as the prophecy she longed to believe whispered through her mind. *When your heart is fully captured, the ability to see and feel will become one gift. Your touch will offer hope to those who have lost it.*

She wanted to say yes, more than they could possibly know. But she wanted to be sure. It would be unbearable to go with them, only to have to resume a life on the road if her mental shields came crashing down and her psychic gifts flared to life in the same way they always had, out-of-sync and useless.

"I'll think about it," she said, urging them forward along the campsite-created streets of the festival.

Miciah let the subject drop though Zoë knew he would ruthlessly press for the answer he wanted when they returned to the RV where she would be helpless against his sensual persuasion. He could make her agree to anything if only he would fill her with his cock, and if Iden joined him...

Liquid heat pooled in her labia with images of them kissing her, their lips touching in the process. A shiver went through her at the remembered sight of finding come on their bellies after they'd pleasured her to orgasm.

She forced her mind back to her surroundings, only to blush when she realized how far they'd walked while she was in a sexual daze. She halted in front of a glass worker, a Sixties-era hippie whose gray hair trailed down his back in a beaded braid.

He wore tie-dye and sandals, as did his female companion, whose hair was white and braided with flowers. "Feel free to touch anything that catches your interest," she said and Zoë dared it, picking up a delicate hummingbird.

It was an abstract creation rather than depicted realism. The wash of colors lent it the illusion of stopped time and captured flight.

"This is amazing work," Zoë said, meaning it. "Where are you based?"

"Albuquerque."

"There's a gallery in Santa Fe owned by Peter Knight. It's on Canyon Road and specializes in glasswork. Have you —"

"We know the gallery," the woman said. "We've been trying for years to get Ethan's work shown there."

She sighed and shared a glance with the artist. "We had an appointment to see the owner last year. A family emergency made us cancel it at the last moment. We haven't been able to get a second appointment. The owner handpicks the artists he shows, but he has galleries all over the world and is only in Santa Fe a couple times a year."

Zoë set the hummingbird down and picked up another piece, surreal lovers entwined, two men with a woman held between them, their bodies blended and touching completely. It was a sturdier piece, though for its added weight, it held the same qualities of time suspended and a precious moment caught in glass.

There was no way she could walk away without it, especially now, after having been in Iden and Miciah's arms. A small, discreetly placed price tag indicated how much the piece would set her back, and that the artist knew the value of his work.

"I'd like to buy this," Zoë said.

The woman rose from her chair and handled the transaction, wrapping the glass lovers in bubble wrap before placing them in a box for safekeeping. Zoë put the box in her purse and with the transaction compete, pulled a business card from her billfold.

She wrote a brief message on the back of the card before handing it to the woman. "Give this to Peter's gallery manager. His name is Lloyd. I can't guarantee he'll put you on the schedule, but it might help."

The woman's partner set what he was working on aside and joined them, taking the card. It was one of the gallery's.

His eyes widened. "You're the Zoë Andreadis who wrote an article about all of Peter's galleries, not just the one in Santa Fe."

A small thrill of pleasure went through her. "I am."

He immediately offered to make a gift of her purchase. Zoë shook her head, that's why she'd paid for it first before offering the card.

Iden watched Zoë's interaction with pride. *She will do well on Belizair*, he sent to Miciah.

Yes. Miciah's voice held the same pride.

After saying goodbye to the artist and his partner, she slipped her arms through theirs once again and they continued on, pausing in front of other artisan camps and shops.

Zoë was open in her admiration and lavish with her praise. "You're a writer?" Iden asked after they'd left a stall dedicated to Native American fetish work.

"A freelance one, though sometimes I'm more of a photographer, with a few words thrown in."

It tied in with what the bounty hunter sent to locate Zoë had said, that she looked to be leaving Auburn and was a wanderer by nature. Iden found himself asking the same question she'd put to the glassblower, "Where are you based?"

"The RV is home." She tilted her head to look at him. "What about you and Miciah, what do you do in Winseka?"

Several possible answers swept through Iden's mind. He analyzed them against what he knew of culture in the United States before settling on, "You would consider Miciah something of a full-time councilman. He spends his days considering the future and what is the best way for us to proceed as a people, while I attend to the needs of those struggling internally."

"In a way, you're both counselors," she said, sounding pleased by what they did.

"Yes."

They continued forward companionably, the hours slipping by and the sun rising higher in the sky. Lunchtime arrived and they stopped at a stand selling something called falafels, then took a seat on the sand to listen to a band play.

Images of the night before assailed Iden, reminding him of his first glimpse of Zoë and how they'd stretched out on the blanket with her beneath a star-filled sky. His cock hardened, bringing with it a tension he heard echoed in Miciah's voice when it pressed into his mind saying, *Time grows short.*

I know.

Around them other couples openly touched and kissed. It took considerable effort for Iden to keep his hands off Zoë — and Miciah — when she tormented him by stroking his thigh and Miciah's as she pointed out two men locked in an embrace and whispered, "I think I'm ready to go back to the RV now."

Panic flared to life inside Iden. They'd be on her in a second if they did, and if that happened, there'd be no way to prevent the Ylan stones from migrating to her bands.

He was spared from answering by a woman's panicked cry nearby and the sight of a man lying on the sand clutching his chest. Without thought Iden went to him.

Already several people had gathered. "I think he's having a heart attack," one of them said. "Someone needs to get to the first-aid tent."

The woman at the man's side sobbed as he went completely limp. "He's stopped breathing! He needs CPR!"

It was against their laws to interfere yet Iden could no more stop himself from placing his hands on the man's chest than he could have remained motionless and watched the man die. He pressed in sharp, hard movements — what the humans expected to see — as he jumpstarted the man's heart with the healing energy of the Ylan stones and regulating its beating until it became steady beneath his palm and the man's eyelids fluttered opened.

"You saved his life," the kneeling woman whispered. "Thank you."

"You're a hero, man," a scrawny, bare-chested teen said, holding out his hand. "Give me five."

Iden did so as Miciah said, *Well done and perfectly masked. Without a confession, even I would have difficulty offering testimony that I witnessed you breaking one of our laws. It's a good thing human knowledge has progressed to include what they call CPR. But I don't think it would be wise to linger here and allow your fame to grow and spread, or yourself to be photographed.*

Agreed, Iden said, rising to his feet and deftly extricating himself from the crowd without giving up his name.

As they left the area, men carrying a stretcher hurried past them. Iden's eyes met Zoë's and the beat of his own heart became unsteady at the emotion he found in them, pride and the beginnings of love.

"I want to be with the both of you again," she said, catapulting him into renewed turmoil. "Let's go back to the RV, or to your camp if it's closer."

Iden pushed as Miciah had earlier. "Say you'll come home with us."

Something unfathomable passed through her eyes before worry settled there. "I can't promise to stay for long."

He stopped and cupped her face. "But you'll come."

"Yes. At least for a little while."

Miciah's mental growl reverberated down Iden's spine. Iden responded by saying, *Her answer satisfies the Council's requirement when it comes to claiming a human bond-mate. All that remains is her agreement to commit to us. Do you doubt we can get that once we're in the transport chamber?*

Let's leave this place now.

Soon, Iden tempered, though he would have happily slung Zoë over his shoulder and rushed back to her RV. *Better to use what time we have to fortify ourselves against falling into bed with her, or giving in to her desire to see us together.*

He risked a kiss before they resumed walking, heading in the direction of Zoë's campsite.

Zoë couldn't suppress a smile at the increased pace and the tension vibrating off both men. Miciah's hand curled around her upper arm possessively. Iden's rested on her back.

They passed any number of artists she knew from other festivals. She limited herself to a wave and a called-out greeting, and found herself laughing softly at the knowing glances she received in return.

There was no way to hide the truth, even if she'd wanted to. Her nipples were hard points against the thin tank top while Iden and Miciah's erections pressed aggressively against the material of their shorts.

"We wouldn't be any more obvious if we just made a run for the RV," she teased.

"Behave," Miciah said, and as if they were of like mind, he and Iden slowed their pace, forcing Zoë to do the same.

It turned their walk into sensual torment. Her cunt lips were so swollen that each step made her aware of their fullness.

The yellow flags marking the zone where she was parked came into view. They entered a section claimed by musicians rather than artists. Ragged tents, beat-up trailers and cars all served as accommodations. The scent of hash and pot was thick in the air.

Clusters of people gathered to listen to those jamming. Some mellow, some manic.

Miciah and Iden crowded closer in a protective gesture that sent a sweet heat through her chest. Rarely did things get out of hand during the festival, even with those who used psychedelic drugs.

"You don't have to—" she said, only to have her words cut off as a red-faced man tumbled out of a tent reeking of alcohol.

He got to his feet and pulled a knife. Before she could do more than gasp, Miciah was on him, dodging a wild stab to render the man unconscious with a touch that reminded her of something Spock would do on Star Trek.

Another man emerged from the tent and Miciah crouched, ready to take him on as well. A woman in a halter top and panties stopped in the doorway, disheveled and red-faced. "Drag him back in, Tommy. He'll be okay when he comes to."

The man named Tommy approached Miciah warily and grabbed his fallen companion by the feet. His gaze skittered to the knife. "Okay if I take it? No point in getting him going again from finding it missing."

"Suit yourself," Miciah said, returning to Zoë's side as Tommy picked up the knife and placed it on the unconscious man's chest before dragging him into the tent.

"Impressive," Zoë said. She placed her hands on Miciah's shoulders and touched her mouth to his. "Looks like you deserve a hero's reward, too. It's a good thing we're close to the RV."

"Behave," he growled against her lips.

She smiled. "Maybe I'll let you punish me as part of your reward."

His arms went around her, crushing her to him as his mouth ravaged hers. She melted against him until Iden's arm wedged between her body and Miciah's, parting them with a reminder of where they were.

She entwined her fingers with Miciah's, the bands at their wrists touching. When she did the same with Iden, her mind spun off in a sensation that brought dread with it.

Reality faded, except for the fast beat of her heart as a scene unfolded in front of her, an adobe building set in a canyon wall, its appearance and isolation heavy with the weight of a long-dead people and forgotten culture.

No! she screamed silently, not wanting to witness some dark moment in either of their futures.

She braced herself for grief, for unbearable pain, the agony that came from a gift she had no control over. But instead of their misery, their happiness filled her as the front of the building melted in a stream of colorful light, revealing a bed with Miciah and Iden on it.

Though she could not see herself, she knew by their expressions that she was with them. Lust joined the happiness, pulsing through her bloodstream like heated gold. Color swirled around Iden and Miciah, a million tiny particles that made her think of the glass humming bird she'd held in her hands earlier, its wings blurred in an illusion of flight.

She stumbled and came out of her trance to find worried faces and the interior of her RV. "You're okay?" Iden asked, touching the back of his hand to her forehead, his gesture reminding her of how he'd saved a man's life earlier.

"I'm fine," she said, pulling her hand from his and placing a palm on his chest, rubbing it over a tiny nipple that went instantly hard.

"Better than fine," she added as the old fortuneteller's words swelled inside her with hope and certainty. *When your heart is fully captured, the ability to see and feel will become one gift.*

She touched Miciah as well. It was impossible not to.

Her fingertips went to his nipple to tug and torment. His hand covered hers as his eyes bored into hers, burning with a fiery hunger that promised to consume her.

Lust rushed in as quickly as the vision had. It became her only reality.

"Let us take you to a place where we'll be assured of privacy," Iden said, kissing her neck, sucking her earlobe before sending his tongue into her ear. "There's one not far from here."

The image of the adobe building shimmered into her thoughts. "We can unhitch my car from the RV and take it."

Chapter Nine

ഇ

If not for his promise to Kaylee, Miciah wouldn't have allowed Zoë to stop until they arrived at the transport chamber. Now it was all he could do to not protest when she got out of the car at the gas station he'd asked her to pull into.

You fear we'll lose her here? When we didn't among the crowds of the festival? Iden asked, his amusement like sandpaper abrading Miciah's nerves.

Miciah ignored the taunt, and the laughter following it when he captured Zoë's hand in his before she could take more than a couple of steps away from the car.

I'll wait here, in case your behavior sends her running, Iden said, suiting actions to words by leaning against the passenger door.

Inside, Zoë asked about bathrooms and Miciah felt an instant panic when she was given a key and sent back outside. He hated letting her out of his sight, even for a second now that they were so close to taking her home with them.

He ground his teeth together and touched his mind to Iden's. *She's safe?*

I watched her check the room before she entered it.

Miciah hurried to accomplish his task. He placed every carton of chocolate ice cream in the store's glassed refrigeration unit on the counter, along with a large Styrofoam chest and a bag of ice.

Zoë returned as he was paying for it. "Dare I ask?" she teased, her fingers sliding down his spine and reminding him of the honey she'd dribbled onto his cock.

Her laugh when she felt a shudder of desire go through him told him she'd meant for him to remember the honey. And since it was seemingly pointless to tell her to behave, especially now, when he was too close to the edge to enforce his command, Miciah busied himself by loading ice cream into the ice chest.

Iden's eyebrows lifted at seeing Miciah's tense features. His smile widened as his gaze leisurely traveled downward and settled on the front of Miciah's shorts. *You were only with her for a matter of moments.*

Let's go.

Iden laughed and slid into the front passenger seat. *To spare you additional agony, I'll sit next to Zoë.*

Miciah didn't protest. He got into the backseat, allowing Iden to direct Zoë from one seldom-used road to another until they finally turned onto a dirt road that ended in a box canyon.

Ancient ruins climbed the canyon walls, all that remained of a disappeared civilization and a time when the Fallon themselves had walked on Earth. Awe and relief surged through Miciah, that Belizair had avoided extinction as the people who'd once claimed this land had not.

"I wish I had my camera," Zoë murmured, her attention on the crumbled ruins rather than the intact adobe building at the rear of the canyon. "How do you know about this place?"

"It belongs to our people," Iden said.

That drew her attention away from the ruins. Her gaze lingered on the bands at Iden's wrists for an instant before going to his face. "Your people?"

Iden leaned in, handling the question with a kiss meant to distract and reassure. "You'll meet them soon enough, after we've taken you together in privacy, as we promised to do."

Miciah scanned the area though he didn't expect to see the bounty hunters assigned to make sure humans didn't stumble upon the transport chamber. At some point in the future, workers would come from Belizair to dismantle this portal and reassemble it in a place where it would be more accessible to those returning with mates. It was only luck that Zoë was camping in the desert and relatively close to it.

When they got to Winseka, he would make arrangements for Zoë's RV to be claimed and her possessions kept safe until they knew which ones held value to her and should be brought to Belizair. The unseen bounty hunters guarding the portal would deal with her car as soon as they knew the chamber stood empty.

Miciah shifted the cooler under his arm and took her hand. Iden claimed the other.

Their anticipation built with each step. She wore their bands and had agreed to go home with them. Now they needed only for her to acknowledge a bond with them, and because binding ceremonies were a private matter, Council law was flexible on what constituted a human female's agreement as long as her free will was not violated.

Iden opened the door and they stepped into a small foyer. The traditional chests for holding clothing were on either side of an archway leading into the transport chamber itself.

A bed was visible through the arch. It was in the middle of a small room, inches off a floor set with Ylan stones. On Winseka and other less remote chambers, plants thrived under a crystal clear ceiling, but here function took precedence over beauty.

The stones in Miciah's wristbands throbbed, soaking in and reflecting back the power present in the portal, calibrating themselves so transport would be possible. With a sense of relief he realized that bringing Zoë here had bought them time. It would take more than an unguarded moment of passion for the Ylan stones in his bands to migrate to those she wore.

His penis spasmed and arousal leaked onto its head when Iden kicked off his shoes and stripped out of his shorts, dropping the latter into one of the chests before grasping the bottom of Zoë's tank top and saying, "Your turn."

Her moan of willing surrender had Miciah gripping himself. He was held motionless by the sight of Iden's thick cock responding to Zoë, bobbing and leaving a glistening hint of moisture against his belly.

They were beautiful together. He'd never thought he'd enjoy the sight of another male touching his mate, but he liked witnessing what Iden and Zoë did to each other.

She let her purse slide off her shoulder and onto the ground then lifted her arms, allowing Iden to peel the thin top off her. The bra followed.

"It seems like it's been forever since we were naked together," she said, cupping her breasts, her fingers plucking at nipples that bore the marks of their attention.

Do you plan to join us? Iden asked, kneeling in front of her, ridding her of both skirt and panties in a single movement then removing her sandals.

Miciah was barely aware of shedding his shorts and shoes. He took up a position behind her, his hands taking possession of her breasts as he kissed her neck and shoulder.

"Say you accept our claim to you," he said, the words tumbling out in his desperation to know she wouldn't escape them.

Zoë gasped and rose on her toes, her breathing growing erratic as Iden's tongue licked along her slit. Her body hummed with desire. It traveled from the soles of her feet upward through her cunt and breasts and nipples, then down her arms so her pulse throbbed against the bands at her wrists.

In the light reflected off the crystal floor, the blue and black stones in the butterfly bracelet shone. They seemed almost liquid, as if they'd absorbed the heat pouring off her skin and become molten.

Her fingers speared through Iden's hair, holding his mouth against her cunt. She felt like primal woman, an ancient priestess in a sensuous fertility rite.

"I love having your mouth on me," she whispered, her breath catching as his lips closed around her clit, sucking it, filling it with blood and sensation until the hood pulled back so the tiny, pleasure-vulnerable head was exposed for his tongue to torment.

She shuddered as Iden's tongue rasped over it. Pressed backward and rubbed against Miciah's hard cock as his fingers tightened on her nipples, his grip merciless, blending pain with pleasure.

"More," she demanded, only to have them stop abruptly, in perfect sync with each other, as if they'd choreographed their response to heighten her need for them.

Miciah swung her up into his arms before she could voice a protest at being denied pleasure. He carried her the short distance to the bed and placed her on it, coming down on top of her.

His cock was hard against her clit. His hands held hers against the mattress as his weight kept her from canting her hips so he would slip inside her.

"Say you accept our claim to you, Zoë."

"Yes," she said, willing to agree to almost anything if he'd fill her with his cock.

She lifted her head so their lips met. Her tongue tangled with his.

He moaned and sweet victory surged through her with the thrust of his hips. Moisture poured from her slit as she tried to place her opening against his cock head.

"No," he said on a pant. "Not until you say the words."

"Not even then," Iden said, sliding his hand between them, his palm gliding over her belly and grasping Miciah's length so he jerked and wet her belly with his arousal.

She shivered in pleasure when Iden stroked her as his fist moved up and down on Miciah's shaft. "Agree to a permanent bond so the three of us can be together always," Iden murmured. "Agree and before this day is over, Miciah and I will become lovers because of you."

It was irresistible plea and unbearable temptation. "Show me now. Let me see a little of what you're promising."

Can you handle it? Iden challenged, more than willing to give Zoë what she wanted, nearly trembling in his eagerness to do it.

Now that they were in the presence of the ancient, powerful Ylan stones brought to Earth by the Fallon, he could keep those in his wristbands from migrating—at least until he orgasmed.

As long as I don't come, Miciah said, indicating the same level of control before easing to his side with Zoë between them and pinning her arms to the mattress above her head so she couldn't make either of them lose control.

Then there's no longer any reason to deny the truth between us.

Iden leaned in and touched his lips to Miciah's, thrust his tongue aggressively against Miciah's, demanding a response, a definition of what they would be to one another, equals or one dominant to the other.

Miciah curled his fingers around Iden's erection, accepting the challenge. His mental growl promising a fight if Iden thought he'd be the one consistently on top.

Iden's hips bucked, driving his length through Miciah's fisted hand. By the Goddess, he'd dreamed of this since he'd first been introduced to the Vesti Council member who'd come to dominate his fantasies until Zoë entered his life.

Raw need coursed through him, the same desire that had made him lie in bed alone, preferring to bring himself off with his own hand as he imagined being with Miciah rather than to unfairly use another man to gain relief.

He moaned, feeding Miciah his hunger. Tasting the same on Miciah.

Lust scorched a path from where their lips touched to where Miciah's fingers held his cock prisoner in a grip that promised exquisite ecstasy even as it denied it. Iden was intensely aware of Zoë, her breathing as fast as theirs, her scent deepening, becoming a lure that would soon make thought impossible and destroy all resistance to what she wanted of them.

Heat poured off her body as she moved restlessly between them, rubbing her soft skin against their thighs and the back of their hands. "Come for me," she whispered, and the image of coating her belly with his semen as Miciah's cock jerked in his fist and did the same, nearly cost Iden his control.

Enough! he said, forcing himself to pull away from Miciah's mouth and claim Zoë's instead, desperate to keep her from commanding them again and making them spend their seed.

Extract her promise or I will, Miciah growled into his mind. *Already there is no time to prepare her for the sight of our true forms. I'm too close now to do more than get inside her and thrust once before the stones migrate. I want to be on Belizair when explanations are called for.*

Then claim her cunt and give me the task of working into her back entrance. I'll key the chamber to transport us in the moment of orgasm, when the stones migrate and fill her bands.

Do it.

If he'd been lying on top of Zoë, Iden doubted he would have had the strength for conversation. Somehow he managed to lift his mouth from hers despite the way her lips clung to his.

"Agree to a permanent bond," he said. "We can't lose you now that we've found you. Trust us to see to your needs, to ensure your happiness. Say the words, Zoë."

He touched his lips to hers again, putting the depth of his commitment and need into the kiss he gave her. She rewarded him by whispering, "I trust you. I want a future together. I can't imagine not having this."

"Then get on top of Miciah. Take his cock inside you, but don't move, Zoë." He brushed his mouth over hers, hoping to entice her into behaving. "Don't make him come. He's too close. I'm too close. Let us take you at the same time so the three of us can find release together."

"I'll be good."

Iden shuddered and felt an answering reaction ripple through Miciah's cock. He released Miciah's length, watched as Miciah immediately gripped himself, using pain to last a few moments longer.

Miciah freed Zoë's wrists and rolled to his back, his cock glistening and belly wet from arousal. Zoë got to her knees and straddled him, her inner thighs slick with honeyed excitement.

Hurry! Miciah said as she pressed her opening to his cock head and slowly sheathed him, replacing his hand with the tight fist of her channel.

Iden stroked her back. "Lie down on him, Zoë."

She obeyed and instantly Miciah grasped her buttocks, spreading them to reveal the puckered rosette of her anus. Iden reached down and opened one of the discreetly placed drawers built into the bed, pulling out a small tube of ritzca oil.

A moan escaped as he coated his cock with it, not daring to apply it directly to Zoë's back entrance for fear she'd begin writhing and cost Miciah his control.

He touched the tip of his penis to her anus. She gasped, panted as the lubricant soaked in, preparing her. Her fingers curled in the bed clothing, the muscles along her back tensed as she struggled to obey, to remain still so they could orgasm together.

"Hurry," she said, echoing Miciah's mental command, her buttocks lifting in a carnal kiss that had him fighting against thrusting hard and deep.

"Patience, beloved," he whispered, sweat coating his skin as he slowly worked his way inside her. "I don't wish to hurt you." *I don't want to lose control.*

Her sob was answered by a guttural sound from his own throat. The pleasure was very nearly unbearable. She was so tight, made even more so by Miciah filling her channel.

Iden doubted he'd last more than a stroke or two, not with Miciah's cock rubbing against his, separated by only a thin, heated barrier. Not with the future he'd hardly dared dream about spread out before them, needing only the hot splash of orgasm and the migration of the Ylan stones to become a reality.

Now, he sent to Miciah, feeling the phantom quivering of his wings. Seeing the glittering particles that would manifest into Miciah's wings spreading out over the bedspread like a gauzy, translucent blanket.

Miciah took Zoë's hands, entwined his fingers with hers so his wristbands touched hers. Iden joined his hands to theirs, touched his bands to Zoë's. There'd be no stopping now, no preventing the stones from separating and filling her bands. No preventing the fiery spewing of seed.

"Ours," Iden said against Zoë's ear, his tongue claiming the sensitive opening.

"Ours," Miciah said against her mouth before plundering it with his tongue, his hips lifting, his cock thrusting against Iden's, and there was longer any way to remain still.

Around them the Ylan stones began to pulse, lighting the chamber in a sequence of color. The heavy throb of unleashed power intensified the moment, the joining of three beings each carrying the Fallon in their genes as they moved in a rhythmic, ancient dance toward a crescendo where they'd become one.

Sensation bombarded Iden. The feel of Miciah's cock and Zoë's skin. The scent of lust and the sounds of it. The exquisite pleasure that transcended the physical, reaching down to fill his heart and soul so he would never ache for any but those he shared a mate-bond with.

He felt the swell of the Ylan stones at his wrists, and then the sweeping joy of completion as his world narrowed to Zoë and Miciah, to the incomparable ecstasy of shared release.

Reality shattered for Zoë. It fractured into a thousand shimmering particles of pleasure only to reform into surreal fantasy.

Wings and a glassed ceiling. Exotic plants and flower-scented air.

Men and a room that were no longer the same.

It would have been tempting to think it was a dream, a psychedelic vision brought on by accidentally ingesting some of the drugs found at the Sol Celebration. Only her own gifts kept her steady, not fearing for her sanity though her heart raced.

Its beat outpaced the fast pounding of Miciah's and Iden's, the three of them on their sides. Their chests pressed against her front and back, their arms keeping her from leaving the bed in a panic.

All is well, beloved, Iden said, the words sounding as clearly in her mind as Miciah's growled "no" sounded in her ears when she startled and instinctively tried to pull from their arms.

"Easy, Zoë," Iden said, this time out loud, accompanying the words with the touch of his lips to her bare shoulder.

She turned her head to look down the length of their bodies, to find the truth of physical sensation and hazy images. Soft wings draped across their legs like a comforter, Iden's the feathers of a bird of prey, Miciah's, like those of a bat but with the texture of well-worked suede.

"This is Winseka?" Zoë guessed, sunlight streaming through a crystal ceiling the adobe building set beneath canyon ruins didn't have.

"Yes," Iden said. "We also call it the Bridge City." And Miciah added, *Our world is known as Belizair.*

She felt their pleasure at her lack of panic as intensely as she'd ever felt a stranger's deep despair. It flowed into her, sliding up her arms and into her chest, drawing her eyes to the bracelets they'd placed on her wrists.

The bands they'd given her now contained the same night-sky stones they wore, black with a galaxy of tiny stars. She hadn't imagined the hum earlier, the subtle vibration of energy against her skin, just as she hadn't imagined the deepening luster in the stones molded to butterfly shapes.

Otis may have found the bracelets while prospecting for gold in the Sierras, but they had their origins in this place. Zoë knew it as surely as she knew she was meant to have them and meant to be here.

She'd dreamed of Miciah and Iden. She'd glimpsed the future when their hands touched earlier.

When your heart is fully captured, the ability to see and feel will become one gift. Your touch will offer hope to those who have lost it.

Being able to make a difference was what she'd longed for, hoped for—why even in her darkest moments, she'd never thought herself cursed. Hadn't a life spent traveling prepared her for this most amazing journey of all?

Iden's lips brushed against her shoulder. "Your mind is closed to us, beloved. What are you thinking?"

His comment surprised her, until she realized that just as her life on the road had prepared her for being here, so had the need to build mental shields. They were automatic for her, a default setting that would allow privacy in a world where telepathic communication was possible.

Underneath Iden's question she felt his worry, and Miciah's rising along with it. There were a thousand things to learn, a new world to explore, and yet they faded in importance against Iden and Miciah's need for reassurance.

They were bound together in ways she didn't fully understand. With promises exchanged and made truth by stones that seemed to be so much more.

"I was thinking that I belong here," she said, rubbing against them, loving the warmth of the hard, masculine bodies pressed so intimately against hers. "With you."

Good, Miciah said, *because we will never let you go.*

This time she felt his possessiveness as well as heard it in his voice. It was consuming, thrilling.

You are ours to pleasure and protect, Iden said, the intensity of his possessiveness no less than Miciah's, though reassurance came with his words, that her happiness was important, vital, more so than their own.

It was impossible to resist them, but then it had been from the first moment she saw them. *So is the plan to stay in bed all day?*

Their answer was immediate. Simultaneous. *Yes.*

She laughed and slid her hand down Miciah's arm, then around, to stroke the underside of his wing. He shivered in reaction, his lust spiking through her, his eyes turning molten gold.

"That reminds me," she murmured provocatively against Miciah's lips. "I believe Iden promised that before the day was over, the two of you would become lovers in the fullest sense of the word if I agreed to a permanent bond."

Miciah moaned, soul-deep and hungry. Iden's teeth found the place where they'd already marked her. *Behave*, he said, punishing her with a bite that guaranteed she wouldn't.

Their lust swept into her like a flash fire, making her ache and burn. *I want you both again.*

And you'll have us, in any way you desire, Iden said.

Once Iden and I escort you to the quarters set aside for us.

Iden's laugh was husky. *Shall we leave the transport chamber now?*

Miciah's hand covered Zoë's breast possessively. *Yes.*

Chapter Ten

ဆ

Gorgeous, Zoë thought as Iden and Miciah both stood, waiting for her to slide off the mattress. She hadn't thought they could look any better than they did the first time she saw them naked, but the wings...

Her channel spasmed mercilessly at the sight of them standing side by side. They were muscled perfection and fantasy creation—and they were all hers.

"Beloved," Iden said, his hand closing around his cock. "I thought you were in agreement with the plan to leave this bed in favor or going to our own."

She laughed, loving the feel of heat and need pulsing off him, the dark, hungry waves of lust radiating from Miciah. "I know, but the two of you are like something out of a wicked, erotic fantasy."

She couldn't resist the urge to tease them by dipping her fingers into her slit then gliding them over her clit, her toes curling as white fire streaked through her.

A low growl sounded in Miciah's throat. He shackled her wrist in an iron grip and pulled her hand away from her mound.

"You've been warned," he said, delivering a spank to her cunt.

The shock of it made her gasp. The feel of it flooded her channel with liquid desire.

His face was taut, his lips a firm line of resolve. His eyes dared her to continue her teasing.

She glanced at Iden. His expression warned he might well administer a punishment after Miciah was done disciplining her.

The thought of it made her wetter. Desire coiled in her belly. Obediently she slid from the mattress. Not to avoid their sensual wrath, but because going to their private quarters seemed like a very, very good idea.

Miciah took her hand. Iden did the same. They led her to a wooden chest similar to the ones she'd noticed next to the archway in the adobe building.

Iden opened it, putting on something that was little more than a loincloth before pulling out sheer, matching harem pants with the same night-sky pattern as the stones in the bands the three of them now wore. He knelt in front of her as Miciah moved behind her, his hands covering her breasts, his fingers teasing her nipples into hard, aching points of need.

It's tradition that you wear this design on our binding day, Iden said, circling her ankle, silently urging her to lift her foot so he could dress her.

She complied, and was rewarded with the sensuous feel of the material sliding up her legs, and by the sweet torment of his lips closing around her clit, his tongue caressing it before he stood and fastened the pants closed at her waist. She moaned in protest when Miciah left her to put on a loin covering like Iden's, then startled when the wall parted, reabsorbing itself to form a doorway.

Two strangers waited in a spacious outer chamber. Both of them had wings similar to Iden's though their white feathers had traces of color. One was standing, like someone waiting for an elevator to arrive, while the other sat on a bench, his head bent as though he were in contemplation.

Zoë crossed her arms over her chest in an instinctive reaction. Her cheeks heated. Both Iden and Miciah closed in on her, sheltering her body with theirs. Their touch brought instant comfort. She had no problem going topless at the beach, but here, now —

The women on Belizair don't cover their breasts, Miciah said, the possessiveness in his voice hinting that at the moment he wished it were otherwise.

Iden brushed his lips against hers. He coaxed her arms away from her chest by guiding her hands to the front of his loin covering, smoothing them over the sheer material and hardened flesh. *It's considered rude to stare at a woman's breasts or a man's obvious erection. But truthfully, the thought of others seeing your beauty and knowing your effect on me brings me pleasure, not shame.*

Miciah's rigid length pressed against her buttocks, his growl sent a shiver of pure lust through her. *And I would prefer our mate never leave the privacy of our home.*

Let's go to our quarters then, Iden said, *and see if you can turn your wish into fact, though I doubt your ability to do it.*

They stepped away from her and Miciah's expression grew suddenly alarmed. Iden laughed. "In your hurry to get Zoë into the transport chamber on Earth you left the chest containing the ice cream in the outer room. Kaylee's gift is on the floor at the foot of the bed."

"My thanks," Miciah said, retrieving it along with the purse Zoë had dropped in her desperation to allow Iden to tug her clothing off so they could make love.

She took the purse from Miciah, her eyebrows drawing together. "What about my car? My RV? The Sol Celebration is over in another week."

Iden gave her a reassuring kiss. *Some of those stationed on your world will already be moving to collect your things and keep them safe until you decide what you wish to do with them.*

A small fission of fear went through her. *Can I go back?*

Miciah's expression grew taut. His body stiffened and she could feel his protest at even the thought of it.

Iden's flinch was very nearly imperceptible, his reaction less volatile. *Give our world a chance, Zoë. Give us a chance before you decide you prefer Earth.*

They made it sound like an either-or situation. Her stomach cramped at the thought of losing them and she let the subject drop—for the moment. There'd be time to revisit it later.

"Congratulations to you both," the man who was standing said to Iden and Miciah as the three of them exited the transport chamber.

I notice he didn't congratulate me on ending up with the two of you, Zoë teased after the man entered the chamber and the door closed behind him.

She felt the hum and energy of the portal coming to life. It pulsed through the stones at her wrists, not just the night-sky ones she'd gotten from Miciah and Iden, but the ones on the butterfly-patterned bracelets.

The second man stood, and at the sight of his anguished face, Zoë forgot all about her exposed breasts. "Forgive me coming to you on your binding day," he said to Iden. "I wouldn't have sought you out if the need weren't great. Phenice is... I'm afraid for her. My efforts to console her are failing. Perhaps you can reach her where I can't."

"I will attend you and your bond-mate," Iden said, his concern traveling down the link Zoë shared with him.

"Go," she said when he turned to her, impressions of a candlelit room with a low altar flickering through her mind.

I'll return to the two of you as soon as I can, he said, touching his mouth to hers before leaving with the stranger.

He'd said he was a counselor, but that didn't fit with the image of candles and altar. *Iden serves the Goddess of the Amato as a priest for his people,* Miciah said, picking up on her confusion and answering her unformed question.

And you?

I serve on the ruling council of Belizair. I represent the Vesti who claim the jungle region as their home.

Zoë's eyebrows drew together. "You consider yourselves two different races," she guessed. "The wings determine who is Vesti and who is Amato?"

"Yes."

They stepped outside into a breathtaking panorama of desert and distant mountains surrounding a rainbow-colored city of crystal. Arches connected the buildings, their colors as varied and beautiful as the tulip-like flowers growing in random patterns everywhere Zoë looked.

Trees reminiscent of palms reached toward a sky that had two suns. Exotic birds strutted in an oasis setting, brightly colored feathers fanned out like peacocks.

"Amazing," Zoë whispered, awed by the fantasyscape around her.

Next to her Miciah stiffened. Mentally she heard his muttered, silent curse as a Vesti boy in his teens landed in front of them.

"The other members of the Council sent me with a summons," the boy said, his eyes continually darting to Zoë and turning it into a struggle not to cross her arms over her chest again. "They wanted me to tell you there is urgent business to discuss. Your attendance is necessary even though you've just returned with your new bond-mate."

"Tell them I will be there as soon as Zoë is settled."

With one last glance at her, the boy launched himself into the air. She felt a pang of envy as she watched him, and a sense of being *less*.

"Never," Miciah growled, reminding her that she'd left the pathway between their minds unobstructed. "You are our future."

Both he and Iden had said as much, in several different ways. Now, with the bond between them, she sensed the words held a deeper, more significant meaning than she'd attributed to them before. But when she would have probed, seeking answers in the same wordless communication that was the essence of her gift of *sight*, Miciah blocked her by shielding his memories and thoughts.

"Later," he said, "when Iden is with us and we can talk at our leisure. He and I will share all that we know with you, everything that we are."

She felt the sincerity of his pledge and the depth of his commitment to her. She also felt how much he hated being called away from her.

The idea of being cooped up and left waiting held no appeal for her, and while she was bold and confident enough to explore this new world alone, as she'd done so many other exotic locations, she could well imagine Miciah's reaction if she suggested it. Iden might be persuaded, but Miciah...

She laughed silently. There was a downside to having a dominant, possessive lover who she suspected would soon have her comparing him to a caveman.

Thankfully his arms were occupied with the cooler of chocolate ice cream. Seeing it gave her an idea of how to avoid being deposited in their quarters with no guarantee that she could figure out a way to escape them. She ran her hand along the leading edge of his wing and felt him shudder with pleasure.

Behave, he warned, the mental connection between them restored in a heartbeat.

Who's Kaylee? she asked, remembering Iden calling the ice cream Kaylee's gift.

Rather than answer her in sentences, Miciah showed her pictures of the human child he'd nicknamed the small general. He shared with her the visit that had led to Iden and him coming to Earth.

"I've got a sister?" Zoë asked, dazed and excited and nervous all at the same time.

"Ariel." He sent a picture of an adult version of Kaylee.

Considering that Ariel's petite, blonde-haired, blue-eyed looks were the opposite of her willowy dark ones, Zoë couldn't stop herself from saying, "Are you sure? We don't look anything alike."

For which I am grateful, Miciah purred. *Everything about you is perfect. You claim Iden and I are something out of an erotic fantasy, yet you are very much the same to us.*

His words, and the images accompanying them, sent heated arousal sliding down her inner thighs to wet the loose, sheer fabric of the harem pants. Need spiked through her, intense and heated.

"Behave, yourself," she said, her voice husky, her nipples so hard and tight that it was all she could do to keep her fingers away from them.

For a split second she was tempted to let him take her to their quarters so she could gain some relief, either from him or from her own hand. But the prospect of meeting Ariel and Kaylee gave her the strength to resist.

She curled her fingers around his arm. "Rather than leaving me alone in our quarters, let's deliver the ice cream now. If Ariel's not busy, perhaps I can visit with her and Kaylee until you and Iden are free. Can you tell if they're home? Can you communicate with them mind-to-mind?"

"I don't share a bond with them. From this distance I can neither tell where they are nor communicate telepathically with them."

She could feel a struggle going on inside him, primitive male versus caring mate. His desire to protect and possess and keep her locked away was like a living flame inside him. It burned and twisted and sent pulsing waves of lust straight to her cunt and breasts. But in its wake came something even more powerful, his need to see to her pleasure in all ways, physical as well as emotional.

He growled. A frustrated masculine sound that signaled his intention to accede to her wishes against his own. With a heavy sigh he said, "We will go to the quarters Ariel shares with her mates and Kaylee. If she invites you to stay, I will leave you with her.

"Generally we walk or fly when in a given region of Belizair. But I need to get to the Council building. I will transport us there."

He transferred the cooler into her arms before circling her with his own. There was barely time for Zoë to blink before the view of desert and mountain and city was replaced by a solid wall composed of a material she doubted could be found on Earth.

She wasn't sure if she was imagining the hum of energy at her wrists and the whisper of *how* to transport that seemed just out of reach of her hearing, or if she was picking up on them through her bond with Miciah. "Will I be able to do this on my own?" she asked.

Denial flashed down the link along with his worry and fear. Accompanying it was the knowledge that none of the human females had attempted such a thing and Miciah didn't intend that *she* be the first to do so.

Zoë closed her mental shields, preferring to save that particular battle for another day. Their relationship was new, despite her dreaming about them and believing she was meant to be with them on Belizair. There would be time to iron out issues of expectations and independence.

Miciah took the cooler from her and set it on the ground in front of where she assumed a door would soon appear. She wrapped her arms around his neck and pressed her naked breasts to his equally bare chest, wanting to calm him. "Thank you for bringing me here."

His hands swept down her back, smoothing over her buttocks as his hard cock ground against her mound. "Don't think you'll leave our quarters anytime soon once we finally arrive there."

She smiled against his mouth. Considering all the sexual experimentation she wanted to enjoy with them, it was easy to say, "I won't."

He claimed her lips then, thrust his tongue against hers in a way that told her just how furiously he intended to fuck her when they were together again. The desire to ignore his responsibilities and forget about delivering the ice cream vibrated through him as the kiss lengthened, taking on a desperate edge.

With a groan he stepped away from her. He touched his hand to the wall.

A moment later the door slid open to reveal Kaylee. She squealed in delight. "You found her! You found Mommy's sister! I told you she'd be your mate!"

Her eyes went to the cooler. She started jumping up and down like a human pogo stick. "And you brought ice cream!"

Kaylee's happiness was completely infectious. It bubbled over Zoë, making her laugh and putting a grin on Miciah's face. "Chocolate," he said. "As promised. Is your mother here?"

"Yes." Kaylee calmed long enough to ask Zoë for her name. As soon as Zoë provided it, Kaylee turned away from the door and yelled, "Mommy, come quick! I've got a double surprise for you!"

Ariel joined them a moment later. Her expression was a mix of curious and welcoming.

"Did I hear the word surprise?" she asked Kaylee.

"Look!" Kaylee said, lifting the top off the cooler and revealing the cartons of ice cream nestled in ice.

Ariel's breath caught on a sigh Zoë understood completely. There were times when the prospect of indulging in chocolate was more enticing than sex.

A glance at Miciah and she laughed silently. In her case, she didn't see that time arriving in the near future.

"This is only part one of your surprise," Kaylee said, grabbing Ariel's hand. "Part two is Zoë. She's my new auntie. That's because she's your sister, Mommy. Your *real* sister. The one you wanted to find before I got sick when I was a baby. The golden lady told me she could be Miciah's match because the genes that mattered were like your genes."

Kaylee bit her bottom lip. "Well the golden lady didn't say *exactly* that. But it's what she meant. I gave Jeqon some of the hair from your locket. He said — "

Ariel curled her hand around the lower part of her daughter's face, covering her mouth as she pressed a kiss to hair that was exactly the same pale blonde as hers. "Hush, baby. Give me a minute to take this in."

"The ice cream is melting," Kaylee said, her voice muffled.

Ariel laughed. Her gaze shifted between Zoë and Miciah, then down to the bands on their wrists. "It's true?"

The wonder and quiet happiness Zoë heard in the question told her she and Ariel would make up for a childhood apart by becoming close friends as adults.

"Yes," Miciah said. "Your father's genes carried the Fallon markers. Jeqon had Zoë located and confirmed she's my match. I've claimed her with Iden, of the Cathetel clan-house."

Tears glistened at the corners of Ariel's eyes. She held out her hand and Zoë took it. "I'd like to spend time with you. Can you stay long enough for a bowl of ice cream?"

Zoë grinned. "I was hoping you'd ask. A little while ago I was in a box canyon looking at Native American ruins and thinking the adobe building set against the cliff wall was some kind of exotic make-out place."

Ariel's eyes widened. "You just arrived here?"

"Yes. Iden was called away before we left the building with the transport chamber in it. Miciah's got an urgent meeting he should already be attending."

"Then you absolutely have to stay with me," Ariel said, releasing Kaylee and starting to bend down to pick up the ice chest.

Kaylee beat her to her. "I'll get it Mommy. You're pregnant."

Ariel snorted. "Pregnant but not weak minded or weak bodied, as I often find myself telling your fathers."

Kaylee giggled and Zoë laughed.

"You and I are going to get along great," Zoë said, turning to say goodbye to Miciah.

He brushed a kiss over her lips. *I will come for you as soon as I'm free, unless Iden collects you first.*

She could feel his reluctance to leave her. *Go. I'll be fine.*

He stepped back, and blinked out. She shook her head. "It's like something out of a science fiction story, isn't it?"

"You're handling it very well," Ariel said. "Now let's open up a carton of ice cream and get to know each other."

Chapter Eleven

ఴ

Iden had counseled so many since the effects of the virus became known. But as he watched Denaus plead with his bond-mate to join them at the altar, doubt over being able to truly help plagued him as it never had before.

Layered over that uncertainty was a thin measure of guilt. In all likelihood, because of Zoë and Miciah, there would be children for him, a son or daughter carrying his blood and his Amato heritage into the future. For Phenice, who'd miscarried the child it had taken her years to conceive, he could only offer the comfort of the Goddess along with his own words of hope.

Tragedy brought some mates closer, but others it drove apart. More and more often now, that was the case, and his counsel seemed only to delay the inevitable rather than mend what was broken.

Males came to him, hoping he could advise them on what to say to ease the suffering of their women, how they could bridge the gap forming between them.

Females came to him, sunk in the depths of a despair that often took hours to pull them from.

Both the Amato and Vesti cultures revered motherhood. Children, even before the devastation wrought by the Hotaling virus, were considered priceless, a gift. And now, stripped of what they had come to value the most in themselves, what many viewed as their most important purpose, to bear and raise children, the women suffered.

The High Priests and Priestesses, who the Goddess and Consort spoke with directly, maintained that those on Belizair would grow stronger for what they endured now. But as Denaus guided his mate to the altar, Iden wondered how much longer the women would suffer before they had tangible proof they weren't forsaken.

Would hope come only to those women without mates, as it had for the unmated males? What then for those who were already bonded?

At Denaus' urging, Phenice knelt on one of the pillows placed around the low altar. The light from the scented candles brought out the gold in her hair and wings, revealed the sorrow clinging to her. She allowed Iden to take her hand, while Denaus clasped her other.

The soothing grace of the Goddess flowed into Iden. Where his hands touched Phenice and Denaus', it tried to slide into them, offering to comfort and shield them from the pain they carried, at least while they were in the temple.

The Goddess' gift wasn't like a pounding wave. It didn't sweep away any barrier that might keep it from reaching the shore and wiping away marks in the sand to leave it smooth and clean. It was a trickle easily blocked and denied.

Denaus accepted the warm flow of comfort, but Phenice denied it, lifting pleading eyes to Iden and saying. "What good does it do to take solace here when it changes nothing? As soon as I step outside, the loss of our child crushes me all over again. All I see ahead of me is nothingness."

"The pain will lessen," Iden said. "Let the Goddess and Consort help you. Let them ease your burden one day at a time. Not long ago, it seemed as though both the Amato and Vesti would disappear, leaving Belizair deserted. But now there's hope for both our races. Grasp that hope, Phenice, let it reignite your own."

Tears pooled in Phenice's eyes. "How can I? Denaus is the only son of his clan-house. They had another mate in mind for him, but he chose me against their wishes. If he hadn't, then he would already be a father. She was pregnant soon after joining in a different bond. He owes it to his parents to petition the High Priests and Priestesses for the separation of our bond so he'll have a chance at gaining a human mate. I can't bear knowing that because of me, he'll never have a son or daughter."

"I didn't desire her, Phenice. You know that's true." Denaus' voice was hoarse with pain and pleading. "Nor did I want a bond that included others. I still don't. You are enough for me, only you, Phenice. Please. Take the comfort offered through Iden. I don't want to lose you."

His tears melted the barrier of Phenice's resistance, allowing the first trickle of peace to slide into her. With a nod she bowed her head.

Iden closed his eyes and sank into a state of meditation, all sense of self and time fading away. He become the conduit of the Goddess whose embrace surrounded Belizair, and of the Consort, Ylan, whose form was Belizair itself and whose life force pulsed in the veins of stone throughout the soil, just as blood pumped through the flesh of a man's body.

* * * * *

Miciah entered the chamber set aside for formal discussion and claimed the remaining open seat. On the table in front of him were three smooth, crystal disks to be used when a vote was taken.

To his left, Isaura, who represented the Amato in the fertile growing region of the west, said, "Our apologies for calling you away from your new mate."

Jati, a Vesti scientist serving on the Council added, "But in a way, your being recently matched is fortuitous." With a small nod acknowledging the Amato scientist who also served on the Council, he continued, "Gabri and I both spoke with Jeqon before approaching the others to ask for an emergency meeting and a decision on an issue that can longer be avoided.

"There was no breach of protocol or ethics in Jeqon having bounty hunters search for the sister of the human, Ariel, who you were first found to be a match for. I do not think anyone would claim you took advantage of your position to secure a mate, or cheated another since Iden is both your co-mate and the closest match to the human female, Zoë. But in the short time you were away from Belizair, two significant matches were made using the experimental protocol. In both cases, a Vesti and an Amato carry the identical Fallon gene sequence matching that of the female. And in both cases, one of those matched is closely related to a Council member. The first is to my cousin, who is an only child. He and an Amato friend have already agreed to form a bond should one of them be matched."

Isaura spoke up, "The second match is to my son. His brother is already in a shared bond but there are no children for any of the females in it."

Miciah felt the heavy weight of responsibility settle onto his shoulders. He understood Jati's purpose in mentioning both Ariel and Zoë before arrowing to the heart of the matter.

How could the Council members take mates for themselves, or allow their relatives to claim them, and not be seen as dishonorable when it came to light that there was more than one possible match? And yet should they deny themselves and those they cared about a chance at happiness and children in order to keep the knowledge that there was both a perfect Vesti match *and* a perfect Amato match secret, knowing even as they did so, that ultimately the truth would be revealed?

With an internal sigh, he closed his mind to thoughts of Zoë, to the joy he'd found and the pleasure he'd experienced. There would be no returning to their quarters until a decision was reached here. "You've already discussed this new information among yourselves?" he asked, his gaze traveling around the circular table.

Jarlath, the Amato priest Miciah often found himself at odds with, said, "Yes. We sent a bounty hunter to locate you and ask you to return. When he couldn't find you, we hoped you were on your way to the transport chamber." Jarlath too glanced around the table. "For the sake of efficiency, is it acceptable for me to provide an overview and summarize the most important of the arguments first, allowing anyone who wishes to expand on a point of view, or clarify one to do so afterward?"

The others nodded in agreement.

Jarlath said, "We seem to agree there are three divergent paths to take, though within those three, there are variations of approach. One option is to control the selection process, alternating the search between Vesti and Amato and then assigning the female to the first male who is a match. Or alternatively, to the male who first provided his DNA, though there have been arguments this would favor the Amato since we came forward in greater numbers initially.

"The second path we might choose is to delay notifying those who have been matched until we can gather more information and study this matter further. Cyan is expected to go into labor at any moment now. Until she gives birth, we won't know the true outcome of what we set in motion, and depending on it, it's possible there will be a huge increase in males submitting their DNA.

"The third of our options is to allow the scientists to notify both pairs of males who have been matched to a female, then work toward a solution as to who can claim her."

"Which is, of course, the most divisive course of action," Javant, the Vesti from the same region as Isaura interjected.

Miciah gave a small nod in acknowledgement of the point. He could guess where the others stood on this matter. His own resistance to rapid change on Belizair was well known. But in the interest of all, not just the Vesti way of life, Miciah ordered himself to keep an open mind, to be willing to listen to the arguments that would be put forth by the others. "Shall we argue the merits and disadvantages of each course of action before taking a vote on which one to pursue and further define?"

* * * * *

Zoë grinned as she passed through Ariel's living room. It was spacious, open, and decorated in a style that could only be labeled as an eclectic collection of museum-type displays—of the natural history type instead of art and ceramics.

Pressed flowers and leaves were held in crystal slabs, reminding her of bugs trapped in amber. Rocks, big and small, graced tables and sat clustered on the floors.

She couldn't resist teasing by saying, "I'm glad you thought better of having specimens in jars of formaldehyde as conversation pieces."

Ariel laughed. "Believe me, if I'd allow it, it would happen. My Vesti mate is a scholar and scientist. But if you were to visit Komet's office, you'd be tempted to call him a packrat."

At the arched entranceway to the kitchen, Zoë did a double take when movement in a shoulder-height tree caught her eye and she saw what looked like a miniature version of a flying squirrel—in green instead of gray—sitting there.

"That's Sabaska," Kaylee said, setting the cooler of ice cream down on a counter. "She's called a banzit. Komet found her when she was just a baby, but he couldn't find the nest she came from. One day she might go back and live in the jungle. Until then Komet and I are taking care of her and trying to teach her the things she needs to know."

Kaylee straightened her shoulders. Her expression grew as serious as a professor's. "On Belizair no one keeps pets. They might take care of animals that need help, or can't live on their own, but they're viewed as a privilege and a responsibility, not as a possession."

"I'm looking forward to learning all about life here," Zoë said, entering the alcove-like room that served as kitchen and intimate dining area.

Kaylee took out bowls and spoons and set them on the table. Ariel put all but one of the cartons of ice cream in a compartment built into the wall.

"You can't imagine how desperately I've been craving this," she said as they all took seats around the small table. "I almost feel guilty indulging without letting the other human women know there's ice cream on the planet. But as soon as I do, it'll be like a locust swarm went through here—not that I'd blame them in the least. I'd do a locust imitation myself if someone else had the ice cream."

"Or a Big Mac," Kaylee said, giggling. "You were practically drooling last night when you were talking to Zeraac about them." She turned to Zoë, adding, "And the night before that, it was Kentucky Fried Chicken. Not many people eat meat here, especially the kind that comes from things with wings. Besides, it costs a lot of money. They don't raise animals to kill, and compared to Earth, there aren't that many Amato and Vesti who fish for a living, or hunt."

Ariel opened the carton to reveal its smooth, chocolately contents. A sigh escaped and her eyes teared up. She wiped at them and sent Zoë an apologetic glance, "Ignore me. It's a side effect of carrying our newest family members."

"Family members?" Zoë asked, taking up a large spoon and filling a bowl with ice cream then handing it to Ariel.

"Mommy is going to have twins," Kaylee said, leaning over the table in anticipation of getting the next bowl. "All the humans here are. Well, except me. And I don't plan to have even one boyfriend until I'm a lot older. The boys here are too bossy."

Zoë and Ariel shared a conspiratorial smile. "Bossy can be fun sometimes," Ariel teased.

Kaylee rolled her eyes as she claimed the bowl of ice cream Zoë pushed toward her. "I don't think so, Mommy."

Zoë filled her own bowl and gave only a passing consideration to the calorie count. With everything that had happened since waking up in her own bed, snuggled between Iden and Miciah, she wasn't going to let the possibility of helping to polish off a carton of ice cream worry her—which was a good thing considering that by the time she and Ariel and Kaylee had finished talking about their lives on Earth and how they'd come to end up on an alien world, they were halfway into the second carton.

"That'll hold me for a while," Zoë said, putting down her spoon and nearly falling out of her seat when she remembered too late that to accommodate wings, it didn't have a back.

Kaylee giggled and said, "That used to happen to Mommy and me all the time, until finally we told Komet and Zeraac that at least *some* of our chairs should be made for humans."

"I'll probably have to tell Iden and Miciah the same thing," Zoë said, her earlier curiosity about Belizair returning. "Are there a lot of humans here?"

Kaylee shook her head no. Ariel said, "How much did Miciah and Iden tell you?"

"Not much. A man, an Amato, was waiting for Iden in the outer room of the transport chamber. Then as soon as we stepped outside a Vesti boy arrived with the summons for Miciah. Before that our conversation was limited."

Ariel's knowing glance sent heat creeping into Zoë's face, and when she felt a brush against her mind, it seemed completely natural to open her mental shields and hear Ariel tease, *Be glad they were called away. Otherwise it might have been several weeks before they allowed you out of bed. The men here—*

Are prime fantasy material, Zoë filled in.

Ariel hid a smile with a spoonful of ice cream. *It gets even better the longer you're with them. The Araqiel clan-house Komet belongs to is apparently known across the universe for the bedroom toys they create.*

Zoë didn't need convincing. She didn't even need toys though the image of Miciah spread-eagled and handcuffed was more delicious than chocolate. She was looking forward to being with Iden and Miciah again. They'd only scratched the surface when it came to her fantasies — or theirs.

Her cunt spasmed as she remembered the sight of strong masculine fingers curled around cocks as they'd lain together in the transport chamber, Iden's on Miciah's and Miciah's on Iden's. Oh yes, they'd only just barely touched on the things they were going to do together. But until then —

She forced her mind away from carnal thoughts by reminding herself that not only was she enjoying getting to know Ariel and Kaylee, but it would be a shame to waste this opportunity to learn about her new world. "Sorry, I got distracted there for a minute."

Ariel snickered behind another spoonful of ice cream. "Understandable. There's a lot to take in."

Zoë resolutely refused to think about hardened, thick cocks operating singly and in tandem. She sent a mock glower in Ariel's direction.

I can't help it. It's a side effect of the pregnancy.

I doubt it. Getting pregnant isn't like a "which came first, the chicken or the egg?" question.

The corners of Ariel's eyes crinkled up in suppressed laughter. Out loud she said, "Can I interest you in going for a walk now that we've finished pigging out on the ice cream?"

"I'd love it. And while we're walking I can bombard you with questions."

Kaylee's professorial expression returned. "Mommy and I can teach you everything you need to know."

Ariel stood and put the carton of ice cream in the refrigerator space. Kaylee followed her example by rising and taking care of the bowls and spoons.

"People don't waste here like they do on Earth," Kaylee said. "That's one important difference. And there aren't any malls or shopping centers. There's just the marketplace where you go to buy stuff."

"What do you use for money?"

"Mostly we use credits. But you can't see them or hold them because they're not real like paper money or coins. A computer keeps track of them. Once you can hear the Ylan stones, and talk to them, then you always know how many credits you have to spend."

"I'm totally lost," Zoë admitted.

Kaylee frowned and walked over to stand in front of Zoë. She held one arm in front of her and touched the band there. "These are Ylan stones. You can't live on Belizair without them. You can't even come here. That's why some of the stones from Miciah and Iden's wristbands had to move onto the ones they gave you. Otherwise you couldn't go through the portal. Zeraac calls it a completely closed planet. Only people who have Fallon genes are allowed because they're the only ones the Ylan stones bond with."

A hundred questions crowded Zoë's mind at the same time. She took a deep breath, knowing the conversation could end up going off in too many different directions to follow if she gave into the impulse to chase each new concept. A memory surfaced, of almost hearing *how* Miciah had moved them from outside the transport chamber to standing in front of Ariel's living quarters. "What do you mean about talking to the Ylan stones?"

Ariel said, "It might help if you think of the Ylan stones as symbionts. They're not alive in the sense of sentient, organic beings. But they're more than rocks and different than the crystals psychics on Earth swear by. Even the Amato and Vesti don't fully understand the Ylan stones, though collecting and studying them is a passion both cultures share. Their uses seem to be endless because they react to the individual who wears them. There are different types of them, though all of them serve as an energy source and power what we'd call nano-computers embedded in the wristbands. It can take awhile, but eventually they form a mental link with whoever is wearing them.

She grimaced and wrinkled her nose. "For me it was a slow process. I couldn't *hear* anything. Then one day something clicked. I realized the door to the outside wasn't opening because it was programmed to open whenever I was standing in front of it, wanting to leave, but because I'd unconsciously sent a command. Once I did it consciously, the link 'went live' for me."

Ariel pulled Kaylee against her and placed a kiss on the top of her head. "For my brilliant daughter, it happened much quicker."

Kaylee grinned. "If you weren't sick and worrying about throwing up because of the babies, you would have figured it out sooner, Mommy."

She lifted her face and got a second kiss before stepping out of Ariel's embrace and saying to Zoë, "You want to try something? Maybe it'll help you *hear*."

"Sure."

"Hold out your arms."

Zoë extended them.

Kaylee's eyebrows drew together when she saw the butterfly bracelets. "Did Miciah and Iden give you those, too?"

"No, a friend on Earth did. A prospector found them when he was looking for gold in the Sierras."

"Oh. They look like something I've seen before." She visibly shook off her curiosity and lifted her arms so they were parallel to Zoë's with the bands on their wrists only inches apart. "One way of knowing about a person is to look at their wristbands. See the saber-tooth cat on mine?"

"Yes."

"That's the device of Zeraac's clan-house. The other animal, the kind-of unicorn is the device of Komet's. But an easier way to know about a person is to touch your wristbands to theirs. That's the way people greet each other here—even if they already know one another. Let's try it and see if you can hear who I am."

"Okay," Zoë said. "Is it all right if I close my eyes so I can concentrate?"

Kaylee gave a very solemn nod. "You hold still. I'll do the greeting."

Zoë closed her eyes, automatically following Kaylee's lead of bands touching and forearms gripped. There was an immediate hum, similar to the one she'd felt in the transport chamber.

This time it seemed more like an attention-getter rather than a reaction to energy. And as if to prove her theory, it faded away, leaving the same whispering sense of knowledge just out of reach that she'd experienced earlier.

Understanding hit Zoë then. The shield she'd learned early in life to erect in order to keep from *feeling* others' emotions and *seeing* their futures was between her and the Ylan stones.

With a thought, she created a mental link like the one allowing her to communicate mind-to-mind with Iden, Miciah and Ariel. Data poured in, not just about the clan-houses of Ariel's mates, but about Iden and Miciah's as well. It was a recitation of lineage, as well as profession and location of clan-house dwellings—a streaming computer dump of information that Zoë finally realized would continue until she put a stop to it.

She shut off the flow of data with a mental command and was left with what amounted to a blinking curser on a screen, seemingly waiting for her to ask something new, or refine her search. It was weird and fascinating and exhilarating at the same time.

"I heard," she said, opening her eyes.

Like a little professor, Kaylee quizzed, "What's the name of Zeraac's clan-house."

The answer was there before Zoë could form the mental question. "Gadreel."

Kaylee's grin put one on Zoë's face.

"You *did* hear," Kaylee said. "Do you have any credits?"

Zoë checked and found she did, though she didn't have any idea what they translated to in terms of purchasing power. "Yes."

Kaylee looked at Ariel. "Let's take her to the marketplace and show her how to buy things."

Ariel laughed. "I'm not sure her new bond-mates will thank us for that."

Zoë reached over and tugged a lock of Kaylee's hair. "I don't think they'd mind if I bought my brand-new niece something special, especially since they have her to thank for finding me."

"And the golden lady," Kaylee said in a serious voice. She looked up into her mother's face. "You believe me about her sometimes visiting me in my dreams, don't you, Mommy?"

Ariel gave her a kiss. "Of course, baby."

Relief melted Kaylee's somber mood and a child's excitement took over. "Can we go to the marketplace now?"

"Yes."

Kaylee began jumping up and down. "I know just what present I want Zoë to buy me!"

Ariel gave a dramatic sigh and looked at Zoë. "Will it do any good to tell you not to spoil her?"

"Probably not."

"Okay. Let's go."

Chapter Twelve

ꙮ

The marketplace was bustling with activity. It was part farmer's market, part exotic bazaar, filled with color and sound and scent, and winged men and women. But if they were an amazing sight to her, then apparently the sight of three humans was equally startling to some of them—and to a few, unwelcome, if their hastily turned backs were any indication.

Emotion swirled around Zoë, making her tense and almost suggest a retreat. It brushed against her mental shields, but didn't seek to penetrate them.

Was it a change in her psychic talent that caused the increased awareness? Or the result of the Ylan stones she wore and the world they were in, where mind-to-mind communication was commonplace.

Probably a combination of all of it, Zoë thought. There was a deep well of sadness here, of anguish and pain, the very emotions that served as a trigger for her gift.

Sweat trickled down her back, cold in the dry, desert heat of Winseka. Her palms grew damp at the prospect of intentionally touching someone with the idea of seeing what lay ahead for them.

Nervousness coiled in her belly along with anticipation as she thought of the fortuneteller's prophecy, the shining hope she'd carried with her for years—that one day she'd be able to use her psychic abilities to help others.

The first condition was met. Her heart was fully claimed. There was no doubt in that regard. How could there be when she could feel the intensity of what Miciah and Iden felt for her? When she returned their feelings and believed with all her heart that the bindings of love and lust would only grow stronger and deeper the longer they were together?

The second condition, that the twin gifts of empathy and *sight* would be joined... She wouldn't know until...she knew.

A hand grasped hers, startling her out of her thoughts and sending a quick frisson of fear sliding through her. She grimaced, old habits died hard.

"This way, Zoë," Kaylee said, tugging her over to a stall containing a variety of musical instruments.

"Please, not a drum set," Ariel murmured just loudly enough for Zoë to hear her.

Zoë laughed. "I can see how that might make me very unpopular at your place."

"This one," Kaylee said, jumping up and down and pointing to a small board with strings stretched across it. "It's just a beginner's instrument, so it doesn't cost too many credits."

On Earth it would have been called a hammered dulcimer. The choice surprised Zoë.

She glanced at the stall owner, "Is it okay to touch the instruments?"

The young Vesti girl shared a smile with Kaylee before answering, "Of course."

Kaylee said, "Samara taught me how to play the *santur* the other day when she was working here."

Just as the choice of instrument surprised Zoë, the name did too. "They're called that in Iran and Iraq, too," she said. "Most people believe this instrument was invented in Persia about two thousand years ago."

Kaylee stood taller, in a way Zoë had come to recognize as her professorial posture. "Or maybe they were invented here," Kaylee said, "and taken to Earth by the Fallon."

"Could be," Zoë acceded, curious about the Fallon at hearing the name again, but deciding to hold off asking until they'd finished buying the dulcimer.

Kaylee picked up the two small mallets next to the instrument and played a simple tune by striking the strings. "This is just one of the songs I already know."

Zoë turned slightly to catch Ariel's eye. "What's the verdict? Will I end up *persona non grata* if I get this for Kaylee?"

Ariel combed her fingers through Kaylee's silky hair. "We've talked about this before. You know Komet, Zeraac and I all agree that if you want to learn how to play an instrument, then you have to practice every day without us telling you to, and you have to use some of your allowance to pay for lessons. For one full year, Kaylee. After that you can quit if you want to, but not before."

"I know, Mommy. I'll practice, I promise. You'll *never* have to tell me to do it."

"Okay then. You can show Zoë how to part with some of Iden and Miciah's credits."

Parting with credits was even easier than dealing with the string of information that had bombarded Zoë when Kaylee demonstrated a greeting on Belizair. It involved agreeing on a price, then touching a single band to the seller's band and mentally transferring funds.

As soon as Zoë's transaction was complete, Ariel arranged for Samara to continue giving Kaylee lessons. The Vesti girl was thrilled and proud to have been asked. She invited Kaylee to keep her company while she manned the stall, so they could work on learning the names of the different strings and save the fun stuff, like playing songs for their official lessons.

Kaylee glanced back and forth between her new auntie and her new musical instrument, so clearly torn that Zoë couldn't stop herself from giving Kaylee a hug and a kiss. "You and I will have plenty of time together."

Kaylee hugged her back then asked Ariel, "Can I stay with Samara?"

"Yes. We'll come back and get you, or one of your fathers will."

They left Kaylee to her music lesson and wandered through the marketplace, pausing at various booths. As they walked, emotion continued to swirl around Zoë, intense and often sorrowful, but also hopeful.

More than once she caught men and women both glancing at her stomach, or Ariel's. Their expressions held such longing that Zoë could no longer ignore the suspicion that had been forming.

It didn't take a great leap to confirm it, at least in Zoë's own mind. Kaylee had said all the human women were pregnant. Looking around, Zoë could find no women with infants in their arms. There were older children in the marketplace, and a few toddlers, but not nearly as many as one would expect given the number of people doing their daily shopping for food.

Zoë parted her mental shields just enough to touch her thoughts to Ariel's. *They need us in order to have children.*

Ariel's footsteps faltered. She worried her bottom lip and gave a slight nod. *Yes. But it doesn't mean we can't find happiness and love here. Seeing you with Miciah —*

Trust me, I'm very happy with Miciah and Iden.

Zoë felt as well as heard Ariel's sigh of relief. She added with confidence, *This is exactly where I'm meant to be.*

Of that, Zoë was absolutely certain. Iden and Miciah weren't responsible for her dreaming about them before she met them. And while they may have come to Earth with the thought of snagging a human mate and making babies, the connection between them was much more than that. True, fucking was very much on their minds, *all* of their minds, but she was fairly certain it was an end in and of itself at the moment.

Have they always brought humans here? she asked.

No. A bio-gene virus was let loose on Belizair. It was created by an alien race known as the Hotaling. Apparently they hoped to gain possession of the Ylan stones, either by killing those on this planet, or perhaps by holding the threat of extinction over their heads in order to get the stones. A few died when the virus struck, mainly the weak and the old. But the most devastating impact was that it caused miscarriages and left the women unable to conceive. So far the only solution the Council scientists have been able to find is to match an Amato male and a Vesti male to a human female carrying the gene sequence of the Fallon – the ancestor we all share. There's something about the combination, a matched pair plus a male from the other race that ends in pregnancy.

And all the women are carrying twins, Zoë said, remembering Kaylee's comment in the kitchen.

Yes.

A Vesti and an Amato? Zoë guessed.

"The scientists aren't sure," Ariel answered, her verbal response telling Zoë the topic could be discussed openly. "We'll know the answer to that question pretty soon. Cyan's expected to go into labor any day now."

"You mind if we sit?" Zoë asked, indicating a vacant bench between two slender, flowering trees, far enough away from the flow of traffic to allow them to converse privately.

"Sitting sounds good. The sugar rush from the ice cream is gone. Now I just want to curl up and sleep." Ariel grinned. "Or maybe go home and have another bowl of it."

Zoë shook her head. "If you polish it off—"

A thought occurred to her then as she remembered the conversation she'd let drop in the portal chamber about being able to return to Earth. True, transporting down to the canyon she'd been in and driving out and back for ice cream would be a pain, but Ariel and Kaylee had come from San Francisco. "Why can't someone pop down for a Big Mac or a Kentucky Fried Chicken meal when the craving hits?"

"Earth is off-limits except to those granted permission, mainly the Council scientists and bounty hunters assigned there, plus the men who have been matched to a human. Even for them, travel to and from is limited since it draws on the energy of the chamber Ylan stones. They recharge naturally, but the more they're used, the longer it takes to renew them. The same is true with the stones in the wristbands when it comes to using them to move between places.

"Our happiness really is important. Komet and Zeraac both think the rules will change over time, and the humans brought here will one day be allowed to visit Earth, as long as there's 'zero impact' when it comes to technology or influencing a world less advanced than this one. That's why the laws were passed in the first place."

Ariel's hand settled on her stomach. Her voice conveyed a wealth of love. "These children are a miracle, not just for Komet, Zeraac and I, but for the planet. Our twins and the ones being carried by the other human women might be the only hope the Vesti and Amato have of avoiding extinction. When you couple how important they are to a tendency in the men to be very protective and possessive, it doesn't make for a high likelihood of racking up frequent-traveler points — even if it weren't against the law."

Zoë didn't have any trouble believing that. And while she wasn't as accepting about not returning to Earth as Ariel was, there was plenty of time to fight that battle later, after she'd explored this world.

"There's probably one other thing I should mention," Ariel said. "Birth control here basically comes down to abstinence or the withdrawal method." She snorted, "Either of which I can pretty much guarantee isn't going to be used by anyone in a mate-bond."

Zoë had a fleeting thought of her purse, still in Ariel's kitchen, and the "emergency" pills she carried as a precaution in case she decided to be spontaneous and leave the RV parked while she went off on a road trip in the car. "Other birth control methods are banned, or they just don't work?" she asked, wanting to make sure she fully understood Ariel's statement.

Ariel tapped the Ylan stones on one of her own bracelets. "Don't work. It's one of the reasons I said, 'think symbiont' earlier. It's more accurate than *stone*."

Worry practically radiated off Ariel. Zoë could guess at its cause, given Ariel's obvious joy at being pregnant. She reached over and took her sister's hand, finding it amazingly easy to think of Ariel that way.

She gave a squeeze of reassurance. "Thanks for being willing to talk openly. I prefer to know the facts up front rather than being blindsided by them later. Nothing you've told me makes me regret saying yes to Miciah and Iden."

Ariel exhaled. The hand on her belly lifted to dab at her eyes.

Zoë gave a dramatic groan and teased, "You're not going to get weepy are you?"

"Hormones," Ariel said. "This is the true reason I'm seemingly out in public without one of my mates. They're having a tough time handling this part of my being pregnant. In another month or so it should pass, or at least it did when I was carrying Kaylee."

Zoë glanced around and saw plenty of women, alone and in groups, with no male guardian hovering nearby. But rather than have what she'd consider a truly nasty surprise later, she asked, "What do you mean, *seemingly* out in public without one of your mates?"

Ariel sniffled and laughed. "Not what you're thinking. Men and women have equal rights here. It's just that neither Komet nor Zeraac thought they'd end up with a bond-mate at all, much less a human one who then immediately got pregnant. They're still in an ultrapossessive, overly protective, *I can't believe my good fortune* state of mind. Truthfully, except for those moments when it drives me crazy, I love that about them. And they're actually getting better about not hovering. At the moment, Zeraac is getting a lecture from Kaylee about which strings are which on her new *santur*, and Komet is browsing through vegetables in one of the shops a couple of rows over from here and trying to decide what to make for dinner since it's his night to cook."

Thinking about the quickly turned backs she'd glimpsed when they first arrived at the marketplace, Zoë asked, "Are they worried something will happen to you and Kaylee? Not everyone can be happy about bringing humans here."

"There's very little crime here. As you can imagine, the ability to communicate telepathically puts a new spin on giving a lie detector test and collecting eyewitness accounts." Ariel grew pensive. "There was a challenge to the mate-bond I have with Zeraac and Komet almost as soon as I arrived here. It came about because of a personal grievance between Zeraac and a former lover, though it took the form of a legal challenge. During the course of it, and afterward, when Zantara sought me out to apologize for her actions, I never felt any prejudice or hatred because I was human. But I don't know how the majority of those on Belizair feel about humans being brought here. I assumed…but then that's always a mistake, isn't it? In a lot of ways, my life here has been insular."

Zoë rubbed her fingertips over the night-sky Ylan stones at her wrist. One last question, then she'd let this go. "Do Komet and Zeraac know where you and Kaylee are because of the bands, or because of your mental link?"

The skin at the corners of Ariel's eyes crinkled in amusement, as though even on such a short acquaintance, she could guess what prompted Zoë's question. "There's no global positioning satellite above Belizair using a built-in tracking device for potentially wayward mates. The Vesti can find theirs, but it's mainly a sensory approach to locating a mate through a serum they inject through their bite. It works by heading in a direction and getting a cold, cool, warm, hot feel when it comes to a mate's trail—or so I've been told.

"The mate-bond does provide subtle feedback in terms of well-being. Even when my thoughts are purposely walled off from Komet and Zeraac, or we're separated by a little bit of distance, they can still send the mental equivalent of a ping, which is what they did the instant they discovered Kaylee and I weren't home. I felt it and responded." Her smile widened. "That's one thing I really love about being here. It's so easy to answer questions by sending a picture or a quick snatch of memory."

"How far apart until you can't touch your mind to theirs?" Zoë asked, trying to keep her fingers away from her shoulder and to ignore the heat in her belly that mention of biting had caused.

"Right now? A couple of blocks I think. Over time it may expand. Or not. Apparently the distances vary widely, though in general nuclear families, bond-mates and their children, have a longer reach when it comes to telepathic communication."

Zoë was tempted to reach for Iden and Miciah, just to see if they were close enough to touch mentally. She didn't, only because it was too easy to remember the anguished face of the Amato waiting for Iden, and Miciah's internal battle to leave her anywhere other than their quarters. She could easily imagine what his reaction would be if he learned she was sitting in an open space, in view of other men.

She leaned back against the tree at the end of the bench, soaking in the warmth and the exotic scent of flower and desert and marketplace cooking. As long as she didn't think too hard about being topless, she could go with it. She'd always loved the feel of the sun's rays on her breasts and on her bare buttocks when she'd worn little more than a g-string at the beach. "If we're going to do this very often, we're going to have to lobby for benches with backs and maybe even some nice padding."

"Excellent idea."

The golden moments of perfect relaxation lasted until a Vesti woman claimed a seat under a nearby tree. Her back was to them, the dark chocolate of her wings only a slightly deeper shade than her skin.

Her posture gave no hint to the nature of her thoughts. She neither trembled with grief nor vibrated with feelings just barely kept in check. And yet a shaft of ice slid through Zoë, taking her breath for an instant.

With a certainty that had always before come through an accidental touch, she knew that inside this Vesti woman, fiery emotional pain had chilled to the frigid numbness and eerie calm often proceeding suicide.

This is it, Zoë thought, glancing down at slightly shaking hands. *This is the moment of truth.*

Somehow she'd imagined being more ready for it. Having this happen after she'd been on Belizair for a little while, or discovering the fortuneteller had been right with a casual touch of someone's hand instead of a conscious act of choice.

The prospect of walking over to the Vesti woman made Zoë's mouth grow dry. She touched her fingertips to the back of Ariel's hand and realized instantly it was the act of her subconscious doing a test run.

Ariel's eyes opened and color crept into her cheek. "Sorry. I didn't mean to conk out on you. One minute I was resting my eyes and thinking about padded benches, the next I apparently slid into naptime."

Zoë touched her mind to Ariel's. *I need to speak with the woman sitting over there.*

Why? Ariel's puzzled expression matched her mental voice.

Deniability — in case things went bad — was the best Zoë could do for her newly discovered sister. She had no idea what was going to happen when she attempted to use her gift. She had no idea how the people on this world felt about such things and now it was too late to ask. *I'll tell you later.*

Curiosity replaced Ariel's puzzlement. It practically sizzled down their mental link. *Do you want me to stay here or go with you?*

Stay.

Okay. But don't think I'm going to let you off the hook for an answer. A couple of days being cut off from the chocolate ice cream supply and you'll be begging to tell me all your secrets.

Zoë laughed. Her fingers curled around Ariel's for a quick squeeze and release. She already loved having a sister.

Before she lost her nerve, or time ran out and Miciah or Iden arrived on the scene, Zoë stood and crossed to where the Vesti woman sat. There was no easy way, but rather than hover, Zoë claimed a spot on the bench next to the woman.

She turned toward the Vesti and held out both arms in the traditional greeting Kaylee had demonstrated earlier. "I'm Zoë."

"I am Acacia."

Chapter Thirteen

ဢ

Zoë couldn't stop herself from tensing as they grasped each other's forearms, allowing the bracelets to touch. She wasn't sure if the same rules would apply as before, if it would require a touch of hands in order to be propelled into the future.

The tightness in her chest loosened when instead of being jerked into a vision scene or bombarded by emotion, there was only the flow of data about familial relationships and clan-houses.

Acacia wore two bands at each wrist, one placed on her at birth, the other when she bound herself to her mate and some of the Ylan stones he wore migrated to fill it. Zoë couldn't tell which band the information originated from, but among the litany of those related to Acacia and her mate, she recognized the name Lyan as being somehow related to Ariel through her Amato mate, Zeraac.

The flow of facts ceased and Zoë had no time to brace herself as she was submerged in an icy despair so complete that it took her breath away and turned her world black.

There was nothing around her, nothing in front her. It was more intense than anything she'd ever experienced before, so consuming that it attacked her core, threatening to extinguish the flame of her personal hopes and dreams.

In self-preservation Zoë fought against the frigid waves of darkness. Some part of her realized that a mental link had formed and Acacia was incapable of closing it.

Rather than draw on her strength to build a shield between them, Zoë used the cold edges of Acacia's pain to slice through the agony of hopelessness. She reached for something good in the future to offer the Vesti woman, and in doing so felt the twining of her two gifts, the instant when they became what the fortuneteller had prophesied—*Empathy* to find those who needed her the most, *sight* to give them a reason to fight the bleak despair and live.

Out of darkness came a vision. It formed tree by tree into a jungle similar to the ones on Earth. A narrow trail beckoned and Zoë could no more avoid stepping onto it than she could avoid seeing what lay ahead.

This time, it was the flow of Zoë's thoughts that led, not the pull of Acacia's emotions though their mental link remained in place.

Zoë thought she was in the jungle region Miciah represented. But then a human woman hurried past, terror on her face, and a moment later three guerrillas appeared wielding machineguns and already bloody machetes. But instead of following the fate of the woman, the vision took Zoë deeper into the jungle, to a small village and the carnage that remained there.

Guerrillas loitered, laughing and smoking, eating and drinking amidst scattered bodies. Men. Children. Women. Many raped before being slaughtered.

The scene was horrifying and heartbreaking, yet familiar from its depiction in the news. It was the conscienceless of war, the end result of centuries of genocide and corruption, greed and hate in Africa.

Fury and pity buffeted Zoë, at not being able to do anything, change anything. Confusion and frustration followed at not understanding what connection this had to Acacia, how seeing it offered hope to replace the Vesti woman's despair.

She could feel Acacia's horror and revulsion, her struggle to close her mind to Zoë's. And Zoë would have gladly turned away from the scene and the knowledge of what had happened there if she could have.

Instead she was compelled into the village, then through it and onto a narrow footpath. A boy, no more than nine or ten, lay facedown, dead at where the trail curved and the village disappeared from sight. Beyond him was another boy, even younger. Both of them had been shot in the back as they tried to escape the guerrillas who'd arrived to turn the last minutes of their short lives into a terror-filled nightmare.

A Vesti man appeared then, shimmering into view on the path between the first boy and the second one. Shock jolted through Zoë, echoing along the mental link that bound her to Acacia, though the Vesti woman's reaction was more intense.

The gray locks of the man's hair tumbled down to his shoulders. And even in profile, Zoë saw his face was wreathed in sadness, his sorrow adding weight to his age.

He stepped forward and parted the dense foliage, revealing a toddler crouched there, soiled and shaking, her face wet with tears. She was oblivious to him, though she flinched at the sound of gunfire followed by the raucous laughter of the guerrillas in the village.

The man turned his head. His gaze connected with Zoë's and their eyes met and held as if the two of them existed on the same plane. Without a word being spoken she understood the *why* — to save this child and give Acacia a reason to live.

He knelt and touched the bangle-like bands on the girl's wrists. With the tip of his index fingers he traced over the swirled design carved into one pair of them in a message for Acacia.

A blink and Zoë felt the forging of a block between her mind and Acacia's. And then she saw the *how* as the man's age gave way to youth and the batlike wings became the iridescent blue and black wings of a butterfly, leaving a being straight out of a fairy tale standing in front of her for an instant before he and the vision dissolved, and she was on bench under a sky with two suns, the bands at her wrists touching Acacia's.

Fierce determination slammed into Zoë as the link opened again. *We must go,* Acacia said. *Please. It is the will of the god. He walks on your world now but reaches to us in our time of need using you as his bridge.*

Zoë's heart thundered in her chest. The god?

Acacia's fingers tightening painfully on Zoë's forearms. *We must go. Now. Or it will be too late. Please. I beg you.*

Zoë's own sense of timing was skewed, but Acacia's urgency resonated as truth inside her. *I don't know how to get to Earth,* Zoë said, trusting she would be able to find the child once she was there, otherwise there would be no point in the vision.

I do. A hesitation followed, then an admission. *What I am asking is against our laws. Your mates can't know what we're about to do. They can't know what we've done once we return.*

Zoë's stomach roiled and knotted at the idea of keeping such an important secret from Iden and Miciah. But to do nothing? Bile rose in her throat at the thought of the tiny girl being found by the guerrillas, a fate worse than being left to die alone in the jungle. She couldn't live with herself if she turned her back not only on the child and Acacia, but on the very thing she'd spent her life wishing for, that she could put her psychic gifts to use and make a difference.

Will they be held responsible for my actions?

Acacia gave a quick shake of her head. *Not if they don't know of them.* She released Zoë's forearms in favor of clasping her hands. *I can move us directly to the transport chamber.*

Let me tell my sister I'm leaving.

Acacia tensed. Zoë said, *Take us to the chamber as soon as I say okay.*

Zoë touched her mind to Ariel's while holding her link with Acacia open. She kept her mental voice light as she said, *At the risk of being cut off from the chocolate ice cream, I've got to abandon you for a little while. Okay?*

They arrived very close to the spot where the Vesti teen had intercepted Miciah. "I will see if anyone is waiting within before we enter," Acacia said, letting go of Zoë's hands.

She hurried up the crystal walkway, sending a command ahead of her so the wall parted to form a doorway before she reached the building. A quick look inside, followed by a wave, and Zoë hurried to rejoin her.

Guilt assailed Zoë as she passed through the outer chamber and stepped into the one containing the bed. Her mind was blocked to Iden and Miciah, but she easily remembered the depth of their commitment, the heartfelt words they'd spoken to her more than one. *You're our life. Our hope.*

But the child is Acacia's hope, Zoë told herself. *And nothing will happen to us.*

Still, she couldn't suppress a shiver as images of rape and murder, of a village slaughtered in senseless, atrocious violence assaulted her as Acacia said, "I am familiar with your world since several of those related to me serve there. What continent?"

"Africa."

Zoë felt a pulse of energy as the portal came to life. It hummed through the bands at her wrists. And this time, Zoë was aware of the night-sky colored Ylan stones, as well as the black-streaked blue of her own, drawing power from the crystals, preparing for the transmutation that preceded transport.

Around them the stones lit in a sequence of color. Pulsed faster and faster in a surreal strobe-light effect that lasted less than a second as they made the jump from one world to another.

We don't dare step out of the chamber and risk being seen by the bounty hunters assigned to guard it, Acacia said. *Where do we go now?*

Acacia's fear and worry rushed over Zoë, along with a desperate sense of urgency. For an instant it sent panic spiraling through her. She didn't even know how to move between two places or operate the portal, how was she—

Zoë took a deep breath, halting the negative chatter. She stilled her mind, trusting the answer to Acacia's question would come to her.

It did.

There was no way to prove it, but Zoë felt sure the knowledge came from the butterfly bracelets and was being filtered through the bands Iden and Miciah had given to her. She shared the coordinates with Acacia and asked, *Will we be able to get back here?*

Acacia's hand circled Zoë's wrist, covering the bracelets on it. The touch made Zoë aware that they were both standing topless in harem-like pants, and Acacia appeared fully human.

Yes, Acacia said. *The Vesti call the Ylan stones your bond-mates gave you the Wanderer's Stars. Most would be drained of energy if used to transport us over such a great distance, but not yours. They will easily allow us to retrieve the child and return to the chamber.*

Okay.

The word served as the same prompt it had when Zoë had spoken it to Ariel. In a blink they were in the jungle, their sudden arrival triggering the warning screams of monkeys and birds.

Ahead of them, on the trail, lay the dead boys. Acacia rushed forward, tears streaming from her eyes at seeing the reality, the finality of their deaths.

Zoë hurried after her, heart thundering in her chest, adrenaline pumping through her system at the possibility the jungle calls of alarm would bring men armed with machineguns and unconscionable intent.

Her fear was realized just as Acacia reached the spot where the winged Vesti had parted the foliage to reveal the child.

A guerrilla stepped into view. He smiled widely at the prospect of raping and murdering them.

And died with those thoughts.

One instant he was standing there. The next he was gone.

Zoë wouldn't have been able to process it at all if she hadn't already formed a mental link to the nano-computers in the wristbands.

On some level she'd been aware of the energy gathering and condensing in them. She'd assumed it was in preparation for the trip back to the chamber. Now she knew they'd been reacting in the presence of danger, bunching to become a weapon capable of sending a blast of pure power.

It had been Acacia's bands, Acacia's command that had reduced the grinning guerrilla to particles so small they couldn't be seen under a microscope—because Acacia knew how and was closer, her arms already lifted. She'd only had to turn slightly so her hands were pointing at their would-be assailant.

Having witnessed it, Zoë could do it if need be. The information firing from her wristband told her how, and warned that the Ylan stones wouldn't allow it on Belizair.

She moved to Acacia's side. Her throat tightened on tears for the two boys whose deaths they couldn't prevent. Her heart wept when Acacia gathered the small girl to her chest, careful not to let the last sight of her world be one of horror.

The child clung, recognizing safety. Acacia grasped Zoë's hand. With their minds linked and her attention focused this time, Zoë saw how the command to move from one place to another was given. She felt the surge of released energy, the power gathered in her wristbands to serve as a weapon turned to another use as they transported to the chamber.

A man waited there. He was dark and handsome—scowling ferociously one instant and apparently shocked to his core the next. His eyes widened and his lips parted. He blinked several times then touched his fingertips to his chest, pressing and rubbing the spot over his heart.

His gaze flicked continuously, making a circuit.

Zoë. The child. Acacia.

Zoë. The child. Acacia.

Until finally his voice and thoughts collided and he said, "Are you absolutely insane, Acacia? Do you seek banishment from Belizair? To come here without permission. To bring a human bond-mate with you."

His eyes dropped to the small girl. "To—"

"Save a child's life, Thaden," Acacia said.

He went completely still. "Tell me you don't intend to return to Belizair with her."

"The god wishes it."

Thaden brushed her answer aside with the wave of his arm. "Now I know the despair crushing the women of our world has driven you beyond rational thought. The god of the Vesti probably no longer remembers his creation of Belizair. He wanders on so those he gave life to can make their own choices. You know that."

"He hasn't forgotten us. In our time of need he reached out. He sent an answer for some of us with Zoë's arrival. I'll show you."

Because the link remained open, Zoë saw the transfer of the vision. She felt Thaden's shock, not just at seeing the image of the Vesti male, but at discovering Iden and Miciah were Zoë's bond-mates. She learned he was Acacia's cousin, a bounty hunter who was on Earth to guard a scientist given permission to study here.

It was pure chance he'd been close enough that the bands at his wrist had signaled Acacia's arrival because of their kinship. Luckier still the man he was protecting and the one assigned to guard the portal were visiting one another and so deeply engrossed in the chess-like gave of Fett that it was easy for Thaden to wait for Acacia's return to the transport chamber.

He was visibly shaken by her revelation. "This will cause trouble on Belizair. More than is already brewing."

His quick, unconscious glance in Zoë's direction added to her certainty that not everyone was thrilled by the presence of human women in their world.

"Nothing you say will change my mind," Acacia said.

Thaden speared his fingers through his hair and tugged. He exhaled on a long sigh. "I won't stand in your way. But it would be better if news of this doesn't get out, at least not right away. There will be those who'll demand you be sanctioned, and sanctioned quickly. There will be just as many who will demand they be allowed to come to Earth and do what you have done. It'll be an impossible situation for the Council. They'll have no choice but to punish you with banishment or by taking the child away and bringing her back to this world until they can deliberate on a course of action for the future."

"Zoë has already promised to keep it from her mates."

The knot that had formed in Zoë's stomach at hearing the possible consequences tightened further. She hated the need for secrecy, hated being torn between wanting to keep Miciah and Iden safe in their ignorance, and her desire to share everything with them.

"I'll keep it from them, for now," she said, speaking up, accepting the necessity of it. "But it can't remain that way for long."

Acacia gave a solemn nod. "For now. So the god might be allowed to offer hope to others, and in doing so, give the seeds of change a chance to grow roots in a culture that has seen very little of it until the virus struck."

Thaden stepped forward, placing his arms around Acacia and the child. "I'll return to my charge. Don't linger here." He gave them a hug, then surprised Zoë by giving her one as well before blinking out.

Murmuring soothingly to the toddler, Acacia knelt and tried to set the little girl on the floor. At first the child clung, desperate to remain in safety's embrace, but eventually she stood though her hands fisted in the material of Acacia's pants.

Acacia touched the two bands on each wrist to the child's bracelets.

Zoë's nerves stretched and vibrated when nothing happened.

Were they wrong after all? Was Acacia to make a life here? Or only to take part in the saving of one so she could see her own had value?

What if the child wasn't a descendant of the Fallon? What if the Ylan stones —

A small portion of them left Acacia's wristbands, as if melting to fill the swirling, tribal pattern carved into the bracelets the toddler wore.

When it was done, Acacia offered open arms and the girl rushed into them. Standing, Acacia said. "From the portal chamber on Belizair, I'll take us directly to my home. It's at the edge of the desert, which will help cover your absence."

Zoë found herself relaxing. A little distance, a little bit of time to reacclimate would be a *very* good thing before facing Iden and Miciah.

"Okay," she said, and moments later they shimmered into a room where two men hovered over a game of Fett.

Both looked up, registering equal expressions of shock. The man on the left stood so quickly that his chair fell over. "What have you done, Acacia?"

The other rose to his feet more languidly, his eyes and smile holding unholy amusement. "I believe that's my cue to leave. I already wear a target on my back when it comes to the Council. Whatever transgressions your mate is guilty of, I don't need to add them to my own."

"Will you take Zoë to Winseka with you, Lyan?" Acacia asked.

The man's eyebrows rose. "Who are her mates?"

"Iden of the Cathetel and Miciah of the Danjal."

Complete and utter silence descended, broken a long moment later by Lyan's shout of laughter. "I'd never thought you a rabble rouser, Acacia, but in this... You do us proud. Change is here. For the good of all of us, it's time we embrace it." Wicked amusement danced his eyes. "I'll return Zoë to Winseka and deliver her safely into Miciah's arms."

Chapter Fourteen

ॐ

It was pointless to continue the debate, Miciah thought. Around and around they'd gone, seemingly for hours, as was often the case when serious matters were discussed. Duty kept his mind from Zoë and Iden, but he found he'd had enough of it. It was time to call for a vote, and then an adjournment since any path they chose would require further discussion and analysis before rules were set in place.

He stood, drawing the eyes of the others around the table. Silence descended. "I suggest we vote."

Javant, whose token had allowed Miciah to cast the deciding votes in the challenge to Ariel's mate-bond, also stood. "I concur, but suggest we take a short break to gather our thoughts."

The others agreed by standing and stretching their wings. Some of the Council members remained at their places while others moved about the chambers. Miciah stepped out into the hallway, mentally reaching for his mates.

The temple was close enough that he brushed against Iden's shields and gained confirmation of his location. Ariel's quarters were too distant, at least for now. But the bond he shared with Zoë through the Ylan stones and the Vesti mating serum hummed subtly, telling him she was alive, and since he knew where she was—safe.

His cock filled in anticipation of collecting her and taking her to their quarters. Only iron-willed control kept him from sliding into fantasies of what they'd do when they got there.

Slowly the others began taking their seats at the table. Miciah joined them.

When all were sitting, Isaura stood, signaling she was prepared to cast her vote. She set aside the top two crystal tokens in the stack in front of her, then pushed the sky blue one forward to the center of the table. "To not tell the males that they have been matched to the same female will only lead to greater conflict in the future."

She sat and Jarlath stood, separating his blue token from the others and placing it next to Isaura's. "I agree. We need to embrace change. It has come to Belizair and because of it, we will grow stronger."

When he took his chair, Luz, representing the Amato in the fertile region to the north stood, saying, "And if we tell them both, are we then to demand the males form a bond with their counterpart, regardless of existing obligations or what their hearts might desire?"

"We will debate further, after the vote," the Amato healer said in a gentle reminder that a statement of reasoning was more appropriate than a question.

Luz took the hunter green token from the top of her stack and placed it in the center of the table. "We continue what we have already begun. The first to be matched claims the female."

Javant placed a similar token next to Luz's. "I agree. Let us continue as we have begun, but perhaps set safeguards into our process so a second match isn't found unless the first one fails to result in a mate-bond."

The tension grew when the two healers set sky blue tokens in the center. The Vesti female spoke for both of them. "We need to have more faith in those of our world. Learning there is more than one match for any human descended from the Fallon will offer additional hope."

Gabri, the Amato scientist, stood. "In the end, I agree with those who have voted to follow a course of action where we disclose fully what we learn when it comes to finding mates among humans. But at the moment, it seems wise to place a brief moratorium on notifying those who've been matched, at least until after the birth of Cyan's twins. We don't know how that's going to impact Belizair, and the refinements we've made in the short time since we discovered that Miciah and Zeraac both had the right to claim Ariel have allowed us to match the gene sequences of others more quickly." He took the middle token, a shiny black one and placed it in the center.

Jati joined his fellow scientist, adding his black token to the center of the table. "Gabri is right. We need time. The females in question can be kept safe. And we shouldn't forget that bounty hunters search for the Hotaling. There is always a chance we will find a way to reverse the effects of the virus."

The Amato Raym took the floor. "We need to remember the women here on Belizair. We need to offer them hope besides what we've found for a few of them, those who are willing to go to Earth and parent orphan children who might one day be matched and brought here. Thanks to Draigon and Kye, who remain on Earth with their bond-mate Savannah, we now know there are human males who carry the Fallon gene sequence. One of them has already been matched, to my niece Zantara, though she doesn't yet know of it because we are waiting for the scientists studying the matter to advise us on how to proceed.

"The birth of Cyan's children holds the possibility of offering hope and causing devastation in equal measure." He placed the black token from his stack with the others in the center of the table. "We need time, a moratorium perhaps extending until we discover if Zantara, by forming a mate-bond with both a Vesti male and human male, can defeat the virus and become pregnant."

Inoke stood. "Our scientists are only just beginning to suspect that the mating serum of the Vesti somehow alters human chemistry, making conception possible. What if Zantara's bond requires her human mate to be so altered for there to be a child? It would require the Vesti in the mate-bond to be in the fever of our kind and use his fangs on another male."

His voice held the Vesti culture's censure of homosexual relationships, causing a knot to form in Miciah's chest with its reminder.

"We can't wait on the results of Zantara's bond, should she agree to enter into such an experiment and take a human male as a mate," Inoke said. "And we can't add to the upheaval already impacting life on Belizair by forcing a Vesti male into such an arrangement."

He voted with the hunter green token to allow the first male matched to claim the female, as did the Vesti representing the fertile region to the north.

All eyes turned to Miciah. In the center of the table there were four votes in favor of allowing the first match to stand, four in favor of making it known when both a Vesti and Amato had an equal claim on a human carrying the Fallon gene sequence, and three for a moratorium.

The knot in Miciah's chest tightened to an ache as he thought about what placing the blue chip in the center would mean for Belizair. If not for the challenge Raym had made against Ariel's bond, Miciah wasn't sure he would ever have learned about his own right to her. He remembered well what he'd felt when he learned Ariel was his match and had already been claimed by Zeraac and Komet. He remembered, too, his first sight of her in the marketplace.

Knowing she could have been his had been agony. Worse yet was being forced to choose whether to cast his vote in favor of the challenge to her bond or to let it stand when he bore the responsibility of being an only son and only child.

He could no longer imagine having Ariel for mate. From the instant Jeqon had shown him the picture of Zoë, she'd become everything to him. But what if Zoë had been found first? And Zeraac identified as the perfect match at the same time Miciah was?

Miciah's stomach tensed, his mind refusing to conjure up images of Zeraac and Zoë together. He couldn't imagine sharing her with anyone but Iden.

Others would protest the lack of choice if it was forced on them. And if not, if determining who could claim the female was resolved in some other manner, there would be challenges, losses and disappointment festering into bitterness, and worse. And all of it would erode the very hope that the females brought with them to Belizair.

He couldn't cast the vote that would set such a thing in motion, nor could he place the green token in the center, not now. Not when this meeting had been called because in the short period of time he was on Earth, two identical matches had been found.

A vote for a moratorium would create one. It would force them into adjournment until they met again in four days, the prescribed time after reaching a stalemate.

He saw no other choice. Change needed to be managed and controlled, minimized.

Miciah stood and placed the black token with the others.

* * * * *

Ariel smiled as she studied her mates. They were hiding their tension well. Or should she say, their aggravation?

To anyone watching them, they were absolutely absorbed in the concert of simple dulcimer songs Kaylee was giving them. But underneath, Ariel could practically hear the question—or rather, the outrageous accusation—circling continuously in their minds.

How could you let Miciah's mate leave with a complete stranger!

Well, how could she have stopped it? She could count on one finger the number of times she'd transported between places since arriving on Belizair. She certainly hadn't expected Zoë to disappear in that manner!

True, Komet and Zeraac hadn't been thrilled by the trip to the market in the first place, which probably accounted for why they'd so quickly abandoned their own pursuits to follow her there. But for the sake of their domestic harmony, neither of them had dared try to forbid her from leaving their quarters.

In no way would she play a part in being her sister's jailer—though in all honesty, she'd *known* Miciah wouldn't have wanted Zoë out in public, not on their binding-day, maybe not for weeks afterward, when the mating fever of the Vesti cooled enough to allow it. Then again, if Zoë'd had any idea just what kind of possessive frenzy going out would stir to life in Miciah, she probably would have *insisted* on doing it.

Ariel looked at Komet and smiled. Considerate scholar he might be, but with the right provocation, Vesti instinct ruled and gentle lover became a lust-ridden primitive—to their mutual satisfaction.

Zoë would be okay, *was* okay. Ariel felt certain of it.

She had puzzled over the events. Her sister's sudden need to approach a complete stranger. The formal greeting that had definitely lasted far longer than was normal and seemed to encompass an intense private conversation.

The best explanation Ariel could come up with was that maybe the Vesti woman was a bounty hunter or scientist and had been on Earth, and Zoë recognized her. It was plausible, but...

At the sound of chiming, Ariel knew the moment of reckoning had arrived.

"I'll get it!" Kaylee said, gently setting the dulcimer hammers aside before heading to the doorway.

Ariel laughed silently, noting how neither Zeraac nor Komet stopped Kaylee. If it was cowardly to let their small daughter greet Miciah, and by doing so, remind him there was a child to consider before venting, then she wasn't alone in her cowardice.

She did get to her feet, and was immediately flanked by her two mates. They were halfway to the door when Kaylee reached it, ordering the wall to recede and form an opening.

Miciah vibrated with possessive fury. He controlled it, even managed a smile when the small general told him about taking Zoë to the marketplace and showing her how to spend credits. But when Kaylee would have tugged him deeper into the living space in order to demonstrate her skills on the dulcimer Zoë purchased, Miciah resisted.

It took every ounce of self-discipline to appear calm, to sound it as he asked, "Where is my bond-mate now?"

She wasn't with Iden. Iden was still at the temple.

She wasn't close enough for their minds to touch. Or if she was, she was purposely blocking her thoughts, a skill she shouldn't be so adept at this soon after arriving on Belizair.

Ariel worried her bottom lip. Miciah saw the answer in her eyes before she spoke it, "We don't know."

Anger and fear whipped through him in equal measure. But he was spared from reacting badly by Zeraac suddenly stiffening and saying, "Zoë will be here within moments."

Miciah's nostrils flared. How could Zeraac know what he himself didn't?

Irrational jealousy came on the heels of the question, stirred to life by the answer. Just as he was the perfect genetic match for Ariel, Zeraac would be the same for Zoë.

Miciah's mind filled with a heated growl as the mating fever of the Vesti ignited. It grew worse when he sensed Zoë's presence and turned to see her approaching in flight, carried in the arms of another male. Not just any male, but Lyan, who constantly skirted the law and whose frequent summonings to stand before the Council and defend himself were legendary.

If there was any consolation, it was in knowing Lyan was mated to a human female and shared her with Zeraac's brother Adan. But that did little to cool the fire streaking through Miciah, turning his blood to flames and his cock into hot steel.

The furious storm of possessiveness raged more violently when Lyan landed far enough away to allow him to set Zoë on her feet and press his lips to hers. "It was a pleasure to make your acquaintance," he said, escaping in a blink before Miciah could reach him and tear him to shreds.

Words were beyond Miciah. Even the need for explanations couldn't override Vesti instinct.

He scooped Zoë up in his arms, and with a mental command transported them to the quarters he and Iden had claimed before leaving for Earth. He didn't make it past the couch in the main living room before placing her on the cushion and coming down on top of her, not sparing her his weight. Not sparing her from the intensity of his emotions.

Fire poured into Zoë, burning away the barrier between her mind and Miciah's. She moaned as his mouth slammed down on hers and his tongue thrust aggressively, parting her lips in a savage claiming.

Lust swamped her. His as well as her own. It seemed like forever since she'd felt his weight, his heat, the raw pleasure that came from being with him.

Blood rushed to her labia, filling her cunt lips, parting them. Arousal gushed from her slit to slide over the tight rosette of her anus and wet the thin pants she wore.

Her clit became engorged, alive with sensation. Agonizing shards of white heat streaked through it as he ground against her, the barrier of their clothing only serving to heighten the need.

Fuck me, she said, turned on by his savage, sexual hunger, by the desperate need to put aside everything that had happened since arriving in Winseka. She wanted to reconnect completely with him, to feel not only the hard weight of his body on top of her, but his thick cock deep inside her.

The command, the words, inflamed him further. He thrust against her, snarled and growled in her thoughts. But rather than tearing their clothing away and shoving himself inside her, he tore his mouth from hers, leaving her crying out and lifting her head in an attempt to capture his lips.

Why were you with Lyan?

Hot waves of jealousy and possessiveness pounded her, making it clear he hated seeing her in Lyan's arms, hated even the idea that any male other than Iden had looked upon her, much less held her and felt her skin against his.

If she didn't trust Miciah, didn't believe with absolute certainty that he was incapable of harming her, the scorching intensity of his emotions would have sent her running. Instead they made her cling, crave.

She was prepared for his questions. But she knew he didn't really want reasoned answers, not now. They wouldn't satisfy his need to be reassured she was irrevocably his. They wouldn't appease the primitive desire to dominate. They wouldn't dampen the scorching flames of jealousy.

It doesn't matter. I'm with you now, she said, and wasn't disappointed by his reaction.

Furious lust rolled off him in waves. His eyes blazed with it.

Everything about you matters to me. Everything you do concerns me.

He pinned her wrists above her head with one of his hands. With the other he took possession of her breast, his palm rough against her taut nipple, sending spikes of need straight to her cunt.

Her channel spasmed repeatedly, like a hungry mouth desperate to be filled. *Please fuck me,* she said, accompanying the words with images though she didn't think he needed the translation.

His hips jerked and she nearly came as his cock thrust against her clit. His lips pulled back in a snarl and a shiver of erotic fear went through her at the sight of the fangs that hadn't been there before.

Miciah hardened further, his cock throbbed against her clit, leaked. The scent of her arousal assaulted him, threatened to strip away what little control he had.

The hint of fear excited him, fed the dark need inside him to see her trembling, waiting uncertainly for the retribution that would come for daring to allow another male to touch her. He'd explain the purpose of the mating teeth later. He'd tell her she was the first, the only female he would ever pierce with them. He'd allow her the enhanced release that came with his bite. Later.

Why were you with Lyan?

I met a female Vesti in the marketplace. She took me to her home. Afterward she asked Lyan to return me to Ariel's quarters.

You knew I didn't intend for you to leave Ariel's home.

So punish me for it, she dared, and all ability to think deserted Miciah when confronted with the truth of what he wanted, needed.

He rolled to his feet. Stripped the black pants from her frame with a savage jerk and tossed them to the floor.

She tried to escape but he was faster, grabbing her wrist and holding her prisoner.

His loin covering joined her pants on the floor. His breath escaped on a moan when he sat, hauling her over his thighs and holding her positioned across his lap with one hand on her back and the other on the smooth, tanned globes of her buttocks.

She wanted this as much as he did. It was obvious in her lack of struggles, in the way her ass pushed against his palm, inviting a spanking.

He gave her what she wanted. What they both needed.

He lifted his hand and brought it down in a sharp spank.

A second, harder one followed. And then a third.

Each blow sent tortured pleasure spiking through his cock.

Her whimpered, panted breaths encouraged him to strike her again and again. Until golden skin blended with rosy heat and his thighs were wet with her desire.

And the wild jealousy was tamed.

He caressed her then, palmed her buttocks before leaning down to trail kisses over the warm flesh. She was his and he adored her, loved her beyond anything he'd ever imagined himself capable of.

"Don't make me wait any longer," she whispered, parting her thighs, tormenting him with the sight of her swollen, glistening folds.

Only the fleeting image of her in Lyan's arms kept Miciah from ending her punishment and joining his body to hers. "Where did you go? Who were you with?"

"I can't tell you."

His calm threatened to desert him. He straightened and delivered another spank.

Zoë moaned, writhed on his lap. She purposely rubbed against his cock to send scorching heat through it. He was as wet as she was, his penis slick with arousal. He was as hungry to thrust into her slit as she was to have him fill her, stretch her, claim her.

The Ylan stones at her wrists pulsed, echoing and amplifying the throbbing connection between them, making Zoë wonder if they were truly the symbionts Ariel had likened them to, if they fed on emotion.

Fuck me, she pleaded, knowing what the sight of her swollen cunt lips did to him.

He spanked her. Denied them both the ultimate pleasure even as the feel of his hand striking her buttock ratcheted up a desire no longer fueled by jealousy or the need to dominate.

Punishing her had centered him. Accepting it had allowed her to let the guilt she carried about keeping the full truth from him slide away, at least for a little while.

"Where did you go? Who were you with?" Miciah asked, not completely ready to let the matter drop.

"I can't tell you that. I can only tell you *why*."

She arched, pressing her hot skin against his open palm. She widened her thighs further, subtly asking him to reward her for her willingness to give him *something* in answer to his questions.

Miciah found it impossible to deny her. Impossible to deny himself when his cock throbbed and ached.

He slipped his fingers into her and nearly came when her sheath clamped down on them.

Once, twice, three times he fucked his fingers into her before forcing them out and away from her wet slit. "Tell me."

"I have a gift. I can sense when others are in emotional pain, especially when it's almost beyond what they can endure. I sensed it in the Vesti woman at the marketplace. I was drawn to her and by the time I left with Lyan, she had a reason to hang on and fight her sadness."

Pride surged into Miciah, caging the aggravation that rose with Zoë's mention of Lyan. That she wanted to help the women of his world, and *could* help them, brought Miciah immense joy.

The gift she spoke of explained why she could so easily block her thoughts. It explained why she refused to tell him who she'd been with and where she'd gone.

What she'd done wasn't so much different than how Iden served the goddess of the Amato. Miciah could accept her need to keep the confidences of others, just as Iden did, just as he himself was required to do as a member of the Council, but that didn't mean he intended to allow her to roam freely.

He leaned down, pressed kisses to Zoë's buttocks as he thrust his fingers into her channel and let her feel the sharp points of his mating fangs against her ass cheek. *You won't go anywhere else without Iden or me accompanying you.*

Are you saying Belizair is so dangerous, I'm not safe alone?

No, but you won't go off with anyone again, or leave our quarters without permission.

In the short time Zoë had known Miciah and Iden, she'd come to love them. On Earth. On Belizair. There was no denying it and she couldn't imagine life without them.

She reveled in the moments when she was a captive to lust, when dominance and possessiveness heightened the desire and added to the pleasure. But that didn't mean she intended to spend all her time lost in that state or anticipating it.

She'd told Miciah what she could. For now, though she still hated keeping the full truth from him.

If her gift came to life in the presence of other women, she'd do what she had to do. And if it didn't, she still wouldn't allow herself to lose all independence.

I'll be obedient in the privacy of our quarters, when it suits me. But as far as leaving without permission goes... You can't enforce that.

I won't need to. You'll agree to it.

Never, she said, offering him a challenge she knew he wouldn't be able to resist.

Never?

The silky, masculine confidence in Miciah's voice made Zoë laugh. *Never.*

He rose, scooping her up with him so she was once again cradled in his arms. Zoë took advantage of the position, rubbing her fingertips over his nipple.

His shudder rewarded her. She pressed her lips against his and whispered into his mind. *Nothing you can say or do will make me agree to become a prisoner, even a well-loved and cosseted one.*

She traced the seam of his mouth with her tongue. *But if you want to try to, feel free. Only there are conditions.*

Miciah shuddered again when her fingertips abandoned his nipple to stroke the top edge of his wing. *What conditions?* he asked as he strode toward the bed, knowing on some level he was falling into a sensual trap she'd set for him.

It didn't matter. He was a Vesti male.

Instinct fed his innate confidence. He could pleasure her so thoroughly that defying him — except in sexual play — would be impossible for her.

Chapter Fifteen

∞

What conditions? Miciah asked again, his tongue twining with hers, his cock leaking arousal in anticipation of finally thrusting into her heated core.

A sliver of Zoë's amusement arrowed straight to his heart.

Turnabout is fair play—where it's anatomically possible, she said. *Anything you do to me, I can do to you.*

Images of being at her mercy had his testicles pulling up tight, burning as they grew heavier with seed. *Granted. Anything else?*

By the time we've both come, if you haven't been able to get me to agree to asking for permission before leaving our quarters, then you won't stop me from going off with any of the women who might approach me for aid.

Miciah stiffened, a growl escaped. Denial flared but was immediately tamped by Vesti instinct. He wouldn't lose this challenge.

Agreed.

His tongue retreated from her mouth, her moan at its loss validating his belief she'd soon concede defeat. He tugged at her bottom lip, sucked it and let her feel the sharp points of his mating teeth.

She shivered and pressed her breasts against his chest, wrapped her arms around his neck as though she wanted to melt into him so they became one being. *I need you inside me,* she said, her voice a hot fist around his cock.

It was ecstasy and warning at the same time. He was close to coming, so close he didn't dare stretch her out on the mattress and cover her body with his. He didn't dare bury himself in her wet heat and try to torment her into surrender with shallow thrusts and stillness.

Miciah forced his mouth away from hers. He steeled himself against temptation as he placed her on the bed, her chest against the mattress.

He straddled her, pinning her so she couldn't roll over. With a touch to a spot on the headboard, a small door opened. A quick tug freed a tether.

He bound one wrist. Then repeated the process with the other.

Zoë laughed as a heady rush of feminine power swamped her. She recognized her bondage for what it was, desperation on Miciah's part. Fear that he would lose.

And he would lose. Too much was at stake for it to be otherwise.

She slid forward and rose onto her forearms and knees, parting her legs to let him see her wet slit and glistening inner thighs, presenting her ass, knowing its rosy glow would remind him of the pleasure they'd both found in its spanking.

Miciah's breathing grew harsher, faster. Lust flowed back and forth between them, filling their mental link with hot urgency and intense desire.

As if he couldn't help himself, he leaned forward and pressed his lips to her buttocks, caressed them with his palms. She felt what it cost him to stop touching her, to turn away long enough to tether her ankles with enough play to allow her to remain on her arms and knees.

He retrieved something from a hidden drawer on the side of the bed frame.

Toys. Too late she remembered Ariel's mention of them.

It was Zoë's turn to pant as he slipped a ring around her clit and it tightened, becoming a sucking mouth. Her hips bucked and she was torn between riding the wild pleasure to orgasm or lying down and writhing until she could dislodge the ring.

Miciah's hand around her thigh eliminated the second option. "Say you'll obey me in all things," he demanded.

She answered on a ragged breath. "Never." And struggled to remember the exact terms of the challenge. Did she lose if she came first?

No. She'd been smart enough not to phrase it that way, even if she'd neglected to think about him using something other than his body to gain her compliance.

Toys might be considered cheating. But Zoë didn't protest, not when she could use his game against him.

She looked down the length of her body and sent the image of it along their mental link, tormented him by interchanging the sight of the ring sucking her with memories of Iden using his mouth on her, of Miciah doing it. She gave in to the sensation, moaning and rocking, totally unselfconscious in her pleasure.

The Vesti were a physical race, but nothing in Miciah's past had prepared him for a mate like Zoë. He locked his fingers around his cock and used pain to keep from impaling her with it.

He couldn't look away from her slick, parted folds. Couldn't close his mind to the images she was sending him, or his ears to the sounds she was making.

It took all his control not to join her as she climbed, crested, moaned in release. It took all his control not to mate with her when her upper body collapsed against the bedding but her buttocks remained in the air, thighs parted in temptation, her glistening slit begging for him to shove himself into it.

He cupped her mound, rubbed his palm against wet heat and removed the clit ring before sliding his fingers into her opening. Her sheath rippled on his fingers, telling him her release hadn't satisfied the hunger to have his hard cock filling her.

Miciah's fist tightened on his shaft as he remembered the last time he'd had her, what it felt like to be inside her when Iden was.

A shudder went through him. He pulled his fingers from her slit and brushed over her back entrance, leaving the evidence of her arousal there before leaning over and once again opening the drawer containing the toys.

She would agree to his demands this time. And when she did, he'd reward her. He'd give her the *fucking* she'd begged for.

Miciah chose an anal toy, a cocklike plug to allow them to recapture some of what they'd experienced during the binding ceremony.

The tube of ritzca oil was already on the mattress. He used it to coat the toy then pressed the plug against the rosette of Zoë's anus.

You're ours to pleasure and protect, he said. *Say you won't leave our quarters or go off with anyone without permission.*

She moaned in answer, rocked backward. A sheen of sweat coated her skin as the oil lubricated her, heightening the need.

She took the toy inside her. Fucked herself on it.

It was a visceral reminder of ecstasy, a savage call burning away all ability to think.

Miciah couldn't stop himself.

He covered her body with his. Plunged into her channel. Thrust.

Once. Twice. And his will was decimated, his control eradicated.

Nothing existed except his mate.

Nothing.

He pounded into her. Their bodies and minds fused together.

And still he fought to get closer, to become one.

Found what he sought when her sheath clamped down on him.

He came.

And came again. Hips bucking as his testicles emptied of seed. His mating fangs sinking into her, making her scream as another orgasm took her.

* * * * *

Emotional weariness fell away from Iden as he entered his new living quarters. It was empty of personal touches because there'd been no time to move their things before leaving for Earth, but it didn't matter. Zoë's presence already made this *home* for him.

The sound of their voices told him Zoë and Miciah were in the bedroom, momentarily sated by lovemaking. Their low, husky murmurs had him eager to join them.

He removed his loin covering and padded across the living space, his cock hard against his belly, his testicles heavy and full beneath it. Pleasure rippled through him in the doorway when Zoë immediately sat, her gaze traveling the length his body.

She licked her lips and his penis bobbed, leaked. Her laugh was pure invitation. *Come to bed*, she said, an intimate command he had no intention of fighting.

Iden closed the distance. But when he would have positioned himself so she was between them, she moved to the edge of the bed. "I've had my turn at being the center of attention, now it's yours."

A glance at Miciah and hunger roared through Iden. He transmuted his wings, turning them into shimmering barely visible particles. It was a feat most found difficult, if not impossible on Belizair, but the Ylan stones at his wrists contained enough energy to do it.

When he was stretched out between Zoë and Miciah, she leaned down, stroking his chest with her hand as her mouth found his. "Perfect," she said, kissing him, her tongue tangling with his.

She smelled of desert blossoms, as did Miciah. They'd showered, as he had at the temple.

Iden moaned when her fingers found his nipple, rubbing in tiny circles until he ached to feel her lips, her bite. His hips lifted off the bed when a masculine hand gripped his cock.

Miciah, he said, their mental link open so it was impossible to hide the desire, the need wrapped up in the name.

It seems like I've been waiting for us to be together like this forever, Zoë teased, ending the kiss. Her expression told Iden that she was abandoning his lips only so Miciah could claim them.

Lust coiled and tightened inside Miciah, building a tense need he wouldn't be free of until he'd ridden Iden and they'd both come. He could no longer remember the reason he'd fought his hunger for Iden as he covered Iden's mouth with his own.

Where Zoë's lips where soft, yielding, Iden's were firm, challenging. Where Zoë's tongue dueled in mock battle, Iden's waged a war that would last a lifetime and always end a draw.

Heat poured into Miciah, Zoë's as well as Iden's. It built until the rub of tongue against tongue was no longer enough.

He was intensely aware of Zoë stretched out on her side next Iden, her eyes dark with desire. She'd made no secret of how aroused it made her to think of Iden and him as lovers.

With a moan Miciah edged on top of Iden, bucked as their cocks touched, rubbed against each other. Exquisite sensation burned along the length of his spine, making his buttocks clench and his wings extend, quiver as they became a suede blanket.

"You two are so beautiful together," Zoë whispered, holding their hardened shafts together.

179

Electric pleasure whipped through Miciah as she stroked. He could feel it echoed in Iden.

Their kiss deepened, intensified. Their bodies moving, grinding, as the need to fuck built.

Unlike with Zoë, Miciah felt no desire to linger and savor. He wanted to find Iden's back entrance and thrust inside until the white-hot ecstasy of release screamed through him.

It shouldn't be possible to need to come so desperately, to want it so badly so soon after he'd spent his seed in Zoë, but he did. His testicles were tight, his skin slick with sweat.

Panting, Miciah pushed himself to his knees. He looked for the tube of ritzca oil and found it.

Iden's heated gaze challenged him to put the oil on his own cock. He squeezed the lubricant on his finger, knowing he didn't dare apply it to himself.

A touch. A brush across Iden's anus. That's all it took.

Iden's face grew taut. His muscles stood out in stark relief. He tried to keep from thrashing but his rapid breathing and sweat-sheened skin testified to the effectiveness of the oil in preparing him, in making him burn for the exquisite agony of being taken by another man.

"Fuck him," Zoë whispered, her command sending a spike of dark, dark pleasure through Miciah.

He glanced at her and nearly came at the sight of her hand between her legs. He shuddered as he imagined her thrusting her fingers into her wet slit as he thrust into Iden.

Miciah gripped his cock and lowered himself back on top of Iden. Zoë's moan joined theirs when Miciah guided himself to the pucker of Iden's ritzca-coated anus.

Raw need gripped him and made it impossible to hold back. Fire engulfed Miciah as he pressed forward in an agonizing inch-by-inch claiming.

He didn't resist when Iden drew his head down, demanding intimacy with the lust. Their mouths fused together, their tongues parrying aggressively.

Remaining motionless wasn't an option for either of them. Neither was gentleness. The hunger was too intense, too long denied and the potent ritzca oil stripped away all denial.

Finally they were lovers as they were meant to be.

It was more impression than words. A soul-deep feeling of completion at being skin to skin, joined in a bond that transcended the physical and encompassed another, Zoë, whose pleasure poured into them, heightening their own, making her a part of what he and Iden did together.

The tight heat and relentless squeeze of Iden's internal muscles had Miciah struggling against coming as shards of icy-heat spiked through him with each thrust and retreat. He delayed the moment of release until Iden's cock spasmed against his belly and he felt the strike of heated semen against his flesh. Then there was no fighting it.

Miciah shuddered and gave in to what his body demanded. He came on a moan, hips jerking uncontrollably.

When no seed remained he rolled to his back, transmuting his wings as Iden had.

Tremors of pleasure continued to go through him as he came to terms with what he'd done and accepted what he'd long fought. He'd found extreme satisfaction in making love to another man, and he would do it again.

There was no desire to cuddle afterward, or curl around Iden possessively as he did with Zoë. But its lack didn't change the intimacy flooding the mate-bond.

Satisfaction made Iden languid though his cock stirred to life when Zoë slid on top of him, replacing Miciah's lost heat with her own. "I don't have to ask if you enjoyed that," she murmured against his lips.

He laughed, his hands smoothing down the length of her spine. "And did you enjoy it, beloved?"

She answered by rubbing her mound against his hardening penis and coating her belly with the seed he'd released. "Very much. Though I think we could all use a shower."

"A shower and an evening meal, then we can return to bed."

Zoë's eyebrows drew together. "Evening meal?" she asked, glancing at the window with the light from the second sun streaming through it.

Pleasure of a different kind settled in Iden's chest, that she'd so easily accepted being brought to Belizair. That she was curious about her new world, and embraced it.

"The third sun will rise in a short while. We seek shelter then, and by custom, it is when we take our rest." He took her bottom lip between his and gave her a playful nip. *Though somehow, I suspect that unless we make love to you at least once in the shower, there will be no rest when we return to the sleeping chamber.*

They left the bed long enough to slowly bathe, to make good on Iden's threat to tire her out with lovemaking, then eat. When they returned, Zoë settled between Iden and Miciah.

Through the archway she saw the windows and walls darken against the harsh glare of Belizair's third sun, and thought fleetingly of Acacia and the child she was hiding.

In the shower, she'd told Iden about Miciah's being called away to a Council meeting, and her subsequent visit with Ariel and Kaylee. Now guilt and worry tried to push their way in and eradicate her contentedness. She blocked them, but not before Iden murmured, "What troubles you, beloved?"

Not wanting to lie, Zoë turned onto her side to face him. She stroked his arm, then the soft feathers of his wing. "The plight of the women here. Who are the Fallon?"

"They were a powerful race of winged shapeshifters. Not only could they take many different forms, but they had various psychic gifts." Iden leaned forward and pressed a kiss

182

to Zoë's forehead. *Not unlike the gift that drew you to the Vesti female in the marketplace.*

A tiny knot formed in her chest, part dread and part hope. "Does that mean there are others here with psychic gifts?"

"Perhaps the healers could be said to have them, though I can't say for certain. Their world is closed off and the weave of their day-to-day lives a mystery. For the rest on Belizair, most have a talent, a leaning. If they pursue it, the Ylan stones they wear can enhance their abilities. In most ways, it's not so unlike what you have on Earth. Effort and dedication are required. There is no substitute for learning and practice, followed by experience."

Iden's answer didn't ease the knot in Zoë's chest. But it presented a theory about the descendents of the Fallon. Maybe after thousands of years of evolution, humans ended up with the psychic gifts, while those on Belizair got the wings.

"Are you saying that my having a psychic gift would be accepted here?"

"Your gift of empathy will be much appreciated," Iden said. "Our women hurt so deeply now."

He spared a glance at Miciah. And against her back, Miciah tensed, as if he already knew that whatever Iden was going to say, they'd be in disagreement about it.

"I don't support the Council's decision requiring humans to remain housed close together in Winseka," Iden said. "Your presence can perhaps bridge the gap between females from Earth and those on Belizair before it widens into a chasm. News of your compassion and the solace you offered will have already spread."

A fist squeezed Zoë's heart at hearing additional confirmation—though after encountering Acacia's male relative in the transport chamber, she really didn't need it when it came to accepting—that not everyone was pleased about bringing humans to Belizair.

The fear and guilt spread to her belly. She had to honor her promise to Acacia, at least until she warned Acacia before revealing what they'd done.

Zoë pushed forward, needing to better understand Belizair. "What if other humans are brought here and they have different kinds of psychic gifts? Like my friend Destiny who can read tea leaves? Or some of the fortunetellers I've met who could prophesy? Or what about someone who can move objects with their mind? Or find something by having a vision? Would they be welcome here?"

She felt their answers through the mental bond. Miciah recoiled while Iden contemplated.

"Let us hope females with such gifts aren't brought to Belizair anytime soon," Miciah said.

There was no fear or revulsion in his voice, but there was a conviction that made Zoë's heart race as she thought not only of her gift, but what she'd done with it in the span of a day — the laws she'd broken with Acacia.

Sensing her distress, Miciah trailed kisses along her shoulder and neck. *You have nothing to fear, beloved. As Iden said, your gift of empathy coupled with your desire to reach out to the women of Belizair and help them will be much appreciated. And though Iden disagrees with the Council position with respect to restricting the human women brought to Winseka, it was done with their best interests in mind. Once their children are born, they may live elsewhere.*

She felt the brush of his mating fangs against her skin and shivered in remembered ecstasy.

By the time you are heavy with our children, he continued, *I imagine many of the restrictions when it comes to newly arrived human bond-mates will have been lifted.*

Zoë hoped what he said was true, though she doubted he meant there would be sanctioned trips to Earth. She wanted to confess the full truth to both of them, but her throat closed up on the words.

The promise she'd made to Acacia held her back, as did the fear of what it would mean if she admitted it. Would she be sent back to Earth without Miciah and Iden? Or would they all be banished, and in being forced to leave this world, her gifts made discordant again so she couldn't use them to help others?

Both choices sent pain slicing through Zoë. She couldn't bear the thought of either loss.

Not wanting to travel further down that path, she veered away, asking, "What happened to the Fallon?"

Iden answered, "No one can say for sure. Most believe that over time, different clan-houses began to favor one form over another. They began selecting their mates with that form in mind, until eventually separate races evolved and the ability to shift between forms was lost."

"So all that's left are the Amato and the Vesti?"

"Here on Belizair, yes. But not all the Fallon favored the look of the Vesti and the Amato. Some forms bear no resemblance to what you consider a human one."

"Meaning there are other worlds where Fallon descendents live?"

"Yes."

A shiver went through Zoë. "Have those other planets been affected by the same virus that struck here?"

"Yes, a few of them have."

Zoë wasn't sure she really wanted to know, but she couldn't stop herself from asking, "Are they — the descendents who don't look human — taking women from Earth, too?"

"Some," Miciah said. "Where we can, our scientists and scholars are aiding them."

A second, harder shiver went through Zoë.

Iden's mouth settled on her ear. He slipped his tongue into it before sucking the lobe between his lips. *Do not rush to fear for other women. As you've found great pleasure in being mated*

185

to men who resemble the angels and demons of human mythology,
there are those of your kind who fantasize about dragons, as well as
alien beings. The Amato and Vesti believe in free will. Despite our
ties to others descended from the Fallon, we will not aid them if their
vision for the future involves enslaving humans.

Zoë closed her eyes as Miciah's hand took possession of
her breast. His palm rubbed over the hardened nipple as Iden
continued to torment her ear with sucks and shallow thrusts.

She allowed them to turn her mind away from the fate of
other women and reacquaint herself with her own fate, one
she was quite content with.

For long moments their mouths and hands worshipped
her with wet kisses and masculine touches, the brush of wings
against her skin. She responded, giving herself over to the
pleasure of being held between them in a cocoon of feathers
and suede, hard muscle and heated flesh.

The warmth and security invited her to surrender to the
encroaching drowsiness and sleep safely in their arms. She
resisted, questions still lingering in her mind, not yet
completely obliterated by the day's activities finally catching
up to her.

Had she really started her morning on Earth?

"Tell me about the god of the Vesti," she murmured.

"There's not much to tell," Miciah said. "We do not
worship him as you do your God on Earth. Ours is a
wandering god, one responsible for the creation of Belizair,
before he moved on to other worlds."

"He was also the god of the Fallon?" Zoë asked, trying to
reconcile the legend surrounding the forming of the different
races with the image of the man who'd shed batlike wings for
those of a butterfly in her vision.

Miciah rubbed his cheek against her hair. "Perhaps. Or
perhaps he was a god created by the Vesti from legends of
those who *were* Fallon. I don't know. It is not a subject that's
held any interest for me. Ariel's Vesti mate, Komet, is a

scholar. He might have answers to your questions. Why do you ask about the god?"

Zoë remembered the fervor of Acacia's claim that they must retrieve the child because it was the will of the god. Uneasiness threatened to slide in and bring a chill with it as she thought about Acacia's impassioned belief that the god of the Vesti now walked on Earth, but reached out to the Vesti in their time of need using Zoë as his bridge.

She fought the cold tendrils of fear by addressing its source directly. "On Earth, religious conflict often leads to war and persecution. What would happen here, if the Vesti started believing their god had returned and was taking an interest in this world again?"

Miciah stroked her belly. "I'm not sure such a thing is possible. We have no priests or priestesses, as the Amato do, to determine the god's presence and make him known to others. Perhaps such a revelation could come through the healers. If so then the potential for conflict would be greatly reduced. I don't know whether to hope for such a thing, or pray it never happens—our world is already struggling with change."

Zoë pushed her tension out on a controlled breath. What was done, was done, and truthfully, she wouldn't undo it if she could.

His answer didn't eradicate her concern, but it didn't add to it. And there was a small kernel of hope in his mention of the healers. There were Vesti among them, and she knew from her visit with Kaylee and Ariel just how important and respected the healers were.

If...*when*...the full truth of her gift came to light, at least there was a possibility that the healers might come forward and support Acacia's bringing the child to Belizair. They'd treated Kaylee on her arrival in Winseka, and accepted her as though she was one of them.

They'd told Kaylee she would always be welcome in the mountain range. It was an amazing declaration considering only those who were called to the healers' enclaves could survive in the mountains for any length of time. All the information Zoë had gathered and pieced together suggested that just as the Ylan stones were semi-living and symbiotic, Belizair itself was a sentient planet.

She stroked the underside of Iden's feathery wing with the back of her hand then caressed the place where it joined to his body. "What about the Goddess and her Consort, Ylan? Are they personifications of creative forces? Or do the Amato consider them real entities?"

Iden's eyelids lowered at her touch. Pleasure purred through both the bond they shared and the stones at her wrist.

"They are either or both, and more," he said. "The answer depends on individual experience and interpretation. But in the end our beliefs are tied to Belizair itself. Harmony with self, each other, and our natural world are what we emphasize."

Zoë didn't quite know how to fit the golden lady—the Goddess of the Amato, who'd apparently appeared to Kaylee—into an equation that contained the butterfly bracelet and the man Acacia thought was the Vesti god.

Time would tell. She was ready to let it all go, at least until tomorrow.

A smile curved her lips. She rose onto an elbow and kissed Iden, then turned and did the same to Miciah.

"This has been an amazing day, considering I was on Earth this morning, and now I'm here. But at least one thing hasn't changed. I started out in bed with two guys straight out of an erotic fantasy, and now I'm ending it in the same way."

"As you always will," Miciah said, sliding his hand downward and cupping her mound as Iden's lips latched on to her nipple.

Streaks of pleasure shot through her when Iden began suckling. Her channel clenched as Miciah rubbed and pressed his palm to her clit.

"I already love you both," she said. "You know that, don't you?"

They did. She knew as much through the bond. But she wanted to say the words. And she wanted Miciah and Iden to acknowledge them.

You're our future, Iden said. *It can't be any other way.*

Which is why you'll learn to obey, Miciah growled, taking her lips with his, reminding her of their earlier battle — one holding the promise of a sensual rematch.

Her laughter was a teasing taunt. *Whenever you're ready to try to teach me, bring it on.*

Miciah retaliated by sliding his fingers into her channel. *You'll sleep now,* he commanded, and began thrusting in perfect sync with Iden's hungry tugs on her nipple, pushing pleasure through her in waves and driving her toward an orgasm that would tumble her into unconsciousness.

Chapter Sixteen

ℬↃ

Chimes announced a visitor shortly after they'd eaten a breakfast of bread and fruit. The sound if it had Iden's eyebrows lifting in curiosity and Miciah scowling in bad humor.

"First our binding day was interrupted and now it appears this one will be as well," Miciah grumbled.

"Perhaps I'd better greet our visitor then," Iden said, pausing only long enough to kiss Zoë before turning away from the wall screen currently showing an image of Belizair.

Reluctantly Zoë turned away as well and followed him, as did Miciah, her reaction to the chimes a mix of her mates.

When it came to learning about new places, she'd always been like a sponge, ready to absorb knowledge. But between lingering in bed quite awhile before getting up to shower after the amazing morning sex, then eat, they'd only just gotten around to demonstrating the screen and using it to give her more details of the world she now found herself in. Still, the people had always been the larger part of her enjoyment, so the chance to meet someone new was as interesting to her as learning more about the various regions of Belizair, and the off-world places those who lived here traveled to.

At Iden's command a doorway formed in the external wall. Two Vesti women stood there.

Zoë's pulse sped up at the sight of them. It didn't slow when they smiled tentatively at her before giving their attention to Iden.

They identified themselves as Miette and Avini as they touched their bands to his in formal greeting. When he stepped aside, inviting them in, they stopped just inside the doorway and cast tentative, hopeful glances at Zoë.

Avini, whose wings were a dark chocolate streaked with lighter brown said, "I am a cousin to Acacia. Miette is a cousin to my mate. We hoped you would join us in the marketplace and…perhaps help us as you were able to help Acacia. Several of our friends are waiting for us there."

Excitement and fear, guilt and hope swept through Zoë — along with the emotions of her mates. Denial and frustration vibrated off Miciah, mollified by his pride at having her sought out by Vesti women. Iden's pride also filled her, as did his amusement at knowing of the challenge over her coming and going as she pleased, and witnessing the results of her having defeated a Vesti male at his own game.

Miciah offered his arms in formal greeting, though Zoë suspected his interest was in learning if they were related to Lyan, and if there was a possibility she'd be once again in the other man's arms. She couldn't help teasing. *If you're worried about Lyan, you shouldn't be. He is mated, to a human who is now pregnant.*

Miciah's mental growl confirmed her suspicion. *Don't think Iden will protect you from me should you return in the company of Lyan or any other male.* His arm curled possessively around her, his hand settling on her belly. *When you're carrying our children, he will reconsider the wisdom of letting you go out unaccompanied by one of us.*

The thought of getting pregnant almost made Zoë regret teasing Miciah. Almost.

Her heart and her mind were at odds on the subject of children. She knew what having them meant for Miciah and Iden, and she knew she'd love the children they created together. But if it were left up to her, she'd put it off for a few years — an unlikely possibility in a world without birth control and where every other adult human female carried twins.

Abstinence was *not* an option. Even if they'd agree to it, *she* didn't have the willpower to enforce it.

Zoë acknowledged Avini and Miette with a smile but didn't offer to touch her bands to theirs and risk a vision. She didn't need the shaft-of-ice sensation that had pierced through her in the marketplace at Acacia's arrival to know she was meant to help them.

Their hope and despair washed over her in waves of equal measure, as did there determination. Having a child, even one not of their own bodies, was a fate they would risk banishment for.

There was no way Zoë could deny the calling of her gift and the promise it held for these women. "I'll come with you to the marketplace."

"And I'll accompany you that far," Iden said. "Then keep going to my former living quarters so I can gather some of my belongings."

An edge of satisfaction slid down the link with Miciah. "I'll do the same."

Zoë laughed softly. *Cheater*, she said, knowing he wanted to see for himself just who was waiting at the marketplace.

Flight would have been faster, but Zoë was content to walk. The geography lesson they'd started continued, without the benefit of the wall screen and map though their descriptions accompanied by mental images were equally effective.

Avini and Miette remained quiet. Their surreptitious glances at Miciah revealed a nervousness that remained hidden otherwise.

Zoë's own nerves tightened and grew taut the closer they drew to their destination. Excitement and worry balled in her gut. Guilt entered the mix, too.

She couldn't keep this secret from Miciah and Iden much longer. It was already eating at her, though so far, nothing they'd told her made confession an easy path.

She'd tackle it later, she told herself as Avini and Miette indicated a table where three Vesti women sat underneath a latticed canopy of delicate vines.

"I'll leave you here," Iden said.

Zoë halted him with a touch to his arm and stepped into his embrace. "I love you," she said, emotion swelling up inside her with a sudden fear for their future together.

Beloved, he whispered in her mind, covering her lips with his own, his hands sweeping down her back and pulling her more deeply into his kiss.

Desire flared hot between them despite the impossibility of acting on it. He tasted of fruit and she sucked his tongue into her mouth, grew wet at the sweet promise of pleasure.

We won't be parted for long, he said, reluctance at being separated at all vibrating through their bond as he set her aside.

He turned toward Miciah, his intention to acknowledge their relationship openly with a parting kiss obvious to Zoë, just as Miciah's reaction to it was.

Miciah stepped back in a subtle denial that wouldn't draw comment from anyone watching. But between the three of them, it was a shout threatening to shatter their newly formed mate bond.

Iden's expression hardened. It was met by an equally stony expression on Miciah's face.

Zoë felt anger and hurt stab through Iden, searing and dark. A muscle spasmed in his cheek and he took a measured breath, as if to push the intense emotions deep inside himself.

A fist squeezed Zoë's heart painfully. She'd thought her sudden fear came from what might happen as a result of her meeting with the Vesti women, now she wondered if her gift had given her subconscious a glimpse of the chasm about to open between Miciah and Iden.

She didn't know what to say to either of them and her stomach knotted as a result of it. There was no time to resolve this. Not here. Not now.

I'll return to you later, beloved, Iden told her before turning away, the rigidness in his posture the only clue to his emotions.

She wanted to chase after him, to drag Miciah along and force them to reconcile their differences. But a glance to where Avini and Miette had joined their friends, and Zoë accepted she couldn't. Their hope and anguish tugged at her with such force she knew her gift required her to put aside her personal fears and worries.

Still, she couldn't leave Miciah without asking, *Why?*

It's not the way of the Vesti to take same sex lovers.

And yet you and Iden are lovers.

What happens in our personal quarters is no one's business but our own.

So many different thoughts whipped through Zoë that for an instant she was left speechless. Then, like Iden, she took a measured breath, pushing the turmoil into recess.

"I'll see you in a little while," she said, turning toward where the women waited.

A growl sounded in her mind as well as her ears. Miciah's fingers clamped around her wrist and he pulled her into his arms.

Savage, frustrated heat poured off him. He grasped her hair and slammed his mouth down on hers.

Denying him wasn't an option. But neither did she intend to surrender. Her tongue battled his, becoming a sword that said more clearly than words that she wasn't pleased with him.

His growl deepened. His wings came forward to form a cocoon of privacy.

She didn't relent. And neither did he until the need for breath forced them apart.

I will follow Iden to his quarters. We will resolve our differences.

It was all she could ask. She didn't know enough about Belizair and the Vesti to insist on the outcome she desired, an unhidden relationship.

Her stomach clenched, reminding her she had secrets of her own. She brushed her lips back and forth across his. "Go," she whispered, promising herself that the next time the three of them were together, she'd tell them the full truth about her gift, and what it had led her to do.

Behave, he said, repositioning his wings so she could step away from him.

She joined the women as he disappeared from sight, heading in the direction Iden had taken.

As with Avini and Miette, Zoë didn't offer a formal greeting as she was introduced to the others. In such close proximity, their emotions threatened to drown her in endless despair. Only their hope she could help them served as a life preserver.

"Would you like something to eat or drink?" Avini asked, assuming the role of hostess.

Zoë didn't think she could handle adding anything to a stomach already knotted and tense. "No thank you."

She willed herself to relax, without success. But didn't chide herself for the lack of it. Despite a lifetime of wanting to use her gift to help others, everything about this was new to her. And the situation was complicated — beyond the obvious.

Zoë took a deep breath and fortified her mental shields as she realized this was a perfect time to learn more about the potential consequences of using her gift. She might not be able to avoid them, but that didn't mean she should remain ignorant of them.

"What will happen when Acacia stops hiding the child?"

"She will be called before the Council," Avini said.

"And banished?" Zoë asked, remembering Thaden's words in the transport chamber and their implication. Acacia had broken more than one law the day before. Traveling to Earth was just the first of them.

Zanya, whose sharp features and piercing eyes would have made Zoë think *high-powered attorney* if they were on Earth said, "It will not come to banishment."

Nisha, whose fragile looks reminded Zoë of Ariel, gave a slight shake of her head. "We can't be sure of that."

"How could they dare banish us?" Miette said. "They plan to allow some of those who want to parent to do so on Earth now that the scientists are looking among the orphaned and abandoned children for any who carry the Fallon marker."

"It's not the same," Nisha countered. "There have only been a handful of female children found. Only one of them is old enough to understand anything about Belizair and the Council has not revoked its rule against revealing our existence to those on Earth. There is no guarantee any of the children raised there will accept the men matched to them in the future and agree to return here."

Etyn, who sat next to Nisha said, "It would be better for us and for the children if they were raised here among us. How can there be free will and true choice when it comes to accepting a mate without full knowledge? How can they know what they stand to lose or gain if they are raised outside of the clan-houses?"

Nisha's shoulders slumped. "I do not disagree," she said quietly. "Otherwise I wouldn't be here. But Zoë asked what will happen when Acacia—or any of us who might be lucky enough to have the god touch our lives directly—makes the child's presence on Belizair known.

"Zoë deserves the truth. We don't know. It is against our laws to go to Earth without permission. Now that the Council knows it's possible to bring a child back through a family bond, because of Kaylee, it's also against or laws to do it unless the child belongs to a human who is being claimed in a mate-bond. To knowingly break those laws means the issue of sanctions *must* be brought up in a meeting of the Council. Whether or not one of the members will call for banishment and bring it to a vote, is impossible to predict."

The misgivings Zoë had suppressed after meeting Ariel and learning the reason for seeking out human mates resurfaced. Anger surfaced with it, not at Miciah and Iden, but at laws making it okay to bring human women to Winseka, but forbidding them from knowing beforehand just what their choice entailed.

With all the focus on avoiding extinction, did anyone consider what it might mean for the humans brought here? Or were they merely a means to an end? Were they represented on the council that ruled? Did they have any voice at all, other than one they might gain through their mates?

She took the opportunity to voice a suspicion. "Not everyone is happy about having humans here."

"What you say is true," Avini conceded. "It is a difficult time for all of us. It has caused old hostilities to surface and gain strength."

"And new fears to be born," Miette added.

"Between the Vesti and the Amato?" Zoë guessed.

Miette nodded. "The Vesti have always mate-bonded in a union that includes only one male and one female. Now our men must share a human mate with an Amato."

"And the Amato fear what it will mean for them," Avini added. "It is against no law, but it is rare for an Amato to enter a bond with a Vesti. Any children resulting from such a pairing have always been Vesti."

Zoë looked around the table. "Is that why there are no Amato with you? Because tensions between the two races make friendships as rare as pairings used to be?"

Zanya gave a decisive, negative shake of her head. Etyn, the quietest of the group, said, "We thought the god meant for you to help us. But you are right to make us see how our differences drive us further apart in a time when the women of *all* races should join together in support of one another. Whether you are able to help one of us or not, I will speak to an Amato friend whose pain is deeper even than my own and ask her to seek you out."

Her eyes held a plea for understanding. "It's hardest for the women. We are all struggling to come to terms with what has happened to us. Some hang on to hope more easily than others. But even that hope is for others, for their unmated male relatives and not for themselves."

"There is uncertainty too," Nisha said in a hushed voice. "We won't know until Cyan's children are born whether they will be winged or not."

"Will they be unwanted on Belizair if they're not?" Zoë asked.

Gasps and horrified expressions met her question. "No," Nisha said, her wings trembling behind her as if shocked Zoë could even suggest such a thing.

"Children, of any race, are treasured here," Miette said. "Our birthrates were low even before the Hotalings struck with their virus. For many it takes years to conceive. It has always been so." She touched the bands at her wrist, one with speckled green Ylan stones, the other with streaked gold. "Most believe it is the price we pay for being able to live on Belizair. The planet will not allow more of us than it can sustain."

Surprised satisfaction made Zoë smile. She hadn't been far off in thinking perhaps the planet was sentient, and the Amato Goddess and Consort might be personifications of it.

She glanced down at the wristbands she wore. The butterfly shaped stones glowed with a deep luster and held a wealth of promise, while the night-sky stones in the bands

Iden and Miciah had given her provided a means to turn that promise into reality when used with her gift.

Was it right to bring human children into this world?

The answer was easy for Zoë. Yes.

She'd seen too much suffering on Earth. Through her eyes as she traveled. In her mind when she'd stayed too long in one place and her gift flared to life.

"What about your mates?" she asked, making eye contact with each of the women. "Do they know why you asked me here? Are they willing to risk banishment if need takes us to Earth and a child is brought back?"

"It won't come to that," Zanya said again, lifting her hand to halt anyone from contradicting her. "If anything, our actions will force the Council to *hear* us when we say we can open our hearts and our homes to children who aren't from our womb.

"All of the Council's efforts have been for the unmated. All that's left for us is to cling to the belief that one day the scientists will understand how the virus works and be able to reverse the effects of it. Or one day our bounty hunters will capture a Hotaling and gain information that will lead to our having children.

"We need hope now. A reason to go on. My mate knows what I intend and he supports me, as will those in my clan-house and his when it becomes known what I've— If the god's eyes are still on this world and he sees fit to lead me to a child my mate and I can raise as our own."

Tears clogged Zoë's throat at Zanya's impassioned words, but her pulse raced as she wondered where Miciah stood on the issue of bringing human children here. If she weren't involved in this, would he be one of the Council members to call for banishment or vote in favor of it?

A fist squeezed her heart as she remembered his reaction when she'd asked about humans with psychic gifts being welcomed on Belizair. *Let us hope females with such gifts aren't brought to Belizair anytime soon.*

Her earlier fear for their future together returned. Panic threatened to swell.

Etyn touched her fingertips to the back of Zoë's hand, drawing her away from the narrow focus of her own life. The quiet Vesti woman placed a pair of tiny bracelets on the table in front of her. "In the clan-house I was born into, it is custom that when a female child enters a mate-bond, the male is gifted with the bands his children will one day wear. It is a symbol of hope, that the union will bear fruit. My father made these and gave them to my mate, Atif, on our binding day. When I spoke with Atif about seeking you out, he broke with tradition by entrusting me with the bracelets. If our need weren't so great, we wouldn't ask this of you."

Zoë took a deep breath and felt calm settle over her, a sureness of purpose, not just about helping the individual women her gift touched, she realized, but in doing something more. Her earlier questions had led to talk of solidarity among the women on Belizair. That movement had to start somewhere—here. And sometime—now. With these women who were willing risk banishment to bring about a change in their world.

She would stand with them, and through the Amato they called friends, spread the idea of unity rather than discord. And down the road, they would stand with her when it came to making sure those who came from Earth had a voice on the council and a chance to return to their home worlds for visits.

"I know something of the Fallon," Zoë said. "I'm told they had various psychic gifts, so I'm guessing that instead of manifesting wings, some of the human descendents ended up with psychic abilities. On Earth I had two of these, though they didn't work together. The first was an emphatic gift tuned to despair and unhappiness. It made it impossible to stay anywhere for very long because my mental shields would give way if I did and I'd be overwhelmed. The second ability was to see into the future when I accidentally touched someone's hand, or they touched mine. Usually what I saw was depressing, heartbreaking, and I couldn't do anything to change what was going to happen.

"Since coming here, the two abilities work together. I was drawn to Acacia in the marketplace but I didn't have any control over the vision. I didn't summon it, it just came. She thought your god was working through me. I don't claim that and I can't promise results, but I'm willing to try to use my gift to help you."

Chapter Seventeen

ஐ

Iden leaned against the smooth arch of the doorway opening into the bedroom of his former living quarters. Hurt and anger had driven him here without stopping, like a wounded animal returning to its cave.

The small room was dwarfed by the bed within. Looking at it, remembering all the times he'd lain on it, stroking himself to completion as he imagined a future with Miciah, only made the emotion filling him seethe like hot liquid in a caldron.

On some level he'd know Miciah intended to keep the true nature of their relationship a secret, and yet he'd thought once they were lovers...

Iden rubbed his chest, trying to soothe himself. In retrospect, perhaps he should have gone to the temple first to regain the full measure of his natural calm. At the moment, he felt far from that state of grace.

He cursed and wheeled away to pace the larger room, hoping movement would help settle him. Instead, memory assaulted him, of Miciah coming to the temple.

I'd like you to claim her with me.

Am I your first choice?

Yes.

You seem to be forgetting something about me.

I'm not forgetting anything.

And you're prepared to accommodate my desires? Or are you hoping our being inside our mate's body at the same time will be enough? That it will stop there?

If she's repulsed —

Then perhaps I'd better wait for a better match.

Come with me to Earth. Meet her.

And if she's as open-minded as the Amato when it comes to coupling?

Whatever happens when we are alone in our quarters, I will accept it as natural for our mate-bond.

Good enough.

But it wasn't good enough, not if Miciah intended for them to live a lie.

Iden's nostrils flared as he thought about what they'd already done together. His hand went to his cock, grasping it through the thin loincloth as he relived those moments when it was Miciah's hand instead of his own.

A shudder went through him with the image of Zoë lying next to them, her eyes dark with lust, her hand between her legs, pleasuring herself as she watched.

You two are so beautiful together.

He grew harder remembering Miciah's kiss, the feel of his cock and the flushed expression of ecstasy as they made love for the first time. He hadn't often let another male top him, but it was different with Miciah.

Arousal escaped, wetting the front of Iden's loin covering. He slipped his hand beneath the material, his buttocks clenching at the feel of flesh against flesh.

The worst of the hurt and anger faded as he stroked himself. Resolve took its place just as chimes announced a visitor.

Miciah.

Despite the mental shields they'd raised in the marketplace, Iden knew who stood on the other side of the wall. Without it being a conscious decision, he stripped away the loincloth as he moved toward where the door would form.

Heat poured into his bloodstream, fueled by suppressed emotion and a pent-up lust that hadn't been allowed expression until Zoë came into their lives.

He felt it mirrored in Miciah. The truth of it pulsed through the Ylan stones at his wrists in a heavy beat that couldn't be ignored.

With a command the wall retreated, forming an opening.

Miciah entered and Iden allowed him a single step, just enough for the doorway to close, replaced by smooth surface. Fury and hurt returned, not in their pure form, but mixed with something Iden had never felt toward another man, a love that seared. Consumed. Refused to be denied.

Words and reasoned argument burned away underneath the onslaught of released emotion. He pinned Miciah to the wall with his body, both of their wings extending, quivering as heat flashed through them.

His mouth crashed down onto Miciah's. Taking, not asking.

A thrust and he'd pierced the seam of Miciah's lips. Their tongues battled, but it wasn't a true fight for dominance.

The words were unspoken but they both knew that in coming here, Miciah accepted he was the supplicant. And it wouldn't end until he was on his knees.

Iden's hands swept downward, freeing Miciah of his sole garment. They both moaned as it fell away, leaving their cocks touching, rubbing, spasming with the intimate contact. Liquid escaped from Miciah's cock head, wetting Iden's skin as well as Miciah's as they ground against one another.

Iden deepened the kiss, making the one he'd intended to give Miciah in the marketplace a pale, pale imitation in comparison. Words tried to form but he ruthlessly suppressed them.

Nothing had ever been easy when it came to Miciah. He doubted that would change, regardless of what happened here.

The savage heat coursing through him was reminiscent of the Vesti mating fever. It burned, stripping away everything but the need to claim a mate so thoroughly that there could be no denial of it afterward.

His fingertips dug into the sensitive area on the underside of Miciah's wings and Miciah returned the touch, nearly sending Iden to his knees as painful pleasure shot down his spine and through his cock.

No! The silent shout gave him the strength to end the kiss, to shift his hands to the top edges of Miciah's wings and force him downward.

It would have been a true battle if Miciah hadn't wanted to go. But Miciah wanted. Needed.

His hand circled Iden's flushed, heated cock. Satisfaction poured into him at the way it throbbed against his palm.

Iden's hips bucked. His breathing was little more than shallow pants.

Suck it, he said, breaking the mental silence.

Miciah's grip tightened in response, forcing a moan from Iden. Iden's clenched buttocks and arched back testifying it was one of pleasure and not pain.

Zoë's image surfaced in Miciah's thoughts, along with memories of the previous night, her arousal-slick fingers plunging into her slit as she'd watched him fuck Iden. *You two are so beautiful together.*

He shuddered. She was the beautiful one, for accepting this.

It's not the way of the Vesli to take same sex lovers.

And yet you and Iden are lovers.

His hand circled his own cock as he leaned forward and took Iden's into his mouth.

The mental barriers standing between them crashed down with the first taste, the first pull of his lips on Iden's smooth, hot shaft.

Iden's thighs bunched, as did Miciah's.

Hips moved in sync. Iden thrusting, forcing himself through the tight grasp of Miciah's hand and into wet heat. Miciah gripping, fucking through his own clamped fist as he took Iden deeper, sucked harder.

Pleasure rippled and surged between them, pulsed and echoed and intensified. Guttural moans, silent and voiced, escaped, joining the sound of harsh, ragged breathing as the need for release built.

Testicles pulled tight in warning as blood roared through Miciah's penis in a searing beat that had him stroking urgently, his heart racing as Iden bucked wildly, a tortured look of pleasure on his face as he came in Miciah's mouth.

Iden's release triggered Miciah's own. Searing ecstasy shot up his spine as hot semen jetted from his cock to coat his chest and belly, leaving him lightheaded in its wake.

He leaned back against the wall and closed his eyes. Slowly his heart rate slowed and his mind cleared.

Reality returned before he wanted it to, with Iden pushing off the same wall where his hands had been braced in order to keep him standing in the aftermath of orgasm.

"You knew I expected our relationship to be openly acknowledged when I agreed to share Zoë with you," Iden said, the edge in his voice not masking either the anger or pain that Miciah could feel vibrating through their mate-bond.

With a sigh, Miciah opened his eyes.

Iden stepped back, crossing his arms over his chest.

His widened stance drew Miciah's gaze to the semihard cock still glistening from being sucked and the heavy testicles swinging beneath it. Despite the spasm through his own penis at seeing Iden on display, frustration edged out the last of Miciah's lingering pleasure, banishing it and replacing it with a hard knot of worry as he remembered Zoë's expression, and his promise to her. *I will follow Iden to his quarters. We will resolve our differences.*

Miciah rose to his feet. "I agreed that whatever happened in the bedroom, I would accept it as natural for our mate-bond. I never promised more than that. What happens in our private quarters is no one's business but our own. I see no reason for it to be otherwise."

"You see no reason because you don't *want* to see one."

Iden stepped forward, crowding Miciah as he'd done on Miciah's arrival. His hand wedged itself between them, forming a tight channel as his fingers closed around both of their cocks.

The touch made Miciah moan before he could stop himself. He hardened at the contact, fought to remain still.

Iden's eyes blazed in a face made all the more beautiful for its hard lines and implacable will. "How many other Vesti males wrestle with this? How many of them sign up for dangerous assignments or live on dangerous worlds because they fear openly acknowledging the cravings of their hearts and bodies on this one? You have the power to set an example, to become a symbol of change."

Resistance swept through Miciah. "Our world is already beset by change. Too much of it, coming too quickly, and with more of it threatening."

"Let it come."

"It needs to be controlled and managed, for the good of Belizair."

"You're a fool if you think that's possible."

Miciah bridled at the words. His lips pulled back in a snarl but Iden only covered them with his.

Tell me you would deny others the chance to have this and know they aren't aberrant for wanting it, Iden said, his hand moving up and down on their shafts as his tongue battled aggressively with Miciah's.

The Vesti don't need some new threat to their way of life! Miciah said. *My openly admitting to being your lover might result*

207

in nothing but my being removed from the Council by those I represent, and shunned by the rest of my race.

Or it might result in more!

I can't risk it.

Won't.

Think what you will.

Iden ended the kiss, his chest heaving. He took a step back, his hand opening so their cocks were no longer trapped against one another. "Coward."

The word lanced through Miciah's heart.

He shut down. Emotionally. Mentally.

Without another word he retrieved the loin covering and put it on, uncaring of the semen drying on his skin.

He turned and issued a command so the wall retracted and formed an opening.

A step and he was outside.

The wall reformed behind him, leaving him alone with is thoughts and his choices.

* * * * *

Zoë turned her hands palm up and reached out, thinking the vision would come in the same way it had with Acacia, after the formal greeting requiring the touching of bands. Instead, Nisha took her right hand and Avini her left, as around the table, the others followed suit until there was an unbroken connection, a unity both in purpose and minds—and Zoë's shields collapsed.

Their despair was like a black sea, but joined together, the darkness couldn't hold against the flare of hope. Individual flickers grew into a roaring white flame, burning away the present so that all knew they were stepping into a not-to-distant future and seeing it through Zoë's eyes.

Blinding light gave way to crowds. To colors and movement and a place Zoë recognized immediately as India.

She felt the collective gasps of the others through the mental link as the winged being they thought of as their god shimmered into existence a short distance in front of them and began walking, drawing them into a red-light district.

They traveled down narrow streets lined with brothels housing caged prostitutes. Most were girls, some as young as nine or ten, though the majority were thirteen to sixteen.

It turned Zoë's stomach and filled her with fiery rage, and yet she knew these girls were just a tiny representation of a sex trade that destroyed lives in the hundreds of thousands.

Enslavement. Rape. Disease. Death. That was the reality for these girls.

They traveled street after street, until the faces blurred though the horror didn't. The god finally stopped at a back entrance to one of the brothels. He turned, his gaze colliding with Zoë's, reaching through her to touch Etyn. A lift of his wings and they were inside in what passed for living quarters. Mats were scattered on the floor, fifteen with little space to step between them.

A woman moaned and cried on one of them, her belly swollen in pregnancy as she labored to deliver a child. It came as they watched, a caramel-colored daughter who brought no joy to the face of the woman attending the birth.

She cut the umbilical chord but made no move to clean the blood-and-fluid-coated child or place her in her mother's arms. "It's a girl child. There'll be no home or future for this one. Better to end her suffering before it begins."

Zoë's breath caught, the woman's words like the lash of a whip. Suede wings stretched out. They blocked the scene and the mother's response, transporting Zoë to a slum.

It was filled with poverty and filth and hopelessness. The crowded conditions meant too many mouths to feed. They reduced the value of a child's life to nothing, to a hell against the paradise of Belizair.

The god stopped again, this time in front of a hovel. He turned, his will reaching through Zoë to touch Avini first and then Miette, indicating order. His wings rose and fell, like a curtain, and they were inside the building where two young girls huddled in a corner, clinging to each other as a man in the same room discussed selling them to a brothel.

They were no older than Kaylee, and perhaps younger. Twins. The god laid his hand on each of them, before moving into the next room. He crouched next to where a naked baby crawled, flies drawn to the filth on her skin.

The scene reshaped into an orphanage. It was crowded, but the children wore clean clothing and were well fed. They played, and in small groups, gathered around teachers who read to them.

Through the mental link, Zoë felt the rapid pounding of Zanya and Nisha's hearts as they hoped the Vesti god would reach for them.

He did, and as he'd done outside the hovel, he focused on them individually to convey order. First Zanya, then Nisha.

This time he walked among the children and entered the building through a door. There were classrooms inside, crowded with more children. A closer look revealed sleeping mats rolled and positioned against the walls for turning a schoolroom into a bedroom.

He continued down a hallway and halted outside an office. Adult voices came from inside but the speakers weren't visible.

When the god made no move away from the doorway, Zoë concentrated on the conversation taking place.

"We can't accept any more children," a man said, "not if we want to feed and clothe the ones we've already taken in."

"So we turn them away?" another man asked, his voice familiar to Zoë though she couldn't place him.

A woman answered, "There's no choice. AIDS is creating more orphans every day and there are few adoptions. This will be home to most of the children here until they're old enough to leave it."

"What about the women I've been talking to?"

"If you've made promises, then you shouldn't have," the first man to speak said, his voice holding a harsh edge. "In two weeks you go back to the United States, your mission for your church fulfilled. They will send money after you tell them what you've seen, perhaps one or two couples will pledge to adopt a child and come here. Good. I wish all the children could find such homes. But by next year, some new cause will have grabbed the interest of your congregation. Their efforts and resources will be directed toward it. It's the way of people, not just Americans, and we are grateful for what help we've received. But we can't accept any more children, not if we want to feed and clothe the ones we've already taken in."

The god shifted away from the doorway and continued down the hallway. Zoë tried to look into the office, wanting to match the familiar voice with a face, but the scene dissolved, forcing her forward and outside, where a boy no older than eight slowly approached the building, one toddler clinging to his neck while a girl of about four hung on to his tattered shirt.

As he'd done in the hovel, the god placed his hands on the boy and the child in his arms, signaling his intent for them to be kept together.

Along the mental link, Zoë felt Zanya's joy. And Nisha's as well when the god touched the small girl before there was a blurring, a lurch that marked a jump back in time, bringing with it a sense of immediacy and a change of location.

Anticipation flashed into Zoë, her own and that of the Vesti women her thoughts were connected to. When the scene around them came into focus, it was obvious they were beyond the slums and the red light district.

They were once again on a crowded street, but here there were more foreigners. Many of them were tourists, the cameras around their necks and dress making it obvious.

The stones in Zoë's wristbands hummed with energy, the same way they had in the transport chamber, making her guess they were near a portal. A man emerged from the building in front of them. He appeared human, but recognition circled through the mental link, starting with Zanya and identifying him as the brother of her bond-mate and a bounty hunter who worked for the Council.

The god pointed then, down a street crowded with cars, bicycles and motorbikes, as well as people. It took Zoë a moment to discern what he was drawing her attention to, but when she did, understanding surged into her.

Mark. She placed the voice of the man in the orphanage to a face then. She'd met him in Istanbul. He'd been traveling the world then, staying in hostels and hitching rides as he tried to make sense of his life after the brother he'd always idolized committed suicide.

He was a block away, crammed into a tiny car. Next to him sat the last of the three children they'd been shown.

At the sight of them, Zoë knew if she acted on the vision, Mark would see her standing in this spot. And because they were friends and he believed her psychic gift was real, he would relinquish the children with him to Zanya and Nisha, and would aid in gathering the others so they could be taken to Belizair.

Awareness of the Vesti women faded then, the link to their minds closing. Zoë turned to face the portal.

The suede wings of the Vesti god became the feathered ones of the Amato Consort, dark features giving way to sun-kissed ones before paling as feathery wings became translucent, and the figure before her ethereal, shining and ageless. His eyes met hers, and this time, the shock was hers as she felt his words in her mind, brushing against her like butterfly wings. *Change is the gift.*

He shimmered and was gone, as was the vision. Reality became the women across the table and next to Zoë, their hands joined in unity. She exhaled slowly and spoke the words they were all thinking, "Let's go."

* * * * *

Coward. The word assailed Miciah at each turn as he paced the length of his office in the Council building.

Despite the hot shower he'd taken in the attached bathroom, he couldn't wash the chill of the word away or melt away the icy numbness encasing his heart. Even with a change of clothing, he couldn't shed the argument with Iden or the memories of what came before it.

Coward. Did Zoë think the same? Would she when he returned to their quarters and she learned that nothing had been resolved between Iden and him?

Pain seared through Miciah, burning away the tight, cold knot his heart had become. He halted in front of a window and looked out at the jagged mountain range separating this region from the one he represented.

He wasn't wrong in his choice. If Iden and Zoë had been privy to the Council's emergency meeting, then they would know just how close this world was to being thrown into greater turmoil.

In two days time the Council would reconvene. They would argue and vote again about what to do when two males were found to be an exact match to a human female.

But that was only *one* of the issues they must wrestle with. There was the matter of Zantara's match to a human male to consider. How best to proceed without raising the hopes of the unmated females on Belizair only to crush them with failure. There would also be the birth of Cyan's children, a blessing that would change their world regardless of the outcome.

It was enough—without him stepping forward and breaking Vesti cultural taboos. Surely Iden and Zoë would understand and agree with his stance if he could somehow

213

articulate his reasons more clearly without breaching his duty as a Council member.

He wasn't repudiating either his love of, or his desire for Iden. But their bond was newly formed. There was no need to rush to make the full truth of it known. Maybe in the future…

Uneasiness settled on him like a chilly shroud with the realization that soon their family members would descend on Winseka in order to meet Zoë. In the privacy of their own quarters, among those they were close to, Iden and Zoë wouldn't accept his denial. Nor would it be easy for him to pretend or hide, even if he wanted to. Glances and casual touches, teasing remarks would make it obvious he and Iden were lovers with Zoë's knowledge and approval.

Amato friends and relatives would think nothing of it, beyond their initial surprise. But his parents…

Miciah rubbed his chest, trying to ease the sudden pressure there.

Tension coiled in his belly at the prospect of facing his parent's reaction.

Coward.

This time the word was self-directed.

He took a deep breath, seeing the terraced patio with plants from the jungle, and beyond it, the desert with its golden sand and smooth surface slowly giving way to the red, rocky mountain range separating the region he'd thought of as home until Zoë entered his life.

He could give Zoë and Iden this much. He could prove to himself that his reticence was due to his concern for the Vesti, who already faced enough challenge to their culture, and not to cowardice.

The decision to visit his parents and confide in them did nothing to ease either the pressure in his chest or the tension coiled in his belly. But it diminished some of his worry over returning to his new quarters and facing Iden and Zoë.

"It's enough. For now," Iden had said in the temple after Miciah agreed to a sexual relationship between the two of them if they found Zoë would accept it.

This too, would be enough.

For now.

Chapter Eighteen

ဢ

The knot of worry already formed in Zoë's chest as a result of her second trip to Earth tightened as she stepped into the living quarters and found it looked no different, save for the purse she'd inadvertently left at Ariel's home that was now sitting on a small table in the main room. Only Iden was home, but without the personal items he'd intended to bring to their shared living space.

He turned from the window and she crossed immediately to him, her arms wrapping around his waist. Uncertainty for the future threatened to overwhelm her. His expression, along with the pain sliding through their mate-bond told her nothing had been resolved with Miciah.

"What happened?" she asked.

Iden rubbed his cheek against the silk of Zoë's hair. He'd agonized over what to share with her and come to no conclusion. But now, with her in his arms, he found he didn't want to think about the disagreement with Miciah and his own harsh judgment.

"This is a matter Miciah and I must work out," he said, softening his words by nuzzling Zoë's ear and tracing its rim with his tongue. *Let's put it aside for a while.*

She shivered as his tongue darted into her ear. Her nipples pebbled against his chest. A low moan followed as his hands caressed her back before pushing the thin pants from her hips so they fell and pooled at her feet. His loin covering followed so they stood skin to skin, their bodies and minds rejoicing at the intimate contact.

This is what he needed, Iden thought as he swung her up into his arms and carried her into the sleeping quarters. He needed to forget, to escape what he was coming to see as his failure, his impatience when it came to his bond with Miciah. He needed to lose himself for a while in Zoë.

Desire pounded through him with each beat of his heart, but it was driven by the need to get as close to her as possible, not just to gain release. *I adore you, beloved*, he whispered in her mind, placing her on the bed and coming down on top of her.

She immediately parted her legs for him, enticing him to join physically with her. He sought her opening, shuddered as he slid into wet heat just as her hands found the place where wings and torso met.

His buttocks clenched as she stroked the sensitive juncture, each one of her touches sending a spike of pleasure down his spine and through his cock. *Slowly, beloved*, he said, trying to control the thrust of his hips, to keep from pounding into her and coming quickly.

Now that he was inside her, he never wanted to leave her snug channel and hot depths. His tongue twined with hers and his breath grew short from the control it took to resist the squeeze and release of her sheath.

The Ylan stones they wore and their mate-bond amplified the pleasure so it hummed through and between them, urging them to greater ecstasy. With a raw moan he left her lips and forced himself to rise onto his hands and knees.

Her cry of protest as his cock pulled from her slit filled him with satisfaction. *I'll give you the release you seek*, he told her, latching onto a nipple, suckling as she gripped his hair and arched her back, silently begging for more.

He loved her breasts. They were perfect, as beautiful as she was. One day he'd have the satisfaction of watching children nurse from them, but until then they'd serve a man's needs, satisfy a man's appetites.

His fingers squeezed and tugged one dusky areola as his mouth feasted on the other, letting her feel the hint of teeth and the hunger of her mate to possess her.

Her breath came in pants, her voice in a whispered, "Please, Iden."

Always, beloved. It's my right and duty to pleasure you.

Reluctantly he left her breasts, kissing downward over her taut, feminine belly. She lifted her hips, presenting him with flushed folds and wet slit.

He lapped, licked, thrust into her with his tongue and savored the sounds she made, the heat and taste of her.

She was so uninhibited, so free in letting him know just how much she liked what he was doing to her.

"Let me do the same to you," she said, catching the tenor of his thoughts and sending him decadent images of sucking his cock as he did the same to her clit.

He'd denied himself before, when they were on Earth. He hadn't dared to risk it when their mate-bond wasn't in place. But this time…

Iden left her cunt only long enough to reposition them on the bed, to allow her the dominant position, her body stretched out on top of his, her face above his engorged penis as he once again pressed his mouth to her plump, slick cunt lips.

Fire scorched through him with the lash of her tongue, the sweet suction of her mouth. Too late he remembered his earlier demand that they make love slowly. Too late he remembered that when it came to behaving, his mate never did.

He shuddered, moaned, helpless against the rhythm she set as she took him between her lips and sucked him eagerly.

His hips jerked and he lost any thought but to apply himself to the task of making Zoë scream in release.

He took control again, fucking her with his tongue, tormenting her with the swirling rasp of it over her clit.

He alternated between heated lashes and hard sucks, his hands preventing her from escaping until she gave him what he wanted—a sharp cry of release as she shuddered and came.

It was agony to tumble her off him and pull from her mouth. He was desperate to spill his seed, but he wanted to fill her channel with it.

The fantasy he'd had earlier as he waited for her to return from the marketplace slid into his mind. He rose to his feet and lifted her into his arms before she could tempt him into covering her with his body and mating with her.

Her laugh was sultry, challenging as he carried her into the bathroom, their bond not allowing him to hide his intentions from her. He placed her on her feet in the shower stall and took up a position behind her, his hands cupping her breasts as his wings spread to their full length.

With a thought the walls became mirrors as water sprayed from the ceiling and sides. "You'll behave now, beloved, or I'll have ropes lowered to bind you with."

Zoë shivered at the threat, at the erotic sight captured in the mirrors. Lust pooled in her belly, need returned like a fever.

She couldn't lose this. She couldn't lose either Iden or Miciah.

Watch as I love you, Iden said, pressing kisses to her shoulder, her neck, his hands caressing her, stroking over her belly, fingers delving into her slit only to retreat and take possession of her nipples.

It was punishment and adoration combined. A carnal demand that she cede all control to him.

Zoë tested him with the rub of her buttocks against his hardened length, and felt the slap of his hand to her cunt in discipline. Fire blossomed in her clit, making her toes curl and her eyes close.

Watch, he said, reinforcing it with another spank followed by the plunging of his fingers into her slit.

She watched, and begged as the image of her winged mate loving her was burned into her memory.

Only when she was shaking with desire did he order her to lean forward and put her hands against the wall. She obeyed, desperate to have him inside her.

He took her then—slowly. But it cost him.

In the mirror there was no hiding his taut features or the trembling of his outstretched wings as he fought to make it last. Just as there was no hiding the ecstasy that shimmered through their bond as his fingers on her clit sent her over the edge and took him with her.

They bathed afterward, sharing soapy touches and wet kisses, lingering in a steamy paradise. And despite all their lovemaking, the need for physical contact still rode them both as they stepped out of the shower.

Zoë allowed herself to be crowded against the wall. She ate greedily at Iden's mouth when he pressed his lips to hers, hungrily sucked his tongue into her mouth.

I can't seem to get enough of you, she said, wanting the reassurance that having him inside her brought as an ache formed in her heart at the thought of Miciah and his continued absence.

Iden's hand cupped her face. *All will be well. He will return.*

The ache spread, creating a place for worry and dread and guilt to fill. For an instant she wavered, wanting to confide in Iden about her gift and how she'd used it, then decided against it, putting it off until she could tell them both at the same time.

She covered his nipple with her palm, distracting them both from what would happen when Miciah came home. He moaned, the heat of his body and the pleasure he found in being her mate seeping into her soul.

Chimes sounded and he pulled away reluctantly. "I fear this is the penalty for serving those on Belizair. Most have a week or more of uninterrupted time when they are newly mated, but between the three of us, it appears we won't go a day without it happening."

They dressed before Iden went to the door and ordered it open. An Amato couple stood there.

Zoë recognized the man as the one who'd been waiting in the transport chamber for Iden to return from Earth. Iden said, "Denaus, Phenice, I will accompany you to the temple if you have need of me. But first, meet Zoë, the bond-mate I share with Miciah of the Danjal."

Zoë went to his side, sudden tension mounting at the prospect of touching Phenice in formal greeting. She relaxed slightly when neither stepped forward or lifted their arms.

Denaus' eyes held uncertainty as they met hers. He took his mate's hand and squeezed.

Phenice said, "I...we...hoped to speak with Zoë, to see if she could help us in the same manner as she did Etyn."

Iden started and his surprise swept through Zoë. She glanced up at him, uncertain what to say.

She didn't have to say anything. Iden inclined his head. "Of course, I can leave to ensure your privacy."

Instinctively Zoë curled her arm around his. "Stay. I'll step outside with them, perhaps go for a walk." She hated having to embellish, regretted she hadn't shared the truth with Miciah after helping Acacia, and Iden after helping Etyn and the other Vesti women.

Iden's eyebrows drew together, but all he said was, "I'll wait for your return. And Miciah's."

Her throat tightened with the reminder that their relationship faced more than one challenge in the name of change on Belizair. She nodded and stepped through the open doorway to where Phenice and Denaus waited.

The wall reformed and awkward silence threatened to descend. Zoë countered it by getting the hard part handled first. "I may not be able to help you."

Sudden tears glistened in Phenice's eyes. She took a breath before nodding. "I—" a quick glance at Denaus, "we know."

Denaus' throat worked, as if he tried to swallow his misgiving. "We ask only that you try."

The worry Zoë experienced in the marketplace returned. They had to know the possible consequences, better than she did, but she couldn't proceed without warning them, "This can't remain a secret. I intend to tell both Iden and Miciah today."

Assuming Miciah returned home.

Denaus stood taller, resolve straightening his spine and chasing the uncertainty from his expression. "We understand and accept the risks involved."

At his side, Phenice nodded in agreement.

Zoë took a deep breath and let it out slowly. "Then we might as well attempt this," she said, holding out her hands.

Denaus took one of them and Phenice the other, their linked hands making it a circle. Zoë had only enough time to hope they would remain standing as they were thrown through a storm of stars in a field of darkness.

Los Angeles. She recognized the skyline in the distance despite it being nighttime on Earth.

They were at the far edge of a gas station parking lot. A breeze brought the smell of the bathrooms. Taillights sped away as freeway noise throbbed through her, pulsing with an urgency that had her looking around, seeking —

Movement caught her eye, moths dancing under the dim light of fading spotlights. They fluttered downward, individuals becoming a solid form, a familiar figure, though this time his wings were feathered. He placed a hand on the dumpster behind the building and then he was gone, blinking out like a star and releasing Zoë from the vision.

She didn't hesitate. As Phenice's whispered words, *the Consort Ylan*, sounded in Zoë's thoughts, she was already giving a mental command, transporting the three of them to stand outside the portal to Earth.

Denaus' and Phenice's hands tightened on hers before releasing them so they could hurry to the building entrance, then through it, pausing only long enough to don appropriate clothing before going into the transport chamber.

"Where?" Denaus asked.

"North America. Los Angeles."

He nodded once and the stones hummed to life. Zoë felt the buildup, but there was no sensation of transport, only the reality of it.

A blink and she moved them from the chamber on Earth to the gas station parking lot. Denaus and Phenice raced ahead of her, unhindered by wings that remained particles.

"Wait," Denaus told his mate as he straddled the dumpster rim then carefully lowered himself inside.

Rats scampered out and away, scurrying from view. A baby began crying. Its cries muted as though it were buried under trash.

Phenice gasped. Her hands went to her mouth, fingers trembling as the light glinted off tear-wet eyes.

Denaus bent over, shifting garbage until he found the infant in a plastic trashcan liner full of bloody, fluid soaked paper towels. Only the fact the bag hadn't been closed and tied had kept the baby from suffocating.

A glance at the bathroom several steps away and the memory of the taillights speeding away told Zoë what had happened here. Denaus separated the child from the trash and found a tiny girl. He rose to his feet and handed her to Phenice.

"Why?" he asked, anger and sorrow in his voice.

"I don't know," Zoë told him. "It's a horrible truth here. There are so many good people who would give anything to be able to have a child, but can't. Then there are others who bring them into the world when they don't want them."

Denaus reburied the bag the infant had been in, covering it with other trash before swinging over the lip of the dumpster and landing next to Phenice. His arms went around her. His face softened in love and wonder as he looked at the child she held against her chest.

Zoë looked around to make sure there were no security cameras before touching a hand to Phenice's back. "Ready?"

"Ready," Phenice whispered.

A summoning of energy, a command accompanied by coordinates and they were in the transport chamber deeper in the city.

Zoë stepped away as Denaus removed tiny bands from his pocket and slipped them on the baby's wrists. She turned her back, granting them privacy as they created a family bond with their new daughter.

They returned to Winseka moments later.

Denaus' arms reluctantly dropped away from Phenice's. "There are no words to express what we feel," he said, and Zoë could tell he was truly at a loss for them.

Phenice reached out and clasped Zoë's hand. "Thank you."

Emotion pounded through Zoë, hers as well as theirs. She nodded, enjoying the swell of good feelings before the now-familiar fear rose to the surface. "I can't keep this secret from Miciah and Iden," she said, reminding them of her intentions.

Resolve hardened both Denaus' and Phenice's features. He said, "The Goddess' hand was in this, as was that of the Consort. The Amato High Priests and Priestesses will support our actions, even against the laws enacted by the Council."

Rather than offering relief, his words tightened the knot in Zoë's stomach. "The Vesti women see their wandering god when I use my gift to help them."

By their surprised expressions, she knew Etyn hadn't told them. But before they could question her further, the baby began crying.

The flash of worry in Phenice's eyes and the hurried glance toward the chamber door told Zoë that despite their resolve and their beliefs, they weren't anxious for a confrontation with the Council. "Go," she said, "I'll find my way home."

"Thank you," Denaus said then murmured to his bondmate, "Let's use the energy stored in our bands to go directly to our quarters."

A nod from her and they were gone.

Zoë considered following their example. She wanted nothing more than to get out from under the burden of guilt that came with secrecy. She wanted her fears for the future to be banished by the feel of Iden and Miciah's arms around her as they told her everything would be okay. But she couldn't return to their quarters yet.

Acacia had to be warned, as did the other Vesti women. In the hurry to India, and the time spent with Mark as they accompanied him on his rounds and found the children they'd seen in the vision, she'd neglected to reveal her intention to tell Miciah and Iden about her gift—today, as soon as the three of them were together again.

Unwelcome realization made Zoë's pulse start to race. Because she hadn't touched her bands to any of those of the Vesti women gathered in the marketplace, she had no way of locating them.

Her panic faded at remembering that the coordinates for Acacia's home were stored. She could go there and ask Acacia to spread the word to the others.

Lyan's face flashed into Zoë's thoughts. Heat spread through her with thoughts of Miciah's reaction to seeing her in Lyan's arms.

At Acacia's home she and Lyan had exchanged a formal greeting. She knew where he lived—and more importantly, that through the sharing of a human woman named Krista with an Amato named Adan, he was related to Ariel because of Zeraac—meaning he was also now related to her.

A small smile formed along with an idea. Lyan was present when she and Acacia arrived with a child who was clearly human. He had a reputation for trouble when it came to following the rules. Who better to go to? He could get word to Acacia as well as to Etyn, Avini and the others.

* * * * *

Miciah found his mother and father engaged in a game of *kantra* on the enclosed porch of their home built high in a Sumerel tree. Small white tiles were laid out on the table between them, lined up in rows and columns, the colors and shapes of the symbols painted in their centers determining where they could be placed. The humans had game very similar to it, called Qwirkle.

His mother smiled in welcome, lifting her face for his kiss.

"Are you winning?" he asked, leaning down and brushing his lips across her cheek.

Her laughter made him smile despite his reason for visiting them.

"Of course I'm winning. Your father might be the undisputed champion of Fett in our home, but he's yet to best me consistently at this game."

Miciah turned and his father stood. They exchanged greetings in the more formal manner, their bands touching as they gripped each other's forearms.

His father's expression was puzzled, leaning toward concern. "Is all well with your new bond-mate?" he asked before settling once again in his seat.

"Jadiel," his mother chided, "Miciah only just arrived. Surely questions can wait until I've had a chance to offer him something to eat and drink."

"I'm fine, Mother," he said, tempted to delay, but feeling too edgy to do so.

The sudden worry in her eyes made him aware of his hand on his chest, rubbing over his heart as if he could loosen the tight fist of tension gripping it.

"What's wrong?" his mother asked, fear creeping into her voice as, like his father, she guessed that only something truly important could make him leave his new mate after only having returned from Earth with her the previous day.

"Nothing is wrong," he said, forcing himself to sit. "I look forward to your meeting Zoë. You'll like her. She's perfect for me in every way. I can't imagine having any other female as my mate."

After a long, probing look, his mother's cheeks colored slightly. "You're finding the arrangement more difficult than you anticipated," she guessed in a lowered voice. "It's not our way to share mates as the Amato do." A darting glance to the other side of the table, and she added, "Perhaps your father could advise you."

Miciah felt heat rise to his face at his mother's suggestion. Her hands took one of his between them, and despite her firm grip, he could feel a slight tremor go through them.

"You must make this work, Miciah," she said. "If you're regretting your hasty selection of an Amato priest—"

"Iden," he said, hearing in her voice that she remained baffled and hurt by his brief message and quick departure to Earth.

Theirs was a close relationship. Under normal circumstances he would have discussed his plans with them, perhaps even argued the pros and cons of allying with any given Amato clan-house.

He'd done neither. Instead he'd sent a messenger.

Too late he realized that this would be easier if they'd heard him speak of Iden before. But he hadn't, and now, in his father's presence, he knew why. He hadn't wanted any hint of his feelings to be revealed.

"Iden," Miciah said, repeating the name, drawing on it as his heart raced and his throat threatened to close off.

His mother's grip on his hand tightened. "You can confide in us. It will go no further."

Of that he was very certain.

There was no good way to say what needed to be said. He kept his attention focused on his mother, knowing he didn't want to commit his father's reaction to memory.

"Iden is more than simply an Amato I must share Zoë with. He and I are lovers as well."

A small gasp escaped his mother, but she didn't pull her hands away in rejection or recoil in horror. She blinked several times then quickly glanced at his father.

Something passed between them. The color that had blossomed in her face with his announcement faded. Her features became set while a look at his father's, revealed a closed-off expression.

"Do you intend to make it known outside close friends and immediate family?" his mother asked.

"Even that many people knowing is too many," his father said before Miciah could answer. "It's not our way."

"Only because no one holding influence has dared to step forward and challenge those ways," his mother said, surprising Miciah with her pronouncement.

His father rose to his feet. "Our son won't be the first to do so. I am prepared to accept that what he does in the privacy of his quarters is his business, though I would have preferred to know nothing of it. But if it becomes public knowledge, his right to represent the Vesti of this region will be challenged and I will support that challenge. The Vesti need stability in this time more than ever before. Already we are being forced to change, to become more like the Amato."

Miciah felt the tight fist around his heart loosen. His father's words closely mirrored his own beliefs.

It could have been worse, Miciah had time to think before his mother stood.

She crossed her arms over her chest and glared at his father. "For those who think as you do, there is *never* a good time for change. And there never will be when it comes to the Vesti who love someone of the same sex. Tyden met his death in the Kotaka Gaming Sector because of it. The shame he felt in desiring men instead of women drove him away from Belizair."

Shock at the mention of the uncle he'd mourned for as child held Miciah immobile. Mute.

"Whether our son decides to step forward and shed light on a truth that has too long been hidden, or remain silent on this matter, I accept it as his choice," his mother continued, unaware of what her mention of Tyden had done to Miciah. "But if his relationship with Iden becomes known, and his seat on the Council challenged, *I* will stand by him. And if you chose otherwise, denouncing your own son for something that is as natural to him as your urges are to you, then I will return to my family's clan-house until such time as Zoë gives birth. Then I will move to be near my grandchildren."

"So be it," his father said before turning and striding from the room.

Agony filled Miciah. It was everything he'd feared for the Vesti—the tearing apart of families over a challenge to their cultural values—only worse. He'd never thought, never imagined his parents fighting, his mother threatening to leave.

Suppressed tears burned his throat. His heart raced as if it would flee his body and escape the turmoil. "I—"

He couldn't think of anything to say. There were no words to repair the damage.

His mother laid her hands on his shoulders. "Your father and I will work out our difference of opinion. Whatever you decide to do, Miciah, know that we both love you."

A muscle twitched in his cheek. He nodded, unwilling to discuss the matter further. She'd already made her position clear.

"I need to return to Winseka." He kissed her goodbye and left, uncertain of the reception he'd get when he arrived home.

Chapter Nineteen

ও

Zoë's heart sank as soon as she entered the living quarters. Miciah hadn't yet returned and Iden sat on the couch, his elbows on his knees, his face cupped in his hands.

She joined him, a touch to his shoulder all it took for him to straighten and pull her onto his lap. Impulsively she leaned forward, opening the purse Ariel must have found by the chair in her kitchen after their ice-cream binge and sent.

Zoë removed the box containing the sculpture she'd purchased at the Sol Celebration. She freed the piece of art from its layers of bubble wrap, tears threatening as the sight of it reminded her of their earlier happiness.

She'd bought it because the entwined lovers made her think of what she had with Iden and Miciah, of time suspended and a precious moment caught in glass. Her throat closed on the thought that like the statue, their mate-bond could be easily shattered. But as she set the statue on the table, she forced herself to see it as a symbol of what they all wanted, to use the image to fortify herself for what might come rather than to view it as a harbinger of pain.

We'll get through this, she said, electing the more intimate way of communication as she wrapped her arms around Iden's neck and pressed her lips to his.

We must, he said, the wet heat of his mouth and the sensuous slide of his tongue against hers keeping worries about their future together at bay. She gave comfort as she sought it, soaking in the heat of his skin.

Her nipples hardened and ached. Blood raced to swell and part her cunt lips.

Her need was answered by the thick ridge of his cock and the tightening of his arms around her. *Take me to bed*, she whispered into his mind, wanting to extend those moments when all that mattered was the pleasure they found in one another.

He stood with her cradled in his arms, never breaking the kiss as he carried her into the bedroom and laid her down, easily stripping her pants away before removing his loincloth and covering her with his body.

This is nice, she said, loving the feel of him, the strength and solid weight, the protectiveness that came with having him on top of her.

Iden abandoned her mouth in order to take her earlobe between his lips and suck gently. *I'm glad you're home. Were you able to help Phenice and Denaus?*

Zoë answered on a moan. "Yes."

Good, Iden said, love for Zoë swelling to fill his chest, his pride in her blocking out the argument he'd had with Miciah and the regret he felt in calling him a coward.

At least this part of their life together was perfect, Iden thought as her hands stroked his back, his wings.

Her stiffened clit pressed against his hardened cock, making need pulse through him. He reclaimed her lips in a slow, thorough taking.

Desperation tried to claw its way back into Zoë's consciousness. She felt its echo inside Iden as both of them forced it down in favor of lingering caresses and murmured sounds of pleasure.

He eased onto his side next to her and she protested the loss of contact, only to arch her back in approval as his hand cupped her breast and his mouth left hers, trailing wet kisses downward. Her legs parted in invitation as he took her nipple between his lips and began suckling.

Sweet waves of pleasure rolled through her with each pull of his lips. It filled her belly and pooled in her labia, had heated arousal escaping from her channel and sliding over her back entrance.

His hand slid from her breast, following the path of desire, pausing on her flat abdomen.

There was a brief flash, the image of her heavy with children. It came from him, accompanied by such intense emotion that her womb fluttered and her sheath clenched.

One day, she told him, hoping for the future together that would allow it.

One day, he agreed, his voice husky in her mind. *I am very content not to share you with anyone other than Miciah.*

Mention of their missing bond-mate sent a painful twinge through both of them, stalling their climb toward intimate union. *We'll find a way to make this work*, she said. *Love me.*

He lifted his face so their eyes could meet. His smile was like a burst of sunshine. *Always*, he said before resuming his suckling, adding the hint of teeth and the decadent swirl of his tongue over her nipple.

Lightning-fast strikes of desire shot downward, spiking through her and making her lift her hips in a silent plea to feel his hand between her thighs, if not his mouth.

Masculine satisfaction purred along their mental link. Her need for his touch adding to his pleasure and feeding his lust.

She shivered when his palm inched lower. Grew wetter in anticipation of him cupping her mound.

Please, she begged.

His fingertips dipped into her flooded channel then glided over her clit. Swirling, stroking, making her hips jerk and her breathing grow fast.

I've ended up with a very demanding mate, Iden said. *It's a good thing I know how to meet her demands. But I have demands of my own. Get on your hands and knees, Zoë. I want to mount you. I want to come inside you and fill you with my seed.*

He lifted his face from her breast and the heat in his eyes was enough to make her obey his erotic command. She rolled over, positioning herself as he'd ordered.

Without being told she spread her thighs, presented her swollen, wet vulva and parted slit. A moan escaped when he rose up behind her and slid his cock into her channel.

Her sheath spasmed, clutched his hardened length. She tried to rock backward, to fuck herself on him but he gripped her hips and held her motionless.

The wall in front of them began changing colors, as those in the shower had done, becoming a mirror. Her breath hitched, as it always did when she caught sight of Miciah or Iden with their wings spread, quivering as they made love. Their sheer perfection and masculine beauty was nearly overwhelming.

You are the beautiful one, Iden said. *Watch as I take what belongs to me.*

He moved then. Slowly at first. Then faster. Harder.

Their pleasure was captured in the mirror, doubled by it.

It built until there was no denying the ecstasy of release.

Orgasm crashed down on them just as Miciah appeared in the doorway. It shuddered through them in long waves of numbing bliss, allowing them to hold against their fears for the future—at least in that moment.

Refection gave way to solid wall, but not before Zoë saw a bleakness in Miciah's eyes, a rigidity in his posture. Her heart stuttered and the warmth of lovemaking dissolved, taking with it the barricade shielding her from worry.

Iden slid from her body and stretched out on his side in a casual pose. His expression was carefully blank, as was his mind.

She left the bed and went to Miciah, stopping in front of him, feeling torn between her two lovers. "I thought you'd be home sooner," she said, placing her palms on his chest, willing him to enfold her in his arms and tell her…

What? That everything was going to be okay? When she'd yet to confess her crimes?

The weight of conflicting emotions settled heavily on Miciah. He'd been so sure of the rightness of his stance, both before he went to his parents' home and afterward. He'd been positive that keeping his relationship with Iden a secret was best for the Vesti and for Belizair. But the moment he'd entered their quarters and witnessed Zoë and Iden's uninhibited pleasure, followed by their reserve when he became the focus of their attention, his conviction wavered.

The wall he felt forming between them hurt. And yet if he intended to keep his relationship with Iden a secret, then that wall would exist every time they were out in public together. And the pain it generated would only fester and grow.

For those who think as you do, there is never a good time for change. And there never will be when it comes to the Vesti who love someone of the same sex.

His mother's words lashed across his soul even though they had been directed at his father. His uncle's death, and the knowledge that he'd experienced shame over desiring men instead of women, tore a raw wound in Miciah's heart.

"How many other Vesti males wrestle with this?" Iden had said. "You have the power to set an example, to become a symbol of change. Tell me you would deny others the chance to have this and know they aren't aberrant for wanting it."

With the pain in his own future confronting him, Miciah truly considered the other males of his race. Men who feared alienation because of their sexuality, who were forced to live a lie because of it.

He pulled Zoë into his arms and buried his face in her hair. "I went to speak with my parents," he said. "I hoped telling them Iden and I were lovers would be enough to appease the two of you."

It was too hard to put the tangle of emotion and thought into words. He brushed against the barriers shielding their minds from his, and knew relief when they allowed the intimate contact.

With images he showed them what had happened. Let them feel his anguish over the fight his revelation had caused between his parents, the strength of his conviction and what had led to his change of heart at returning home.

Iden left the bed and joined them in the doorway. He pressed his chest to Miciah's back, his arms reaching around Zoë so Miciah was held tightly between them.

All the pain and guilt, the remorse he'd hated facing over his failing his mate crashed into him. He'd been blinded by his own desires, by his impatience and by his sureness that he was right. He'd struck out when hurt rather than trying to understand Miciah's position.

His heart ached as a result of the injustice he'd done, to the suffering he'd caused. "I regret calling you a coward. It was unfair of me. I am not Vesti. I cannot truly appreciate what it means for you to break with your culture in the matter of taking a male lover. It was wrong of me to judge it a simple thing."

"You were right in challenging me to stand for all Vesti, to become an example. I won't deny you in public again."

"I will give you some time to accustom yourself to the idea of it. And endeavor to wait until you've said you are ready before giving in to my inclinations in public. The Goddess and Consort willing, we will be together for a lifetime."

With the mention of the Consort, Zoë's joy in their reconciliation disappeared under an onslaught of worry. She'd promised herself she'd tell Iden and Miciah everything as soon as she could. But now that the time had arrived, she didn't want to ruin this chance at shared intimacy and closeness.

A few minutes more won't hurt, she told herself, pressing a kiss to Miciah's chest and wanting to recapture what they'd had before things became so complicated. "Let's take a shower together," she said, already imagining them coming together there, their pleasure caught on the walls like a scene from an erotic movie.

Iden's laugh turned the knot in her belly into a molten coil of need. "I believe our bond-mate has acquired a fondness for mirrors."

Miciah's answering chuckle lifted the heavy weight of worry from her heart. His cock jutted against her stomach, begging to be freed from the confines of his clothing and join them in nakedness.

She eased backward, drinking in his expression as she found the fastenings and undid them, sending his loincloth to the floor. She cupped his testicles with one hand, loving the way his eyes turned into dark pools of lust. With the other hand she took possession of his hardened penis, thumbing the silky-smooth head.

He throbbed against her palm and she wanted to go down on her knees in front of him, to take him in her mouth as Iden fucked him. Before she could, a decadent vision rose in her thoughts — one she hastily blocked from both of her men.

They'd find out soon enough.

"Shower," she said, stepping backward, her hand still wrapped around Miciah's thick shaft.

"Don't think you'll always be able to lead me around by my cock, Zoë," Miciah growled, the heat in his voice telling her he had no objection to it, *this* time.

As soon as they stepped into the shower stall, the doorway closed and the crystal clear walls became smoky-gray then shiny silver. Warm water rained down on them and misted from the sides, wetting skin and feathers and the soft suede of Miciah's wings.

Zoë crowded him, running her hands up and down his chest, stopping to tweak his nipples as she sent a private image to Iden.

Devious, Iden said, but complied by moving to stand behind Miciah.

"Remember what happened after Lyan brought me back to Ariel's home?" she asked.

Dark heat flared in Miciah's eyes. It was followed immediately by a shared image of her draped across his lap, her buttocks reddened in punishment and her thighs glistening with desire.

"I'll have to ensure I'm present the next time you need a spanking," Iden murmured, his voice like a tongue lapping at her slit.

Behave! she told him before turning her attention back to Miciah. "I'm not surprised at all by what you choose to focus on. But I think there was more. Do you remember agreeing to this?"

Turnabout is fair play—where it's anatomically possible. Anything you do to me, I can do to you.

Miciah stiffened and glanced upward, where two thin ropes now descended at Iden's silent command, but he didn't protest when Iden bound his wrists and the ropes reversed direction so his arms were raised above his head.

"Perfect," Zoë said, scraping her fingernails against Miciah's belly to emphasize his helplessness. "Have you ever let yourself be bound before?"

Iden laughed. "I can't truly imagine it. Can you? His resistance to change is rooted in his desire to remain in control."

Miciah shuddered and arched his back in response to a touch from Iden that Zoë couldn't see. "Transmute your wings," she whispered, cupping his testicles again, massaging his heavy sack. "I want to be able to watch in the mirrors when Iden takes you while you're tethered."

He did as she asked and she found it incredibly erotic to see him vulnerable, human-looking, with Iden standing behind him, wings spread like an angel descended to deliver punishment or pleasure.

She rewarded Miciah by leaning in and taking a small, masculine nipple between her lips, sucking it as Iden's hands stroked downward, one settling on Miciah's stomach while the over formed a fisted channel around Miciah's cock.

It'd be fair to use a ring on you, she teased, *and let it work you the same way the one you put on my clit did. But I don't think I can deny myself the pleasure of putting my mouth on you while Iden grips your shaft and takes your ass.*

Miciah shuddered, pulled against the ropes as though he would free his hands and force her to her knees. "Do it," he said, dominant despite his helplessness.

In a minute. It wouldn't be fair to rush.

Miciah's hips jerked as her fingers captured his other nipple. Squeezing, rubbing in time to the pull of her lips and strike of her tongue to its twin, to Iden's hand moving up and down on Miciah's shaft.

It was agony and ecstasy for all of them. With their mental link fully open, there was no separation of sensation.

Miciah's moans became Iden's, and hers. The further swelling of Miciah's cock was equal to that of Iden's, sending more blood to Zoë's already parted cunt lips, to a clit that was engorged, the hood pulled back to expose a tiny, vulnerable head.

She touched herself and felt lust jolt through both of her men.

"No!" Miciah said, struggling against the ropes again. "Let me put my mouth on you, Zoë."

His heated words were accompanied by images. Her on the shower floor, positioned on her elbows so she could watch. Him on his forearms and knees, his face between her splayed thighs as Iden mounted him and took him from behind.

Arousal gushed from Zoë's slit. She plunged her fingers into her channel, tempted to free him.

"No," Iden said, preventing her from giving in. "Miciah is not in control. Get on your knees, Zoë. Touch yourself as you pleasure him."

She obeyed, sinking down in front of Miciah and taking the thick, throbbing inches of cock in front of Iden's fingers into her mouth.

Iden stroked her cheek with the hand that had been resting on Miciah's abdomen, then reached over, pressing a dispenser set into the wall so lubricant pooled in his palm.

Miciah's hips jerked in reaction, in anticipation, fucking him deeper into Zoë's mouth.

She lashed him with her tongue then pulled back. He continued thrusting, their bond allowing her to feel his desperation as he attempted to reclaim the lost territory, to once again be as far into her mouth as possible.

He panted, buttocks clenched and jaw locked against begging.

She relented. Sucked until he was moaning, shivering between them and close to coming.

She released him then. Leaned back to savor the sight of his swollen, needy cock still grasped in Iden's fingers.

"Tell us you need this in order to be complete," Iden murmured, drawing Zoë's attention to the mirror, holding it there as Iden closed his fist around his own cock, coating it with lubricant and pumping up and down slowly.

"I need it," Miciah said through clenched teeth.

Iden laughed. His eyes met Zoë's in the mirror. "What do you think? Good enough?"

"Yes."

His hand left his cock. He held it in front of a spray of water, and when it was clean, pressed another dispenser only long enough for a few drops to coat his fingertips.

He touched them to the rosette of Miciah's anus. And by Miciah's low groan and corded muscles, by the bucking of his hips, Zoë knew it was the ritzca oil. Heating him. Preparing him.

Zoë's gaze remained riveted to the mirror, watching as Iden positioned himself at Miciah's opening, his wings spread and glorious behind his back.

Arousal beaded on Miciah's cock head. She pulled slick fingers from her channel to rub and stroke her clit.

"We take him together," Iden said, knowing that the climb to ecstasy would be quick. "Put your mouth on him."

Zoë leaned forward, obeying him. And Iden knew it was worth the years of waiting to have this, to have them both.

Between them Miciah moaned as Zoë's hand covered Iden's, their fists tightening on his cock to keep him from forging deeper into Zoë's mouth as Iden pierced him, filled him.

Iden echoed the sound at the hard squeeze of Miciah's muscles around his length. He began moving in a rhythm shared by human and Vesti and Amato alike. Watched as Zoë let Miciah fuck through her lips, matching his thrusts with fingers shoved into her slit as their pleasure built, combined, crested in a release that left all three of them shuddering, bound so intimately together that it felt as though they were one being.

Iden freed Miciah from the tethers and Zoë rose to her feet. She wrapped her arms around Miciah and him, just as he did the same, leaving them standing as they had earlier when they reconciled.

For long moments Zoë clung to the shimmering waves of pleasure, wanting it to last forever. She clung to the present as though doing it could keep the future at bay. But slowly the lassitude left by release was replaced by the heavy burden of guilt and worry.

She had the courage to confess, but not the strength to pull from their arms. "I need to tell you the full truth about my psychic gifts," she said. "And the laws I've broken since coming to Belizair."

Their tension was immediate, sharp. Their bodies stiffened with it. But rather than push her away, their arms tightened around her. Possessiveness and protectiveness surged down their mental link.

"Whatever you've done, we won't allow harm to come to you," Iden said.

Miciah brushed his lips over her ear. "We won't be parted from you. Tell us."

It was easier to do without words. Zoë focused her thoughts, first showing them images from her life on Earth and how her gifts had manifested there, forcing her to stay on the move. She showed them the long ago visit with the fortuneteller and May's gift of the butterfly bracelets. She let them feel her sureness of purpose at arriving on Belizair before moving on to her encounter with Acacia in the marketplace and all that had happened afterward.

"After leaving Phenice and Denaus, I visited Lyan," she said, breaking into speech. "His bond-mate Krista was home. Zeraac was there as well, visiting Adan. They promised to get word to Acacia and the other Vesti women. By now they will think I've already told you everything."

Miciah growled at the mention of Lyan. Iden laughed softly. "Why am I not surprised to hear he's involved in this trouble?"

Despite his lighthearted reply, Zoë's stomach was still a mass of knots. "What happens now?"

"We act quickly and decisively," Miciah said. "We request the Council meet informally and allow them to see your memories. If Ariel and her mates are willing, we present Kaylee to speak about her vision and the golden lady who had her approach Jeqon about locating you."

"Agreed," Iden said. "If you hadn't already acted on behalf of the women of Belizair, then I would advocate approaching the Council members individually. But Miciah is correct, stepping forward with the full truth now, before rumors of it begin circling, is the best course of action. Let's finish our shower and send word requesting a meeting."

"Do you think I'll be sent back to Earth, along with the children? And the others banished?"

Iden's expression turned fierce. "Let them try."

Miciah's arms were like a steel band locking her to him. "Regardless of what the Council decides, we won't be parted from you."

Chapter Twenty

ᔕ

Zoë's palms were sweaty as she stepped into the council chambers. There were eleven chairs gathered in a half circle. At the outer edge, an Amato man and the Vesti woman seated next to him smiled at Kaylee, while several of those near them glared at Kaylee's Vesti father, Komet, their eyes dark with emotion, as if his presence stirred up a wealth of pain and something more, hatred.

Zoë shivered at seeing it, and Iden, following her gaze said, *It was Komet's clan-house, the Araqiel, who unknowingly brought the Hotaling virus to Belizair. But if the Araqiel are to be blamed, then we all are, for enjoying the sex toys they produce and for welcoming their innovativeness when it comes to creating them.*

An Amato male who Iden silently identified as Jarlath, a fellow priest, waved a hand toward the wall and the chairs lining it. "Since this is an informal meeting, please, secure a chair and take your place in the circle."

It took a moment to do so, and Zoë was glad to sit despite the lack of a chair back. Her heart was thundering and her legs were shaky.

Iden recaptured her hand. *All will be well, beloved.*

Miciah took her other hand, entwining his fingers with hers before standing. "Thank you for agreeing so quickly to a meeting. If the matter weren't urgent, we would not have requested it. I will get straight to the point. Since we last gathered, there has been an unseen change taking place on Belizair, one offering the mated women a reason for casting off their despair.

"Whether it is will of the Vesti wandering god, or that of the Amato Goddess and Consort, or all three of them, since

244

coming here our bond-mate Zoë has broken our law with respect to travel to Earth. She has aided others in breaking it in order to bring human children back to Belizair."

Shocked gasps greeted his announcement. Several Council members rose from their chairs, only to be guided into reclaiming them with a touch to their wrists by those sitting next to them.

Miciah glanced at Ariel, who sat between her mates with Kaylee on her lap, then continued, "When Ariel told me of the children on Earth who were abandoned and orphaned, I came to the Council and proposed that we have our scientists begin looking for those with the markers of the Fallon. We agreed to allow the Vesti and Amato willing to go to Earth and raise those children to do so in the hopes the children might one day come here as shared mates. A few of you suggested we bring the children as soon as they were found. I was opposed, as were the majority of the Council members.

"Since then my views have changed. I have seen our world, and also the plight of our females through Zoë eyes. But rather than speak for my mate, I will cede the floor to her and allow her to show you the full truth of what she has to offer those on Belizair."

Zoë stood, forcing steel into both her legs and her spine. She took a moment to breathe deeply, to wet a suddenly dry mouth. She looked at the Council members individually, making sure she met their eyes before beginning.

"I don't claim the deities of the Vesti and Amato are acting through me, only that I have a gift, and a willingness to use it to help the men and women of your world as well as the children on Earth. I will allow you access to my memories in a few moments. You can judge them for yourselves."

She paused, met their eyes once again. "But as a human, brought here without knowing the true cost of my choice— that I would, if I obeyed your laws, never be able to return to my world again—it's also my right to make a judgment. To point out that in keeping the human women and our mates housed in buildings set aside for us and requiring we remain in this city, you segregate us and help build animosity toward us. You claim it's for our own good, but there are no humans on your Council to hear our voices, to protest what we might find an injustice or hear our concerns should we begin to wonder if we are merely a means to an end, ultimately, nothing more than broodmares brought here to save the Vesti and Amato from extinction."

Her words were met with murmured protests and flared nostrils, by the tightening of Iden and Miciah's hands on hers. She squeezed their fingers in reassurance, then continued, "My point in speaking on these things is to challenge the Council's way of thinking, that somehow change can be controlled and cultures kept unblended. I don't believe either is possible, not if you involve humans in your plans to avoid extinction."

She sat and Iden stood. "Zoë succeeds where I fail the women who come to me at the temple. I can offer only temporary strength and solace, but she can give them more. She is a gift to Belizair. One brought here at the Goddess' will, but that is Kaylee's story to show you from her memories, if you'll allow it before exploring Zoë's."

Nods from the Council members indicated they would. The Amato priest, Jarlath, said, "With so many of us present, it might be best if I facilitate the sharing of memories. Is that acceptable?"

In answer the Council members began joining hands so a circle was formed by all those sitting, just as it had been when Zoë was with the Vesti women in the marketplace.

Jarlath directed his attention to Kaylee. "Do you know what to expect?"

"Miciah told us on the way over. He said go right to the first important thing, which is when the golden lady visited me while I was sleeping, then fast forward like a movie, but only show the good parts. And if you need to see something else or think I'm leaving something out, you'll direct my thoughts there."

Jarlath's soft laugh wasn't the only one. He smiled and said, "Shall we proceed?"

With the physical connection to Iden and Miciah, and their mate-bond, it was easy for Zoë to hold the mental link open, and Kaylee's memories flowed through it seamlessly, from the dream of a woman wreathed in golden light whose melodic voice urged Kaylee to look through her mother's things to the reality of her actions afterward.

If Jarlath directed the images, then his touch was so subtle Zoë couldn't detect it. It was only upon seeing the conclusion—with Kaylee's visit to Miciah's office—that Zoë heard Jarlath's prompt for her to begin.

As she'd done in the shower with Miciah and Iden, Zoë began with images from Earth. Her discordant gifts and what they cost her. The long-ago visit with the fortuneteller leading to her certainty of purpose when she saw Acacia in the marketplace.

Zoë heard gasps, but apparently Jarlath's facilitation suppressed outside emotion, so only what was contained in the memory was present in the mental link. From Acacia's deep despair through the meeting with the Vesti women, she showed them all of it, wanting them to see and hear the depth of suffering, the willingness of the women to risk banishment in order to become mothers.

She showed them India. And concluded with Denaus climbing into the dumpster to retrieve a newborn.

Jarlath didn't prompt her for more and she didn't offer it. The unclasping of hands around the circle signaled the end of the shared mental link.

You did well, Iden sent along their private bond.

Miciah carried her hand to his lips and kissed the back of it. *You are a gift. Not just to the two of us, but to Belizair.*

Jarlath claimed the floor by standing. "I had no doubts before. And now, having witnessed events through Kaylee and Zoë's memories, I am more positive in my beliefs than ever before. Belizair is being reshaped—be it by deities or the will of the planet itself. A formal meeting to decide on how to proceed is inevitable, but I will urge that we embrace Zoë's gift and the change it brings to our world."

He sat and another Amato immediately stood. *He's one of the healers,* Iden whispered into Zoë's mind. *The Vesti female next to him is also a healer.*

The healer said, "In this I am in full agreement with Jarlath. Belizair is being reshaped. The healers of the enclave are unanimous in saying the mountains welcome Kaylee, a child of Earth, in a way they do so few others. If the Goddess and Consort are so willing, then we should take it as a sign to bring other human children here, and accept that Zoë's presence in our world is meant to aid us in locating those who should be brought to Belizair."

The Vesti healer took the floor next. "Whether the male appearing in Zoë's visions is the Vesti god or the Consort, Ylan, we would be foolish not to embrace his choices."

A female Amato was the next to stand. "Belizair is being reshaped. I can not disagree with Jarlath's statement. But serious laws have been broken. Unless we want to become as lawless a world as those found in the Kotaka gaming sector, then we can't ignore that fact. At a minimum we should convene a formal meeting—immediately—and banish the women involved, at least until we have time to study this matter and revise our laws accordingly."

She sat and one of the Amato men who'd reacted negatively to Komet stood. Miciah tensed, identifying him as Raym.

"I agree with Luz, not only for reasons of law but for something more, something no one has yet to speak about directly. What if the children Zoë locates through her gift also carry psychic abilities? Are we prepared to introduce such talents on Belizair? We need time to contemplate this larger question. I for one am not sure those with such talents wouldn't ultimately destroy our society as they have done on other worlds. At a minimum, the women should be banished from Belizair for a short time, until the children can be evaluated and guidelines set in place. Perhaps it might also be wise to keep Zoë apart, or chaperoned, if she is not yet with child."

Both Iden and Miciah surged to their feet. Anger pulsing through their shared link.

Before they could say anything a Vesti male who'd taken Raym's place as speaker held up his hand. "Please. Sit. At your request we gathered informally and have remained so despite this being a matter serious enough to warrant an immediate, formal session of the Council. Let each of us have our say. It's to your benefit to know where we stand."

Iden and Miciah conceded, reclaiming their seats though their bodies vibrated from what they viewed as a threat to their mate-bond.

So far there are three in support of what I've done, Zoë told them, wanting to ease their agitation. *Four if Miciah gets a vote. There are only two wanting sanctions.*

The Vesti left standing said, "It might be years before we know the answer to the questions Raym has posed. Are we willing to deny the already mated and those who want to bond outside the Council programs the opportunity to become parents? True, serious laws have been broken, but with the management of Zoë's gift, the decision to bring children here or raise them on Earth could be made on a case-by-case basis, looking to the needs of both child and adoptive parents. If the Council demands punishment for what has already been done, let it be in fines or service, not in banishment or threats of it."

Zoë pulled Iden and Miciah's hands onto her lap and held them there, back-to-back. *That's five. Almost half the Council is on our side.*

An Amato took the Vesti's place as speaker. *Gabri,* Miciah said. *One of the scientists on the Council.*

"Javant is correct. It might be years before we know the answers to the questions Raym has posed about the children having psychic talents. Luz is also correct in reminding us that serious laws have been broken. In a time of great turmoil, it is more important than ever to maintain order. To set the precedent of allowing individuals to choose which rules to obey and which to ignore will lead to disastrous results. We should banish all those involved to a nearby planet, but allow them visitors. This will give us time not only to test the children but to prepare our world for change."

Before he could sit, the teenage Vesti messenger who'd arrived as Miciah and Zoë left the transport chamber on their mating day burst into the room. "Cyan's in labor!" he said. "Those attending her don't think it'll be long before she gives birth."

As one, the Council members got to their feet. "She's at home for the birth?" the Vesti healer asked.

"Yes, she didn't tell anyone she was in labor until just a few minutes ago."

Those gathered became a flow of people leaving the room—only to step outside the building and be forced to an abrupt halt.

Hundreds gathered. And the sky contained even more, women of all ages and men, descending on the Council building.

For an instant Miciah thought they arrived because news of the imminent birth of Cyan's children had spread, but he dismissed the idea just as quickly. It made no sense for them to gather here instead of in the courtyard outside the quarters Cyan shared with Laith and Rykken.

He scanned the crowd and a jolt of surprise went through him at finding some of the human children from Zoë's vision playing among those of the Amato and Vesti, their behavior both a testament and a lesson on the importance of adaptability.

Out of the corner of his eye, Miciah saw Lyan. He growled silently before he could stop himself and heard Zoë's laughter in his thoughts.

That's very Pavlovian of you, she teased before asking Lyan the very question on Miciah's mind. *This is your doing?*

It took very little effort on my part, Lyan said.

Miciah looked away from Lyan and had a greater shock when he saw his parents standing together, their hands clasped. His mother was smiling, her eyes dancing with love and pride. *We've come to stand with you, in all ways,* she sent him.

On some silent signal those crowding into the courtyard began linking arms, further blocking the path of the Council members. Amato and Vesti stood intermingled with human women — some of those from Earth close to delivering children and some barely showing their pregnancies.

He wondered who would speak for this crowd, and bit back a cheer when Iden said, *Aren't those two women Raym's mates? And those on either side of them related somehow to others on the Council?*

Yes, Miciah said, allowing himself to feel a measure of relief for the first time since Zoë's revelation in the shower.

One of Raym's bond-mates spoke then, directing her words to all the Council members. "We are here to support Zoë. Know that if you banish her from our world, we will follow her. She's a gift to us, a shining beacon not only of hope, but one illuminating the need for us to put aside fears and hostilities with roots in the past and come together as one people."

A cheer went up as soon as she finished speaking, followed by a chant. *Zoë! Zoë! Zoë!*

Emotion swamped Miciah. The gathered crowds'. His own and Iden's. Zoë's.

Tears streamed down her face as she stepped forward and lifted her hand for silence. When it formed all she

251

managed to say was "Thank you," the words heartfelt and choked.

Raym used the quiet to announce, "The Council will meet formally with respect to this." He paused, his mind brushing against Miciah's and the other Council members in order to reach a consensus on when, and whether to make the meeting open to all. But before it could be done, Kaylee spoke into the lull, "Mommy, if the Council members start taking turns talking again, we're not going to be there when Cyan has her babies."

Surprise spiked through those gathered. Zoë laughed and found her voice. "I think Kaylee has a point."

To the crowd she said, "We were heading to the courtyard outside Cyan's quarters for the birth announcement. Why don't we all go and wait together? What better way is there to celebrate the joining of three different races for a shared future on Belizair?"

Another cheer went up as Vesti, Amato and human alike surged in an unstoppable wave that collected Miciah and the others within it.

"I remember, Auntie Zoë!" Kaylee said as they were propelled forward.

"Remembered what?"

"Where I saw the stones and the butterflies on your bracelets before. It was when I was in the mountains with the healers. The caves they live in are so ancient that the walls have symbols and words and pictures the Fallon carved into them. The healers only understand some of what's on the wall, but there were pictures of a man there, the one you see when you have a helping vision.

"It was like a story. He started out big, without any butterflies around him, but as he went different places, or maybe it was because he got older, he got smaller and the butterflies were left behind him, like a trail on the wall, until finally he became one of them. Maybe. That's how I would tell

252

the story. The healers might know what the pictures really mean. But I think he must have been important to the Fallon."

"It would make sense that the stones in Zoë's possession are tied to the Fallon," Iden said. "With few exceptions, Ylan stones of any size can't be removed from Belizair unless they're in our bands. The ones on our wrists become nothing more than dulled chunks of rock if we die off-world. When the Council reconvenes, we will mention what you saw, Kaylee, and the healers can confirm it. It will strengthen the argument that Zoë's presence here is no coincidence."

The crowd swept in and filled the courtyard outside Cyan's quarters to overflowing. "Any minute now," became a murmur rushing through those gathered, heightening the buzz of excitement and feeding the sense of anticipation and hope.

Miciah glanced around, absorbing the emotion and noting the expressions. What if the Council's desire to keep things hidden until they knew the final result had prevailed? What if those on Belizair had been denied a chance to experience this? Be a part of it?

Unbidden, an image from earlier slid into his consciousness, of him standing in the shower, his wrists tethered and arms raised above his head as Zoë scraped her fingernails against his belly to emphasize his helplessness. *Have you ever let yourself be bound before?*

Of Iden laughing. *I can't truly imagine it. Can you? His resistance to change is rooted in his desire to remain in control.*

Change couldn't be managed or controlled, or even stopped. Miciah understood now, and didn't fear what lay ahead.

The Council needed to trust those on Belizair with the full truth when it came to discoveries impacting their chances of becoming parents. They needed to let the people experience the hope as well as any disappointment that may follow, and to believe that regardless, their society wouldn't disintegrate and become like some of those on other worlds.

He looked around, seeking out some of the other Council members, and when their eyes met, he thought he saw the same realization there.

A sudden hush drew his gaze to an open doorway and the healer standing in it. "Laith and Rykken will step outside momentarily to introduce their new daughters."

The announcement was met with tears and hugs and softly spoken words, with an increased fervor of anticipation as each of those gathered imagined Laith, Rykken and Cyan placing the bands on their newest family members, willing the Ylan stones on their wrists to migrate—and waiting for the wings to manifest—if they would at all.

Time slowed. But couldn't be measured in heartbeats because those raced.

Zoë's hand tightened on his. And on Iden's.

I can't take much more of this, she said.

Iden's amusement was a warm balm. *At least by the time our children arrive, there will have been plenty of others born before them, and hopefully many more brought from Earth. We'll only have to contend with hovering family members and friends.*

The door opened again and two men stepped out, each with an infant held against his shoulder so their wings were revealed. Feathers streaked with brown and gold for the one in the Amato, Laith's arms. Dark chocolate suede for the baby Rykken held.

The fathers' faces were wet, their expressions holding both love and wonder. But they were in like company. There wasn't a dry eye in the courtyard by then.

"We present our daughters," Laith said. "Asha and Amala. Both mean Hope."

"Which is Asha?" a woman in the crowd called just as another asked, "Which is Amala?"

Rykken and Laith shared a grin then carefully exchanged the children so they held babies whose wings were different than their own—for an instant.

Like the man in Zoë's vision, there was a blurring, a reshaping, dark suede giving way to feathers, feathers giving way to dark suede—and once again, the babies' wings matched those of the father who held them.

Stunned surprise was followed by exultant joy, by a whispered phrase, spoken reverently. *The Fallon return.*

Laith and Rykken remained outside a few minutes longer, allowing those gathered to absorb what they'd witnessed before they retreated into their quarters.

"Change is the gift," Zoë whispered, repeating the god's words as her eyes lifted to meet Miciah's.

"As you are," he said, claiming her lips and kissing her thoroughly before turning to Iden, his hand settling on Iden's waist. "As our mate-bond is."

Iden's eyebrow rose in query and challenge. "Now?" he asked, his voice holding amusement as well as desire.

Miciah answered with action, by leaning in and touching his mouth to Iden's, the passion flaring between them obvious to any watching.

You do know how to set an example, Iden teased, meeting the thrust of Miciah's tongue with his own, both of them shivering with pleasure as Zoë's fingers stoked the edge of their wings, her touch signaling to all her acceptance of a bond defined by love and not by race or gender, by a looking forward into the future and not a clinging to the past.

Epilogue

This is home now, Zoë thought as she walked through the marketplace with Iden and Miciah. She'd longed to be able to stay in one place, to be able to use her gifts to help others. But who would have guessed that what she wanted would be found on another world? One that resembled a paradise— For the most part, she amended as she felt Miciah's subtle flinch as an old Vesti man looked at him with disgust before turning away, his action making her heart ache on Miciah's behalf.

Don't, beloved, Miciah said, carrying her hand to his mouth and pressing a kiss to the back of it. *Some will never accept the choice I made but I have no regrets.*

Even if it costs you your seat on the Council?

Iden laughed softly. *You worry unnecessarily. Despite his break with tradition, there is a more important consideration. You, Zoë. Now that the Council has decided on a policy of full disclosure and formally asked for your help in aiding those on Belizair who wish to bring human children here, there won't be a challenge lodged against Miciah.*

She felt how certain Iden was in his judgment. She felt a fainter echo of it in Miciah, though she also felt his resolve. He would fight any challenge but would concede defeat gracefully if those in the jungle region no longer wished him to represent them.

"How bad is the fine the Council leveled on us for my breaking the law?"

It was Miciah's turn to laugh. "Considering the alternative was banishment, and that the credits will go toward paying those bounty hunters in pursuit of the Hotaling, it is nothing."

Iden carried her hand to his chest and rubbed the back of it over a hardened nipple. *I am sure you can make us forget the surrendered credits. But now that I think on it, perhaps a more private punishment for breaking the law is in order.*

Heat shot straight to her cunt as images crowded her mind, this time of her draped over Iden's lap as Miciah watched while she was spanked. *You might be right,* she said as arousal escaped her slit, and snickered as Iden and Miciah began walking faster with a sudden need to get back to their quarters.

Anticipation surged through the mate-bond. She was just about to suggest they transport when they were halted by a call from behind.

What now? Miciah growled. *Are we never going to be allowed uninterrupted time together?*

They turned to find the Vesti Council member Javant approaching from the air. Despite Miciah's grumbling, his curiosity matched Zoë's and Iden's since they'd just left the Council building after most of the day spent there in formal hearings.

Javant landed a few steps away. He gave a nod to Zoë and Iden before focusing on Miciah. "I am leaving for Earth to inform Zantara that she is a match for the human named Kelleher, and to discuss the possibility of forming a bond with her. There are no guarantees, but the scientists think it likely that just as it takes both a Vesti and Amato to claim a human female, Zantara will need a Vesti male as a co-mate if there is to be any possibility of children from the union.

"I wanted to thank you for the courage you demonstrated in the courtyard following the birth of Cyan's children. Because of it, I was able to admit that while my desire for a female mate is strong, the thought of a relationship such as the one you have with your mates is acceptable to me, should Zantara's human match desire it."

Javant took flight after delivering his message. Warm pleasure filled Zoë's chest as she watched him speed toward the transport chamber. The butterfly-shaped Ylan stones at her wrists hummed, and in that instant knew hope on Belizair was soon to blossom into happiness for the unmated females.

Also by Jory Strong

ဆ

About the Author

෯

Jory has been writing since childhood and has never outgrown being a daydreamer. When she's not hunched over her computer, lost in the muse and conjuring up new heroes and heroines, she can usually be found reading, riding her horses or hiking with her dogs.

Jory welcomes comments from readers. You can find her website and email address on her author bio page at www.ellorascave.com.

Tell Us What You Think

We appreciate hearing reader opinions about our books. You can email us at Comments@EllorasCave.com.

Why an electronic book?

We live in the Information Age—an exciting time in the history of human civilization, in which technology rules supreme and continues to progress in leaps and bounds every minute of every day. For a multitude of reasons, more and more avid literary fans are opting to purchase e-books instead of paper books. The question from those not yet initiated into the world of electronic reading is simply: *Why?*

1. *Price.* An electronic title at Ellora's Cave Publishing and Cerridwen Press runs anywhere from 40% to 75% less than the cover price of the exact same title in paperback format. Why? Basic mathematics and cost. It is less expensive to publish an e-book (no paper and printing, no warehousing and shipping) than it is to publish a paperback, so the savings are passed along to the consumer.

2. *Space.* Running out of room in your house for your books? That is one worry you will never have with electronic books. For a low one-time cost, you can purchase a handheld device specifically designed for e-reading. Many e-readers have large, convenient screens for viewing. Better yet, hundreds of titles can be stored within your new library—on a single microchip. There are a variety of e-readers from different manufacturers. You can also read e-books on your PC or laptop computer. (Please note that Ellora's Cave does not endorse any specific brands.

You can check our websites at www.ellorascave.com or www.cerridwenpress.com for information we make available to new consumers.)

3. *Mobility.* Because your new e-library consists of only a microchip within a small, easily transportable e-reader, your entire cache of books can be taken with you wherever you go.

4. *Personal Viewing Preferences.* Are the words you are currently reading too small? Too large? Too… ANNOYING? Paperback books cannot be modified according to personal preferences, but e-books can.

5. *Instant Gratification.* Is it the middle of the night and all the bookstores near you are closed? Are you tired of waiting days, sometimes weeks, for bookstores to ship the novels you bought? Ellora's Cave Publishing sells instantaneous downloads twenty-four hours a day, seven days a week, every day of the year. Our webstore is never closed. Our e-book delivery system is 100% automated, meaning your order is filled as soon as you pay for it.

Those are a few of the top reasons why electronic books are replacing paperbacks for many avid readers.

As always, Ellora's Cave and Cerridwen Press welcome your questions and comments. We invite you to email us at Comments@ellorascave.com or write to us directly at Ellora's Cave Publishing Inc., 1056 Home Avenue, Akron, OH 44310-3502.

erridwen, the Celtic Goddess of wisdom, was the muse who brought inspiration to storytellers and those in the creative arts. Cerridwen Press encompasses the best and most innovative stories in all genres of today's fiction. Visit our site and discover the newest titles by talented authors who still get inspired - much like the ancient storytellers did, once upon a time.

Cerridwen Press

www.cerridwenpress.com

LaVergne, TN USA
11 March 2011
219787LV00002B/80/P